A Play for the

End of the World

A PLAY FOR THE
END OF THE WORLD

Jai Chakrabarti

ALFRED A. KNOPF

NEW YORK

2021

THIS IS A BORZOI BOOK PUBLISHED BY ALFRED A. KNOPF

Copyright © 2021 by Jai Chakrabarti

www.aaknopf.com

LIBRARY OF CONGRESS CATALOGING-IN-PUBLICATION DATA
Names: Chakrabarti, Jai, author.
Title: A play for the end of the world : a novel / Jai Chakrabarti.
Description: First edition. | New York : Alfred A. Knopf, 2021. |
Identifiers: LCCN 2020045419 (print) | LCCN 2020045420 (ebook) |
ISBN 9780525658924 (hardcover) | ISBN 9780525658931 (ebook)
Subjects: LCSH: Holocaust survivors—Fiction. | GSAFD: Love stories.
Classification: LCC PS3603.H33548 P58 2021 (print) |
LCC PS3603.H33548 (ebook) | DDC 813/.6—dc23
LC record available at https://lccn.loc.gov/2020045419
LC ebook record available at https://lccn.loc.gov/2020045420

Jacket art: *Gris Foncé (14)* by Katrien de Blauwer
Jacket design by Janet Hansen

Manufactured in the United States of America
First Edition

For anyone who's crossed a border

in search of home

sooner would a crow turn white
than Poland be Poland again
we were told and also
that the Lord God had gone away
as far as america
and wouldn't be back

—FROM "CHILDHOOD 1940" BY JERZY FICOWSKI

CONTENTS

❧

Part 4

AUTHOR'S NOTE

On July 18, 1942, weeks before the deportations to Treblinka, the Polish-Jewish educator, medical doctor, and author Janusz Korczak staged a play at his orphanage in the Warsaw Ghetto. The performance was an adaptation of a Bengali play, *Dak Ghar*, by Rabindranath Tagore.

Dak Ghar literally means *"The Calling House."* Nowadays it's translated as *The Post Office*. Rabindranath Tagore wrote *Dak Ghar* in a village in India in 1911. A couple of years later W. B. Yeats produced an English version. The play was then translated into many languages, and eventually a Polish copy ended up in the hands of Janusz Korczak, known to his children as *Pan Doktor*.

The play is about a dying child living through his imagination while quarantined. Pan Doktor chose to stage the play to help his orphans reimagine ghetto life and to prepare them for what was to come.

PROLOGUE

Warsaw—July 18th, 1942

The set has been assembled. A piece of cawed wood that is to mean *window*. A watercolor Hanna has painted of the sun that is to mean *sun*. A bed they've borrowed from the boys' dorm—no easy feat dragging it up and down the stairs for each rehearsal—that is to mean *child's bed*. Wooden blocks Misha carved to mean *child's toys*. And nine-year-old Jaryk is dressed like a boy from India, at least what they'd imagined a boy from India would look like: a pillowcase fashioned into a turban, a prayer marking on his forehead.

From the dressing area Jaryk spies much of Jewish Warsaw gathered in the great room of the orphanage. Szlengel opens with a poem of which he'll remember the lines *"What does it mean: afar? . . . How to explain the word to a child?"* Afterwards the old piano is carted out, and Szpilman plays Chopin.

He waits behind the makeshift curtain, drinking the music in. Last night, they weren't sure if they'd be able to stage the production at all. So many of the other cast members had come down with food poisoning, no one knew from what; maybe it was the stale eggs, someone said, or the vaccine they'd been given days earlier. All night their stewards Pan Doktor and Madam Stefa tended to the children with saline drops and lime water. By morning the worst of it passed, and he and his dearest friend, Misha, built the makeshift dressing area, no more than a long curtain hung from the ceiling, which he now stands behind, waiting to make his entrance.

Pan Doktor introduces their play. It's from India, Pan Doktor says, and it's called *The Post Office*. "How do you help a child in this world? How do you teach him about what's to come? The afterlife?"

The play's about a boy, Amal, who has an incurable disease and must stay indoors on doctor's orders. All day Amal watches the world through his window and imagines the King will soon come to visit him. He makes friends with the villagers through his window, sees other boys playing outside, and invites them near his house, offering up his toys just so he can watch them play in the dirt. This is what first caught Jaryk: how generous it was to let other boys play with your favorite things.

Amal is visited by a whimsical wanderer—a *fakir*, one of the words of Bengali he's learned. The Fakir teaches him how to play in his mind, how to imagine a faraway land across the mountain with waterfalls. Jaryk has never seen a waterfall and, like the boy in the play, can only imagine what one is. Misha has tried to describe the rush of water against the mountain face, though really, what could Misha know about such things?

Pan Doktor finishes his introduction, and Jaryk goes onstage, feeling as if he's been cast under a spell. When he lies on the bed, it's as if he is no longer himself, half starving, afraid of Pan Doktor's health, of what the black boots will do next. Instead he is a boy in a village in India, somewhere between life and death. He is dignified, and he is human. He is majestic, a child. All eyes are upon him as he readies to speak—

AMAL: Uncle! Well, hullo!

THE GOOD UNCLE: Amal, my boy. Let me have a look at you.

AMAL: Surely today you will let me play in the courtyard, Uncle. The sun is out and I wish to see the mountain, and I wish to hear the call of the King's men.

THE GOOD UNCLE: I'm sorry, my dear, but you're under strict orders. We'll need you to be inside. I have many books for you to read, so you may turn out a scholar, unlike your uncle.

AMAL: But I have no wish to be a scholar. What I want is
to be—

(Jaryk pauses. He looks around the dining hall, where chairs have
been placed in the clamshell formation that is to mean *theater*.
There is his teacher Esterka, who is mouthing his line: *"What I
want is to be—a squirrel."* A squirrel, what a strange thing to want
to be, but no matter, he knows the line. He knows the feeling of
wanting to be something else and somewhere else. To be in the
woods again, away from the walls of their city-within-a-city. To be
in the wild. Yes, he knows that feeling. He knows his lines, most
of them anyway.

He sees Pan Doktor and Madam Stefa in the audience. Pan
Doktor has to sit on account of his bum knee, and Madam Stefa
stands beside him. Can it be that she winks at Jaryk? Misha is off
to their right, a toothpick in his mouth. Jaryk is not sure if Misha
is glowering at him, or smiling, or both.

What he wants is to hold this moment for as long as he can,
for time to lose its wheels, for all of Warsaw to be held in step, for
then he can keep the feeling he has now. This certainty of being
part of a family, of being held so firmly there is nothing he can do
to disavow this love. Who knows when it will be taken—what they
have built together—who knows when the black boots will come?

There is Esterka again, encouraging him. No better teacher will
he have than her. No better father and mother than Pan Doktor
and Stefania.

Jaryk rises to his full height so he can deliver his call to the far-
thest corners of the room.

In four days the Germans will begin the deportations of Jewish
Warsaw to the death camp of Treblinka; not even Pan Doktor's
orphanage of two hundred children will be spared.

But on this night they are in the thrall of the theater, as if they're
all children in India, as if over the mountain lies the waterfall with
its constant rainbow, as if this and all the bounties of the earth
await them just beyond the bend—)

PART I

The Wanderer

Morning in Calcutta. The Foreigners queue was filled with longhaired imitators of Ram Dass, a flock of missionaries, and young businessmen pursuing the promise of an urban India. The other line was crammed with locals carrying suitcases stuffed with a country in gifts. All were eager to move past the chain-smoking customs officer and be on their way.

Except Jaryk wasn't in a hurry. A heaviness in his knees held him at the *Wait Till Call* circle until a mustachioed guard with a shoulder-slung rifle prodded him forward. Jaryk paused at the immigration booth with his green suitcase, a sturdy, ugly piece of luggage that was seeing its first taste of the East. It was Misha's suitcase, so he carried it with no small amount of pride.

"Purpose of visit?" the immigration officer asked him.

He was here to retrieve and carry Misha's remains back to Brooklyn, but no one would understand that. "Tourism," he said. "Sights of the country."

He was stamped and cleared and followed the herd out of the frosted doors of the airport. Outside, the air was a dense concentration of humidity and heat. As soon as his shoes touched the asphalt, he felt he'd come overdressed. Under the humid cover, the crowd swelled and dispersed, swelled to disperse. At first, it seemed like a single leviathan, colorful and noisy, but then he spotted a pattern. Lines of men and women waited to greet their loved ones while other lines queued to enter the airport. The family members shuffled nervously, checking each face, until the match was found;

then, not a moment wasted: the whole group would absorb the arrived, and all together they'd head for the road.

He watched his fellow passengers make their way to the taxi stand. Their journey was first complicated by the ambush of men hawking marble statues and shawls, further complicated by the group of boys and girls who smiled, crooned, and cried their way to American dollars. Once the tourists made it through, they were swallowed by a row of taxi drivers, each crying out his own warring price.

When they'd last been together in New York, Misha had told him the first day would be difficult, but this was more. This was the madness brought on by too many people. He took off his shoes and socks and waited in the shade until all the passengers had left. There was no hurry; he was good at waiting.

It took an hour, but the arrivals crowd eventually thinned out. He was left with the hawkers, who sat on the opposite curb and passed a cigarette around. The panhandling children drew a square of hopscotch in the middle of the road, and the winners of each round ate candies they'd begged off a matronly passenger on her way to the taxi stand.

The hawkers noticed him and yelled something in his direction— a curse, most likely, guttural and foul—and laughed and enjoyed their cigarette and cards. It was still too hot for shoes, so he stayed barefoot, though as soon as he left the shade his soles felt like they were on fire. *This too shall pass.* The mantra came to him easy and free, and he held on to it as a group of children surrounded him. One prodded him in the belly and giggled. He tried to smile back, but he didn't have it in him. Instead, he handed out the ballpoint pens he'd brought as alms and, when they wouldn't leave, all of the American coins in his pocket.

When he saw a taxi pull up to the curb, he skipped toward it. This driver was better dressed than any of the other men he'd seen, and he wore an air of superiority, as if he didn't need the business at all. "You are going to burn your feet," the driver said in a crisp British English. He was middle-aged, with a protruding belly, thick glasses cut square, a dark corduroy jacket patched at the elbows, and white, nylon slacks. Why he wasn't sweating through his clothes was a mystery. The driver cocked his head and asked, "Where can I take you?"

Jaryk took a strip of paper from his coat. It had become sweat stained to the point where he could barely make out the letters. "Sudder Street," he said.

As they turned off the airport road and onto the bypass, a patch of cloud opened up. At first, it was only a bit of sweet rain. Through the half-open window, he let his fingers get wet in it, but at the next major intersection, with no warning, the adjacent clouds joined in to make a full monsoon. The stray dogs on the street hid under canopies; the traffic slowed in a single heartbeat; a line of coconut trees swayed in the same direction; five women on the sidewalk, all in red saris, took off their shoes and sprinted. This was the India of the flesh. His sweat proved it, the stink released by the rain proved it, that smell of rot and burning bamboo.

"Are you staying with family here?" The driver squinted and searched for the house number on Sudder Street.

"No, it's just a guesthouse."

They found a boarded-up building with a sign in English, *New Guest Stay*, hanging off the second-floor balcony like a loose tooth. "This was in the guidebook and I called," Jaryk said. "Are you sure this is the right street?" The rain had persevered until the streets were ankle-deep with water. With a suitcase and a sore back, he didn't like his odds. Jaryk flipped through his guidebook and pointed. "Okay, what about *this* place? The Park Hotel?"

"You can pay for Park Hotel?"

From the way the driver was looking at his clothes, Jaryk suspected the place would dig a hole in his budget, but he didn't like the accusation of limited means.

"You know, sir," the driver continued, "there is one place, more authentic, with cheaper and better living. Not so far." The driver took off his glasses and smiled. Jaryk focused on the outline of the man's face: it was a perfect oval, a shape that made him want to trust.

"Authentic," he said, against his better judgment. "I like that."

He had agreed, but after a while it seemed they were heading back toward the airport, toward the open stretches of land that had made the city seem not like a city, and several times Jaryk almost asked him where they were going, only to let jet lag hold his tongue.

They swerved off onto a narrow dirt road. The driver said, "We are almost arrived."

Down the road a zigzag of mud huts. Bare-chested men under the shade of banana leaves. By the tube well, a row of women waiting to draw water, saris soaked, and by the trash dump, a hangout the driver identified as the suburb's only phone station.

Children played in the mud, footballs bounced knee to knee. He recognized a weariness in these boys and girls, a lethargy in how they shuffled from the road to make room for the car. They looked like they were used to being hungry, and when hunger was present trouble was never far behind. Still, he was a head taller than any grown man he'd seen. If things got murky, he could hold his own.

The driver began whistling a tune, and as he moved from melody to melody, the rain eased up. Now it was the quiet sun above them again, boiling the roof of the cab. Jaryk thought about what he had left behind, which was Lucy. Lucy, and not much else. By now, she would have found his apartment empty, along with his letter. She would've called Rabbi Samuel and the rabbi would tell her what little he knew, or maybe she wouldn't call anyone at all— that was the darker possibility: she'd come to loathe him without knowing the whole story.

The driver slowed to a stop. They had reached the end of the road.

"We are arrived," said the driver. "P. K. Pal Guest House."

The house before them had outgrown itself: it was three floors of brick, and the top two levels looked to have been afterthoughts. While the foundation was the same sturdy whitewash stone Jaryk had seen in so many other houses along the road, the second floor was a light shade of rose, and the third level, which jutted out at a nearly perpendicular angle to avoid pressing against the limbs of a nearby coconut tree, bore no resemblance to either, being a roof-less structure with holes to mark future windows.

"This looks like someone's house," Jaryk said.

"It is the house of P. K. Pal. I am Prosanto Kumar Pal, and some-times, when the feeling is right, we take guests." Prosanto Pal smiled and revealed a row of teeth so perfect they could only be false. "For fifteen rupees, you get a large room plus the cooking of Mrs. P. K. Pal. But please, if you do not want, I can drive you to the Park Hotel for no extra cost."

Jaryk fingered the loose stash of rupees in his pocket. He couldn't afford any sort of fancy hotel. Fifteen rupees and home cooking were sounding more and more like the right choice. Also, there were the children who ran out from the arms of their mother. A boy and a girl. The girl with two long pigtails and pink sandals. The boy with thick glasses a size too big; when he ran to his father, he held on to them with one hand.

Mr. Pal received their hugs and reciprocated with kisses. "Let me introduce my beloved, Mrs. Aditi Pal, and my little ones, Avik and Priya."

"Please, please come inside," said Mrs. Pal, who was at least a decade younger than her husband and more attractive, with her aquiline nose and queenly cheekbones.

For a moment the wariness Jaryk had felt dissipated, though a darker feeling took its place. Would he ever have what Mr. Pal had? He joined the Pals in their living room, which was spacious but lacking in furniture. As lunch was prepared, everyone sat on pil-lows around a marble table. Mrs. Pal kept her head covered, ran in and out of the kitchen, and began to cook something that reeked of pepper and spice. "Smells delicious," he said, though spicy food had always felt like a burden on his tongue.

Aditi Pal drew her sari close to her hips but gave him a cautious smile. Her husband sat on a wicker mat reading the paper, rocking a little as he read. With his free arm, Mr. Pal worked a hand fan to create a breeze for Avik and Priya.

"This flood of men-women-children," he said to Jaryk. "They will be the ruin of us. Surely even Americans know this. First we have peasants revolting in Naxalbari, wanting their own plot to till. Now, since Bangladesh is its own country, there are Hindu immigrants from across the border. Just like the Naxals, they all want their own land, but where is the room?"

Jaryk didn't respond. He'd heard the news, at first, as if it were the weather report of a foreign country: the year before, March of 1971, Bangladesh found nationhood; people fled, either into or out of the country. In the streets, there was murder and there was celebration. *The New York Times* covered all of it, but mostly on page 12. It wasn't till Misha became serious about their India plan that he'd begun to pay more attention.

"But enough politics. I hope you are feeling free here. I have hosted Americans before. They come with long hair. Ask about dharma. Is that why also you are here? For religion?"

"No, I'm not much for God," Jaryk said. "And I'm not really American."

"But your last name, don't mind, I saw it on your luggage, is *Smith*. Is that not American?"

He remembered that winter when he and Misha had crossed over from Europe into the country that had seemed till then to be only a fable—*America*—where an officer with too little time on his hands had asked him to state his name and Jaryk had glanced at the man's name tag and repeated it back, thinking a new last name key to a new life. The officer had blinked at hearing his own name but had complied, writing it into history: *Jaryk Smith, originally from Warsaw, Poland, arrived in the United States of America, Mar. 1946.*

"When I came to America, I chose my own last name," Jaryk now explained. "*Smith* sounded right for the job. Originally, I'm from Europe."

"Oh," Mr. Pal said, seeming a little deflated by the news. "Perhaps then you are here for business? We see European men in suits, more and more, these days."

"No, it's not that, either. The truth is that I'm a *fakir*, an every-year wanderer." Behind Mr. Pal's questions, he could feel the tide of a stranger's curiosity, so with every question, he felt himself tightening. With Mr. Pal, there was no reason to go beyond the polite give-and-take.

"Ah, I see, a fakir." Mr. Pal announced the word, the profession, with great seriousness. "Please note, Mr. Smith, I am not only a taxi driver. I am also a graduate of Calcutta University. Honors in philosophy. These eyes—" Mr. Pal took off his glasses— "are so poor because of the many books I have read in my time."

Jaryk lumbered over the information. Mr. Pal had airs and he drove with his face too close to the windshield, as if he were getting the hang of the road, but what did Jaryk know of Indian cab drivers? What did he know of India, for that matter? But he said to Mr. Pal, "I assumed as much. You struck me as a scholar from the first."

As Mrs. Pal brought out the meal, the children grew quiet. Mr. Pal passed him rotis and bowls of lentils and scooped the first pieces of chicken onto his plate. "You are our honored guest," he said.

Jaryk had little experience eating with his hands, so he watched Mr. Pal attack his chicken with thumb and forefinger before he tried it himself. There was an added flavor this way, but it was messier and more time-consuming. While Mr. Pal lent a certain dignity to the process, Jaryk's wrists were soon stained with the turmeric-infused sauce. He tried to use his left hand to clean the right, but it didn't help. No problem, he told himself. When in Rome.

"Have you decided how you shall tour our beautiful country?" Mr. Pal asked.

"I'm going to Shantiniketan," he said, searching for a napkin.

"Shantiniketan?" Mr. Pal said. "It's a little remote, but I suppose there is an appeal because of Tagore's school. Also, the natural surroundings."

"And what shall you do there?" Mrs. Pal said.

He didn't want to talk about Misha with strangers. Instead, he said, "I'm going to see a play. *The Post Office*, by Tagore." As soon as he said it, he felt a tightness in his throat. How remarkable that he was finally in the land of Rabindranath Tagore! He'd read the man's poems over the years, back in his youth performed one of his plays.

"Ooh, Baba, I know that one," Avik said. He raised his arm as if he were answering a question at school. "It's about the boy Amal and everyone who comes to visit him because he can't ever leave his house and he has all these visitors and he thinks the King is going to visit him and in the end the King sends a messenger, but he still dies."

"Oof, Avik, you are too much energy," Mrs. Pal said.

"But you are coming all this way," Mr. Pal said, "to see a play by Tagore?"

"That's right," Jaryk said. "And of course the nature, too."

Mrs. Pal murmured something about the cleanliness of the air at Shantiniketan, but when he looked at her, it was as if she did not believe him. He sensed disapproval. It must've been how she'd narrowed her eyes at him, as if squinting might ferret out the truth. She reminded him of another woman, also a caregiver, someone who scared her children as much as she loved them, who, it was so rumored—and he had believed it with his whole heart at the time—could read a misbehaved child's thoughts. *Ah, Stefa*, he thought. *Old mother of mine.* He hoped to see her in the next life.

Jaryk stretched his arms and permitted himself a yawn. "Would you show me to my room?" he said. "I feel I've been awake for days."

····················

The concrete foundations of the Pals' house were exposed on the third floor, where beams pointed to the sky without the benefit of a roof. As he lay on a cot in the open air, Jaryk fell into sleep feet-first. Cobbled stone at his feet, he relived his first vision of Warsaw. It came in fragments, as if memory had slid a sponge over Grzy-bowski Square, where the donkey carts hurried their produce. He could smell the berries and the grapes, which were turning, which the seller announced as *"just perfect"* though no one was fooled, not even the most pious with their side locks in the wind counting time. There was Pan Doktor standing in the middle of the square, bathed in autumn light.

Soft hands brought him back to the evening sun of Bengal, and he looked up to find Mrs. Pal nudging him gently. It was the first time he'd studied her face. She was delicately featured, with thin lips and queenly cheekbones, and were it not for her large, ungainly eyeglasses, he might have considered her beautiful. He shifted his attention to the insides of her palms, the lines stained with years of turmeric. When she pinched his shoulder, he began to discern her words.

"Your face," she was saying. "It burns. Also, it's well past supper time."

He must have slept for hours. He touched his nose and felt the heat rising from the flesh. His forehead throbbed as if someone had poured hot soup over the temples. Tomorrow, his sunburn would hurt. His face, the length of his exposed arms.

"Wait," she said. "There is an Ayurvedic solution." She left the room and returned with a jar in hand and her two children. "Priya, Avik," Mrs. Pal instructed, "put the healing cream on Uncle."

At first both the boy and the girl giggled, but after they checked their mother's expression, they set to work. Avik took the jar from his mother's hands and shook it. The mixture was gelatinous, the texture of frozen coconut oil and the color of ripe mustard, and there were seeds on the surface of the balm that seemed to move of their own volition, from one side of the mixture to the other. Priya took the jar from her brother and poured a dollop on Jaryk's forehead. It cooled him; he felt it down to his feet, as if the girl had actually touched a cube of ice to his heels, but no, she was rubbing it studiously over his face, while her brother was applying the balm to his arms.

"You have many muscles," the boy said, approvingly.

The Pals left, and he fell back into a dreamless sleep only to awaken again around midnight. Someone had arranged a mosquito net above his mattress; he could hear armies of insects just outside of the nylon mesh. By his pillow, there was a tomato sandwich he devoured in three bites.

When he ventured out of the Pal house, he took his flashlight, but he didn't need it. The pale, squalid moon supplied enough illumination for him to read the name stickers on the rusted bicycles the Pals had chained to a coconut tree: *Priya, Avik,* and separate ones for *Mr.* and *Mrs.* The cloudless sky encouraged the rhythm of dimming and flickering stars. He walked toward the faint light in the distance. On either side of the road, there were farms of long-eared corn and rice. When the wind picked up, he could hear the air course through the corn stalks before it touched his skin. The wind cooled his sunburn, but behind the breeze was the promise of tomorrow's deluge.

The phone stand was a kilometer up the road next to the municipal hangout, and even at this hour several bare-chested men milled about, pinching tobacco out of a rusted jewelry box. The whole area smelled of late-stage banana and burnt rice.

It would be afternoon in America, and the woman he loved would be working her caseload, or she might be stopping for tea, a ritual she allowed herself no matter how busy the day. He had left her a letter and nothing more. *"Don't do anything stupid,"* she'd said, and he hadn't listened. Here he was now—on the island of his mistakes.

Her anger was quick to rise. Her tiny body, its lovely bones, her perfect red fists. She'd never struck him, though he imagined that's what she'd do when they next crossed paths. "Things change, Lucy," he said to no one in particular.

The men who passed the tobacco around gave him a look, and he thought that he didn't mean what he'd just said: *"Things change."* He didn't mean it in the slightest. He had been born on the eve of the greatest war, and if you took apart his mind you'd find a map from one continent to another, uncover new ways to describe hunger and the fear of the dark woods where he'd hounded out his eleventh year of life—but this much could be said: he didn't, for even a moment, believe *he'd changed.* He was still the same boy who could run faster than the whole village. So what if he had more scars? His history had surrounded him the way Stefa's quilts had warmed his shoulders, but he believed that none of it had made him a different man.

"Sorry to disturb you," Jaryk said to the men. He wouldn't try to call Lucy now; he doubted if she'd want him back.

....

When Jaryk awoke the next morning, he found the Pals' children beside his bed reading Misha's guidebook, a red glossary of Indian sightseeing, backpacker-style. Misha had written in Polish on nearly every page, and in the margins Jaryk had discovered a whole itinerary of desires. On the back cover Misha had planned a route from Shantiniketan to the hill station of Darjeeling, then back again to Shantiniketan, where they were to be honored guests in the performance of the play; but the morning of their flight, Jaryk hadn't shown up at the airport. His phone had rung a dozen times, but he'd remained in his apartment.

Surely, Misha had been furious, storming through the queues

with his wounded pride, eventually finding his seat, with the one next to him empty. He'd never been able to say no to Misha, but India—and time away from Lucy—had seemed out of the question.

Mrs. Pal had saved him the trouble of coping with an Indian breakfast. He was given a plate of toast and boiled eggs in silver cups.

"From the elder chickens," Mrs. Pal explained, pointing toward a shed in the back of the house.

As Mrs. Pal retreated into the kitchen, Mr. Pal greeted Jaryk and explained he'd risen early for his morning exercise. He said, "Yoga for the body is also yoga for the mind."

Jaryk showed him the guidebook's map of West Bengal, over which Misha had written "*Start Here*." "How far is it to Shantiniketan?"

"From here, by car, in the traffic of this country, which is as predictable as what Indira Gandhi will do next, I would say, excluding unusual obstructions and stops for sightseeing and so forths, it would be about five hours."

"Could I bike there?" Jaryk asked.

"As in bicycle? What on heaven for?"

"Even if it takes days, I'd prefer that." He'd experienced a moment of nostalgia remembering the old, rusty two-wheeler from his youth; what's more, being on bicycle would give him time to dwell on Misha's passing. He'd try to understand the weave of his life without his friend to guide him, maybe even understand something about Lucy, why he'd left the only woman he'd ever loved.

Mr. Pal seemed shocked by his line of reasoning, but he accommodated Jaryk, showing him a route that ran parallel to but still avoided the main thoroughfares. He drew stars next to hotels where Jaryk could spend the night, and they negotiated a price for Mr. Pal's own sturdy bicycle.

"The hotel owners are my friends," Mr. Pal said. "I will call for you in advance."

When Mrs. Pal discovered he'd be leaving them, and by cycle no less, she spoke to her husband in a stream of rapid Bengali. "This is madness," she then told Jaryk. "Consider yourself more carefully. Mr. Pal can arrange by car."

"Thank you for your hospitality," Jaryk said. "But I should get going."

The children watched solemnly as he tied Misha's suitcase onto the back of their father's bicycle. No one spoke as he checked the tire pressure and greased the chain with a bit of mustard oil. He felt buoyed by the promise of solitude and the journey that lay before him. He shook hands with Mr. Pal and mussed little Avik's hair.

"Remember one thing," Mr. Pal said. "Our people are basically nice except when they are not. Do your best to be kind. All the hotel owners will help you, and for the others, chances are good."

Mrs. Pal handed him lunch in an earthenware container. When Jaryk protested that he couldn't carry any more, she found a way to secure the container with the knot that held the suitcase in place.

"Goodbye," he said.

"God bless," the Pals said as one.

....

It felt like a kind of flying, the dawn and the house of the Pals behind him, the wind gusty at his back, the few morning cows inching out of his way. He pedaled furiously on the quiet dirt road. The suitcase, which at first had felt like an extraordinary burden, became weightless the faster he went. He passed the municipal dump with still-burning cigarettes in the slew of trash, passed the rice fields with their canals of rainwater, passed the few shanty huts that had survived yesterday's deluge, and then he found himself, once more, at the road to the city. He followed Mr. Pal's directions and turned right onto the Koshba bypass, a major thoroughfare he would need to remain on until he reached the less traveled village roads. At this hour, there was little traffic. In the middle of the road, a man pushed a two-wheeled vegetable cart with egg-plants balanced against squash and pyramids of cucumber. A column of scooters swerved their way past. By the side of the road, bamboo burned. The farmers in the fields paused, mid-motion, scythes raised, reins dropped, just to stare. At first he waved back, but it seemed nearly everyone, including the group of schoolboys who passed him one by one on bicycles, were intent on staring. He wished he had a hat. As he pedaled, the rice fields merged into suburban housing—rows of nondescript gray plots that reminded him of pictures he'd seen of postwar Polish developments.

Around seven thirty in the morning, less than an hour into his trip, the traffic picked up. Alongside taxis already full with passengers, buses entered the bypass. Rickshaws with garishly painted rears honked and sped. Pedestrians ran across the street. They were cursing at him, but he couldn't go faster. He'd already shifted to the side of the road, but no matter how little space he occupied the buses managed to squeeze right next to him, so that he could smell the breath of the passengers leaning their heads out of the windows to gawk, then the diesel in a plume of exhaust. It wasn't until a bus fendered with the words "MAKE NOISE" ran him off the road that he questioned his plan: jet-lagged, alone, equipped with no more language than what was in the back of the guidebook, and facing traffic like he'd never seen. But the nearest stop on the Pal itinerary was still an hour's ride away, so he angled his bicycle back onto the road and resumed his slow progress, pedaling so carefully he could've reached for the cups of tea being served at the kilometer markers.

It was almost nine o'clock when he neared the turnoff to Calcutta proper. He would need to cross through the Howrah neighborhood before heading north. It was a massive intersection with a concordance of Ambassador cars and rickshaws and motorcycles all elbowing for room. Perhaps, if he'd been in a taxi, he would have marveled at the chaos, but as it was, he could only do his best to avoid the zigzag of vehicles. One motorcycle began to tail him, honking. He looked back at the driver to say *"It's not my fault,"* but couldn't get the man's attention. In the middle of the intersection, a policeman in a white uniform stained with turmeric and pollution tried to direct the traffic, but the blowing of his whistle was little more than another noise.

The motorcycle behind Jaryk revved up and struck his rear wheel. He fell to the ground, a few feet short of an oncoming rickshaw. Misha's suitcase came loose along with Mrs. Pal's lunch—rice and lentils strewn across the concrete. It took him a moment to stand, and by then the motorcycle driver had fled the scene. Above the honking, people began to yell. He couldn't understand the words, but he thought it was about his predicament. When he touched his throbbing forehead, he came away with blood on his hand.

The policeman in the center of the intersection ran to him, waving his baton majestically, the whistle in his mouth producing unexpected volume. "Halt!" he was saying in English. "All halt!"

....

He was taken to the Calcutta Police Hospital. The cut above his eye was bandaged by four medical staff (one to hold the gauze, another to apply pressure to the wound, a third to place the bandage, and the last to supervise the whole endeavor). In a dark room that smelled of mold, the deputy chief of police offered him a cup of tea.

"So sorry," said the officer. "The traffic is poor because of the protests. The last of the Naxals, you know. There are still a few bad apples out on the streets."

Misha had spoken about these Naxals, named after the little village where all the trouble started. They were mostly boys in Calcutta and the surrounding villages who'd been rounded up in prisons. The root of the problem, Misha had said, was land and who had the right to own it. So far it'd been a shadow war fought by peasants with bows and arrows against SWAT teams with automatic weapons. *A few bad apples.* No government tolerated a brewing revolution for long.

Jaryk consented to sign a series of forms, after which he was rushed into what was called a "visitor's room." The room was equipped with only a latrine and a cot.

When he told the deputy that he was heading to Shantiniketan, the deputy had responded, "But a foreigner on a bicycle, in such a climate of government activity, could not possibly be heading in that direction. We simply have too many disturbing peoples out there. When you're well again and have secured proper transportation, we shall bid you goodbye."

He was left alone in the cell, where he now lay, feeling the effects of sleeplessness claw into his body, feeling the ache in his temples where he'd hit the concrete. A band of ants crawled toward a sugary piece of something in the near corner. There were no windows in the room, only a single fluorescent light that seemingly blinked at will. How had he ended up here—a prison in the heart of Calcutta—with nothing but an ugly green suitcase to keep him company?

He knocked on his door until an attendant came for him. "Could I speak to the deputy?" Jaryk asked. "I'm feeling fine. I'm ready to leave."

"Sorry, sir, but that is not permitted. The deputy, sir, has gone home for the day, but he has left instructions to keep you secure."

"Just let me know when the deputy is back," he said. "I'd like to be on my way soon."

The attendant left with a bow. Alone, Jaryk skimmed through a handful of pages in Misha's guidebook. Strange that the idea of India—all of Misha's planning, his joyous scribbling on pamphlets from the embassy and his one proper guidebook—had come upon them the same season as Lucy, her brilliant grip. It had felt then like a convergence of good things.

....

Over half a year ago Jaryk had first seen Misha's guidebook, but they hadn't spoken much about it then, because there was something else on his mind. For that something else, one early evening

in November, he arranged to meet Misha after work. At Fulton
Market, the last of the fish had been sold or sent to the freezer,
and groups of men were plunging their thick boots into the water
to release the day's smell. He followed Misha's lead and, shoeless,
toed the East River; it was cold, and he had to take his feet out
after a moment, though Misha kept his in. He winked at Jaryk and
asked in Polish, "Should we go swimming?"

They shared the sandwich Misha had saved from his lunch and
allowed the sun to wane. When the lights on the Empire State
Building came on, they dried their feet on burlap bags that served
as breakers and made their way to a nearby bar, Seven and a Half
Dimes, where a beer cost seventy-five cents and men of every rank
gathered to drink for cheap. Junior hands scooted out of the way
when Misha walked to his spot near the woodstove; a fire was
quickly kindled.

Jaryk knew the faces of many of the men Misha worked with.
When Jaryk was nineteen, Misha had found him his first job at
the market, running the slop buckets, collecting the entrails from
filleted fish and dumping them into a giant container, whose purpose was a mystery no one discussed. Afterwards, at the bar, they
would drink one or two beers, and Misha would speak about the
biggest fish they'd carted in that day—once, a marlin that weighed
over two hundred pounds, and another time a tuna so plump it
sold for a limb and a half. When it was just the two of them, they
could speak Polish, but tonight Jaryk kept quiet.

Rebecca, the owner's daughter, collected their empty glasses.
"You'll have another, won't you?"

Without waiting for an answer, she left and returned with
another round on the house. After handing Jaryk his beer, she
pinched his cheek. He flushed at the touch, but when Rebecca
winked at him, he didn't take the bait. Another time, he might
have left Misha for an hour. Walked down into the basement to
engage in half an hour of fierce play with Rebecca, who, a decade
older than him, was still equipped with a remarkable figure and

an astonishing libido. Afterwards, he'd check the books. Rebecca feared her wealth would be lost suddenly, so she gave him the post-coital duty of making sure the ones and zeros were well aligned. Soon, he would have to tell Rebecca that the basement was forbidden for him—at least, for half of its pursuits.

"You've had the look on you the last hour," Misha said. "Something about the job? They not treating you right?" Misha flexed his hands in front of his face. He wasn't even fifty years old but had already developed the first signs of arthritis in his fingers and wrists. In this country, he'd always worked the wharves, everything from cleaning the docks to helping hoist giant octopi onto weigh scales. Once, a fish hook had gotten lodged in the middle of his palm, and it had taken a doctor eighteen stitches to sew the wound, but he'd come back to work the next day, doing everything he needed to with one good hand.

"Remember when you told me to get married," Jaryk said. "We were sitting right here." Months had passed since that conversation. He wasn't sure how much Misha remembered of that night. It had been the week leading up to the Fourth of July, and the crowd at Seven and a Half Dimes was thin. Someone had put Celtic music on the jukebox, and several Irishmen step-danced around the tables. Earl Minton, who ran inspections at the fish market and who was to be married the next day, was hoisted up on a chair and carried around as if he were a bag of bait. At first Earl encouraged the attention by yelping in his highest register, but the jostling caught up to him, and thick into the night he looked seasick; when the men wouldn't keep their hands off him, it was Misha who glowered over them until they sloughed away, Misha who found Earl's coat and put it back over his shoulders. After that, though, Misha went from beer to whiskey to rum. Gifts mostly from the regulars who loved him, but still. Too often, Misha would mix his booze and leave himself slurring and dangerous. Jaryk had to take him home.

At the doorstep, Misha had clubbed Jaryk lightly on the chin and said, "I want you to find a nice woman, and I want you to have a family. Two fat boys. Will you do that for me?" Jaryk rubbed his chin and helped Misha up the stairs, but he took Misha's words seriously—he always had. The steadiest girl in Misha's life had lasted only six months. Ann Lazar, who despite her genteel name, had enough steel in her to skin a chicken with her bare hands. She kept Misha right for months, but Misha's head was never right for love. If either Jaryk or Misha were to start a family—and every day their chances were dimming—Jaryk would have to be the one to do it. There were stories Misha wanted to pass on. All that wisdom from Pan Doktor. That was what he was asking of Jaryk.

Now at the bar, Misha pulled at his beard and gazed into the distance. Finally he turned to Jaryk and asked, "Let the cat out of the bag already. Is she a looker?"

"It's serious," Jaryk said. "I want you to meet her."

Misha whistled under his breath. He made his eyes as large as the mouth of his beer glass, sticking his nose close to Jaryk's face. "Well, it's about time."

Jaryk worked at a synagogue on Seventy-Second Street and Amsterdam, keeping the books. Nearing his twenty-fifth birthday, having tired of work at the fish market, he'd answered an ad in the paper for a bookkeeper. Since he enjoyed doing sums, counting change, and weighing portions of fish, he felt qualified for the job.

The rabbi had interviewed him by presenting three mathematical challenges. He still remembered the final question involved figuring the number of angels who could stand on top of a wedding cake that had a radius of two and a quarter feet. "How small are the angels?" Jaryk had asked, and then computed the measurements so that they could all fit snugly atop the icing.

The morning after Jaryk told Misha about Lucy, he gave himself a task. The synagogue was over a hundred years old and had endured the tenures of two Kabbalistic rabbis who did not care about its upkeep. The current rabbi, Samuel, had said on the last Shabbat, "It can be dark in here," and while he'd meant it in the context of religious light—the kind you had to persistently cultivate, as if faith were a difficult plant—Jaryk had understood it more plainly. The grand chandelier had burned its last bulb, and the congregation relied on a series of steel-toed lamps that had been placed between the rows like vigilant soldiers.

Long ago, someone had climbed the twenty feet and replaced each old bulb with a new, but in the many years he'd worked here—fourteen, to be exact, the rhythm of time passing through a succession of holidays—he'd never wanted to make the effort to do it till now. He went down to the basement, where they kept odds and ends from over the years, and found a ladder and a box of replacement bulbs, which he tied to his belt. He put on his sunglasses to withstand the brightness. Slowly, he climbed all the way up, the bulbs tinkling like small jewels.

When all the bulbs had been replaced, he returned to the pews with aching shoulders. In the strange brightness, he could see the dust his feet had released, but it seemed beautiful, the candor of that room, with the five books of Moses in every row; and the bimah, the fray of the wood where the rabbi rested his elbows and spoke of God—that, too, had its splendor.

All their years in New York, Misha had never entered the synagogue. Were it not for the paying job, Jaryk, too, might have stayed away, but he felt in this chamber, now brightly lit, that he was grateful for his life. He prayed for the first time since he'd been a child, the words out of his mouth difficult yet familiar: for what was to come with Misha and with Lucy—that they would all know equal happiness, neither too much nor too little of life's ordinary pleasures.

....

A few days later, after he'd finished at the synagogue, Jaryk met Misha at Seven and a Half Dimes to play pool. Two of the pool table's corners were creased enough to impose their own physics to the game. Newcomers at the bar were often confounded by the way balls spun near the pockets, but on this table Jaryk could make a shot from just about any angle, which meant that the few times he'd played pool on a proper setup, he'd mishit more often than not. It didn't matter that Misha had played on this surface as much as he had—Misha treated the cue ball as if it needed a good, solid whacking, and it was not uncommon to see his shots engage a crease and volley onto the barroom floor, rolling between legs of tottering patrons and scores of abandoned peanut shells, leaving it to Jaryk to find and retrieve.

But Misha was never a sore loser. He was always a few points behind Jaryk, but he didn't mind. He'd once announced, "It's okay to lose to your friends," and Jaryk, guilty of being the one with the perennially better aim, had felt relieved of a burden.

He'd been bringing up the matter of Lucy in small doses. Despite what Lucy believed, he'd been preparing Misha for months. At first, he just introduced the idea of her, a *something serious*. Then he talked about her place of employment. "So she listens to people complain all day?" Misha had said incredulously. Afterwards, he talked about her father, whom he had a fear of meeting, an army man from the South.

"She told her father about you? A forty-year-old Jew?"

He didn't think she had. But then, he'd been telling Misha about Lucy regularly; maybe, she'd done the same with her father.

Misha hit the cue ball into the eight ball and both nearly tumbled into the same pocket. Jaryk didn't take the next shot, though he had a clear view of a strike that would likely end the game. "Will you meet Lucy for dinner?" he asked.

"Will she like our food?" Misha asked, earnestly. "Can she hold her liquor?"

....

They walked along the water, around which the financial district was tucked like an errant elbow. The cold had come early, and the East River was besieged by an early freeze, a thin skein of ice that wouldn't hold the weight of a boot. But they had an affinity for the cold, walking in the early frost with a liminal sense of pride. The cold made them remember the cobbled and unhurried streets of their youth, where for much of the winter the stones were buried in snow.

They headed to the *Dockside Players Field*, where men from the wharves played roundup baseball year-round at a park the city had left to wither. The bleachers they'd built by hand were covered by snow, but the men had shoveled the field clean, exposing much-maligned sections of summer-planted grass. The dozen or so players on the field now were operating with an efficiency brought on by the cold.

There were rapid-fire volleys of chatter between catcher and pitcher, a musical banter Jaryk had long since learned to ignore. Where in professional leagues, the same conversation would have been had through a series of hand signals, on the *Dockside Players Field* it was paraded in the open. *Ninety-five west, lone man deep, fire in the hole!*—odd, made-up phrases that signified a constantly shifting vocabulary of pitches.

Jaryk understood the game reasonably well, though he was sure both he and Misha missed some of the intricacies, but that didn't matter—not now in the middle of an autumn that already felt like winter, watching his old coworkers run gregariously in thick jackets from one leather stump to another—nor had it mattered in the summers they'd shared here, when the grass had been tended green not by the city but by players who loved the sport too much to let their field wither. Jaryk imagined bringing Lucy. He could see her easily bored by the pace of the game. He could see her wandering from the bleachers to the hut that served as a concession stand to coax stories from the old bruisers who tended bar. In minutes she'd likely charm one of Misha's old friends to tell her his whole life's story. He'd seen that before, how she'd get people talking about their oldest wounds.

"You in, old man?" one of the men called out to Misha. A terrible batsman, Misha was more beloved for his sense of humor on the field (and his propensity for half-Polish, half-English curses) than for his athletic prowess.

"I've got a lecture to go to," Misha said.

"Fancy, you. Well, what about the Flash?" the same man asked.

Jaryk's nickname on the field had been earned after he proved how fast he could run the bases. It was a skill he'd cultivated many years ago, when the whole orphanage had gone to a summer camp on the outskirts of Warsaw and Misha had taken him under his wing, had trained him to outsprint the other boys.

Jaryk said he'd be game another time, and they walked toward West Street. Across the water, smoke rose from the mouths of shoe factories. A tabby cat stopped to smell Jaryk's boot, then darted away. They squatted at the edge of an abandoned pier and listened. Fish were preparing for the winter. A trident of seagulls skimmed low just above the water, then flew away. Behind them they heard, then saw, a drunk zigzag his way down toward the pier, and they gave him space. More and more in the city you had to look out for danger. Everyone knew someone who'd gotten mugged or worse. It hadn't happened to them, and sometimes Jaryk thought it was because the lowlifes could smell all the rot he and Misha had lived through.

"I know you won't come to the lecture, but aren't you at least curious what it's about?" Misha asked.

"I'm dying to know," Jaryk said with a grim smile.

"It's called '*Art in the Ghettos.*' All the ways our people made poems or songs. Who knows, maybe they'll even talk about our play."

Misha saw the ghetto as history they should never forget and the art they'd made there as something that mattered. He liked to talk about Avrom Sutzkever of the Vilna Ghetto, who'd once composed a poem hiding in a coffin—that somehow poetry helped him survive. Misha was always looking for meaning, and he'd developed an appetite for history. In the sallow light of Seven and a Half Dimes, Misha would recount what he'd learned about the migration of the Sephardic peoples, about Sandy Koufax's roots, about the Gershwins, and Jaryk would listen, thinking it was not art that had saved Sutzkever but endurance and luck.

"I'll drop you at your place first," Misha said. "It's been a while since I've seen how you princes live."

In the two years he'd lived on the Lower East Side, Misha had come to his place only a handful of times. Landing this fifth-floor walkup on Orchard and Broome—a swamp in the summer and a drafty cell in the winter—had helped him feel like he'd finally become an adult. Before, he and Misha had always lived together: in Poland, when they were wards of Pan Doktor's orphanage, and then in New York, in a series of crammed buildings in Brighton Beach, where English was hardly ever spoken. He didn't miss it. All those friends of Misha's who'd crash into their apartment at all hours, stink up the place with cheap booze and stories from the old country.

Now, Misha inspected Jaryk's apartment, the room that was living room plus kitchen, and pronounced, "Something changed." It wasn't obvious—Lucy hadn't started to leave her things—but he supposed there was a neatness to the place: back issues of *Life* piled, not strewn; the kitchenette table sanded and polished; the torn bedspread replaced with a new one that was just as plain blue. That he had not objected to the rearrangements was more a testament to Lucy's care than to his flexibility. What Lucy had altered, she'd done in fine stages and in partnership; for Jaryk, who did not enjoy domestic turbulence, even the loss of an old bedsheet had felt at first like bereavement but then, ultimately, in ways he did not yet understand, like an immense liberation.

Lucy was out with her coworkers; she'd said she was a fifty-fifty for coming over if it didn't get too late. But he didn't mind if it did get late. Chopin was playing on WQXR. The station's programing would go until midnight (finishing with Mozart and *A Little Night Music*), at which time he'd turn the dial to static, read a few of his prized Tagore poems, and then fall asleep to the sound of the almost-ocean. To catch the station properly and listen to any of his favorite Romantic composers, he had to place the radio near the doorway, which meant he had to bring his chair into the hall; he'd grown accustomed to sitting in that sloping, narrow hallway, listening to sonatas, though when Lucy came, it interrupted the evening schedule—pleasantly. When he opened his fridge, he found evidence that his bachelorhood was diminishing: a head of lettuce, carrots Lucy had peeled and sliced, a few boiled eggs for the week, and what was left of the turkey they'd roasted the night before. Before Lucy, the fridge sat mostly unused; he would eat at Misha's or stop at a deli on the way home.

"It is she, isn't it?"

Jaryk nodded. They pushed the bed aside and climbed onto the fire escape through the window. Jaryk's Ukrainian landlord was smoking on the balcony, her sizable girth pinioned between the grilles of the railing. She met Misha's grin with a disapproving glare and retreated inside. From the fifth floor, the city below felt emptied of its worries; a kind of translucence had come over the night.

"I need to tell you about our plans," Misha said.

"Our plans?"

"Yes, but first I want you to meet this professor. I'm bringing him out to the bar tomorrow. Be there," Misha said.

Jaryk didn't think much about the conversation, but the next day, as he entered Seven and a Half Dimes, he found Misha seated in their regular corner with someone he didn't recognize.

"Meet my friend from India," Misha said in English, as he pushed a pint of beer Jaryk's way.

Misha's new friend wasn't a regular at the bar. He was entirely too well dressed, in a sharp red blazer. Plus, he was an Indian man in a pub where everyone came from the same few parts of the world, and he was smiling in a way that said he didn't belong. Here patrons smiled only when they were buzzed and laughed only when they were drunk. There were exceptions to this rule, of course. You could laugh for a particularly good story. You could smile with teeth to greet an old friend. But it was too early to be drunk, and no one was shouting a good story.

Misha's new friend continued to beam at Jaryk. "I'm Professor Rudra Bose," he said. "I came to know Misha through the JCC lectures. I'm spending the semester at Columbia."

"So, I was at the lecture," Misha said. "'Art in the Ghettos, 1940–1942: Szpilman, Szlengel, Sutzkever.'"

Whenever Misha talked about that time in their lives, Jaryk could feel his pulse quicken. Sometimes, a low-grade nausea would come and stay for hours after. His body remembered even when he wished to forget, and this was a terrible fact—how memory had mapped itself onto his bones. When they'd first lived together in Brooklyn, Jaryk tried to convince Misha never to talk about their time in the orphanage, but Misha wasn't deterred. Jaryk's best recourse had been silence. Eventually, Misha would move on—he always had.

"Afterwards, this skinny Indian guy proposes to me."

The way Misha spoke reminded him of the difference in their ages. Just ten years apart, but it had meant that when they arrived in New York together, Jaryk would learn English well enough to carry just a hint of a faraway accent, whereas Misha would struggle to master the spoken language, his phrases sounding stilted more often than not. The oddness of the way Misha had spoken—the idea of one man proposing to another—had distracted Jaryk, but the professor didn't seem to notice.

"When I learned that Misha and you had been in the play that I'm producing, I had the revelation of my life."

Misha held up a flyer that said: *Commemoration of the Staging of Tagore's The Post Office in Warsaw Ghetto, Thirty Years On. Presented by Visva-Bharati University, Shantiniketan.* "And he wants us to come. You and me in India."

"I'll have another," Jaryk called to Rebecca.

"Don't order me around," she said, taking her time to refill his glass.

He wasn't looking at her, though. He was studying the professor, whose left eye was twitching as if there were a speck of dust in it.

"So, what do you think?" Misha asked. "You and me and the play in India?"

Performing *The Post Office* in Warsaw had been a pivotal moment of his childhood. Trying to remember the performance now, he felt weightless, as if the bar that contained them was ready to crumble from all the years of wear and snow, all the bodies it had soothed with drink, though when he looked at Misha, his large, nocturnal eyes blinking with the fullness of his curiosity, he felt again the wood of his seat hard under him and saw still-newly-married Earl Minton flirt with a girl out of his league.

"Did you ever wonder why Pan Doktor had us perform that play, Jaryk?"

He wished Misha would stop talking about the play. His hands were getting cold, though enough customers had crowded into the bar to make it feel like there was a second furnace.

"Come on," Misha pressed. "If we didn't have the play to pass time, what do you think we would have done besides complain about how hungry we were? Anyway, it was the only way Pan Doktor knew to teach us about how a person should die, how dying could be something we didn't have to fear. We were going to the land of the King, he said. We could stay who we were until the end and even after that, we could still be boys and girls. Not Jews, not poor people, not hungry people, just people."

The land of the King. He still remembered how Pan Doktor would talk about the afterlife like it was a paradise of culinary delights. Cream cakes, toffees, mandarins dipped in honey. Not even a line for bread.

He licked the inside of his beer glass, an old habit, and looked around for Rebecca. She wasn't anywhere to be found, but the professor was still there, watching them as if they were specimens in his lab. At least his eye had stopped twitching.

"Why go to all the trouble, Professor? I bet there are people who know the play inside out where you come from."

"Oh, there are plenty of Tagore scholars," the professor said. "In fact, I'm one of them. That's not what I'm lacking. What I need are men who lived through the disease we're living now."

"C'mon, brother, I know you read the papers," Misha said.

He tried to jog his memory. Not so long ago he'd read something about Communists trying to stage a revolution in a village in India. Was that right? He remembered reading about how the villagers carried bows and arrows to meet police armed with rifles and grenades. "Are you a Communist?" he asked the professor. In truth, he'd no issue with the philosophy.

"I used to run laps with Mao in my pocket," the professor said. "Not anymore, though. I don't care for all that austerity, all that railing against the finer things in life. I like my down pillows and my old, beautiful records. That's not the problem. The problem is that in my home state young men are disappearing. The problem is that police are shooting protestors at public rallies. I can't tell you how many students I've taught who've ended up in jail, or worse. And there is this little village I've come to love. It's rather idyllic, except for the fact that mercenaries are trying to take it away from the poor peoples who crossed over the border, searching for a new place to live."

"We can help," Misha said. "The play meant so much to us. Finally, we can pass that on."

What did Jaryk know of persecuted youth in India or villagers evicted from their land? Once, in the Polish countryside, he'd walked across a field to scrounge for roots, only to discover that he was crossing over a large, unmarked grave, that all around him were belongings men, women, and children had left before they'd been shoveled into the earth. A doll the size of his hand, a man's pocket brush, a lady's leather boots. He'd been alone then. There'd been no Misha to tell him which way to run.

This time, Rebecca filled his glass without his asking. Maybe she could see he'd fallen into a bind.

"Well, what do you think?" the professor asked.

"I think India is the other side of the world," he said after a pause.

"And they sleep on snakes," Misha said, and laughed. His full-bodied laugh made their table shake.

The professor joined in. "I'll bring you pictures of our village. There are deer, but very few snakes. Of that, I promise."

....

Misha had nurtured the dream of India as he had tenured the vision of their lives in New York. Even as Jaryk resisted the professor's invitation, Misha had cultivated the project, making visa and passport appointments, writing letters, and arranging their itineraries. But these last few months, Jaryk had seen less of Misha than he'd ever had. He'd been with Lucy—that had been where his time had gone.

Now Jaryk was in India, stuck in a cell with a bandage on his forehead and without a plan. An attendant knocked on his door to deliver a plate of food, and he realized it was already evening, but he wasn't hungry. Maybe he was ignoring something. Perhaps the effort of keeping both Misha and Lucy away from his thoughts had subsumed his simple wants: a meal at mealtime, or a proper bed. He allowed himself to return to one moment with Lucy, so small he doubted if she still remembered it. It'd happened in the modest glory of an autumn day, half of the leaves spent, the other half abiding still in the wind, the time in their relationship when he hadn't yet exhausted his best clothes, outfits he'd purchased at a yearly pace, only to let them sit in sleeves of plastic for lack of having any occasion to wear them. They were walking downtown along Broadway just before sunset when Lucy stopped in front of the garden at Trinity Church, where a slanting pine sheltered rose-bushes and honeysuckle was the only weed. A fence the height of Jaryk's chest protected the garden. "Lift me up," she said.

Before he could refuse her, Lucy had climbed the fence herself, navigating with ease the problem of her skirt and the sharp ends of the gate. They sat on a bench past dark, his head resting on hers, consuming her smell. Her mint-sweet breath, which even then he had understood was her way of covering a vestigial habit. He had just asked her to do a difficult thing. "Quit smoking," he'd said, and would have added, "for me," if he'd had the gall, and she almost had. It felt grand: the fear that came with love, the immense sway it provided over another human being.

He missed her, yet he didn't allow himself to miss her. *His first duty,* he'd told himself, *was to Misha.* Sometimes she would come to him like a sharp pain, a hook in the eye. But now he'd failed Misha, abandoned him to his end. How could he not return to find his friend's ashes, the last of his things?

Jaryk wondered what Lucy was doing without him. It had been a gamble leaving her. Were they even a couple anymore? He couldn't be sure. Every day they'd been together, for a year, it felt like she chose him anew. What they'd built was strong; but with a woman who made a daily choice, who could be sure? How many times had he thought of her? How many had she thought of him?

When the attendant came to take his dinner away, Jaryk told him, "I'd like to make a phone call, please." The attendant looked at him blankly, before running out of the room and returning with a quadrangle of eager policemen.

He repeated his request. "A phone call. International."

The youngest of the policemen translated for the others, then rephrased his request. "You are requiring the use of the phone. This is permitted."

It was with a phone call that he'd learned of Misha's death:

"So sorry . . . Massive heart attack this morning . . . You must come straightaway."

He'd heard it all mutely and finally said, "Hold on, I'm coming for his remains."

Now the policemen led him to the hospital's main switchboard, where the formal dispositions of the British were preserved, with orderly rows of middle-aged women punching codes into a machine that blinked and dialed, with the supervising men in the corner drinking tea from gently stained porcelain cups. After a few rounds of translation, he was given a line to America.

It would be early morning in New York. He imagined her in her bed, for once letting the noise of the city keep her up; she would be wearing her faded blue pajamas and one of his flannel shirts. He regretted what he had done, first having let Misha go to India alone; now, with Lucy, he'd left her without a goodbye.

"Hi, you've reached the Gardner residence. Please leave a message."

Her answering machine with his voice greeted him. It was her idea. She'd wanted his voice, at the lowest octave, to repel the city's freaks. He found himself jarred by his echo, the seriousness of his own voice. What could he say?

I want you to come . . . I want you to come be with me . . . be with me, here

But he could not bring himself to say any of these words, to ask her to interrupt her life for him. He held the receiver until a policeman told him that the line had gone dead.

"Fine," he said, allowing himself to be led back to his room. It wouldn't strike him till later that maybe this had been his last chance.

Pan Doktor's March

Sometimes Pan Doktor believed it was better to pretend it was all a story, that what happened to them—what was happening, each day—was better suited to the plot of a play that given enough time would turn toward redemption. In the latter acts the stale bread would turn into freshly baked cake, the black boots of the Germans would become roller skates, and all the walls that had been built would fall as quickly as a curtain falls after the final bow. Then he would cry unabashedly, dirtying his glasses with tears.

There's a part of him that still refuses to believe that this day begins the last chapter for all who've emerged from the orphanage into the August light, which slopes over the roof of their house, shines on the soot that silts the path, falls into the eyes of the little boy who holds his arm and squints at the onlookers. Everyone who's left of the neighborhood is out to witness their march. He passes the flag of King Matt the First, Pan Doktor's patron saint of children, up to the front of his procession, and together they all walk. Someone starts a song.

Only a few months before, he was meeting friends at a secret university. There's a philosopher in their midst who's convinced him of the way the world works. Everything you do in life is a kind of moral choice, says the philosopher. Waking up in the morning, deciding whether or not to brush your teeth, how many sips of vodka you have at night. How they walk to the cattle cars is also a choice, he decides. They've trained for this as they've rehearsed the lines of their theater. He had thought that his fame earned from his old radio show and the books he'd written would give them cover. He had believed the Germans would not come for a house of children, would take everyone but them. The problem with a moral choice is that it is never in isolation, always made surrounded by multitudes, he's told the philosopher, and what if the multitudes win—what choice then remains?

He leads two hundred children the morning of August 6th, 1942. They sing a song, but he focuses on walking without a limp, his bum knee struggling against him with each step, and nods at the Jewish policeman who nods back at him, stone-faced. One little boy holds his hand, and that is enough. To live with any sense of fullness you must be willing to bewilder yourself, embrace the confusion of a world that is always falling away from you, a little at a time. That, finally, is his contribution to the secret university: a little bewilderment can go a long way.

(Sometimes when he looked into the mirror he saw the great fire, other times just a little smoke. Sometimes when he tried to make peace with his heart he'd cry uncle—was there something else he could've said or done, some pleading by which they could've all been saved?

No, it was best to think of everything that happened to them as part of someone else's theater, even that play they built together—a play within a play. These were the games to cheat the Germans. You just had to convince the old Samaritans, like Igor, that this was how the world worked. Just a few weeks before when Igor had been trying to persuade him to flee—)

IGOR NEWERLY: There's no room for poetry when you're marching for death. I told you to leave when you had the chance.

PAN DOKTOR: You do not leave a sick child in the night . . .

IGOR NEWERLY: . . . and therefore you do not leave them now. It is by being together they can be less afraid. I know. I know all this. And yet, I was hoping for a better ending.

PAN DOKTOR: Who said this was an ending? Even the moon is

falling out of our orbit, a little at a time. Even the moon is
heading toward its own recompense. Now, see them salute
us. See them all rise as the children walk down Grzybowski.
Even the rain will stop for us now. No one can take away
that we walked together, that we were family till the end.

IGOR NEWERLY: You would've had oranges and pies with
cherries and meat every night had you listened to my words.
Now look at how the dust rises. Not even the rain will save
your soul, and if anyone escapes this horrid day, they will be
marked for all their lives.

Sixty Miles East

Sometimes Jaryk relived a day in his childhood he kept under lock and key. *Umschlagplatz*, which meant, as he'd been told, *a collection point*, the town square with thousands packed into too little space, awaiting the trains. For them it was to be a train with one hundred ninety-two children. The officers had counted, and so had Jaryk. In the three years he'd been at the orphanage, he'd learned not only how to count but also how to multiply and even divide larger and larger numbers. It was a good way to pass the time, to not think of the hunger, which would spread like a sneeze from child to child. Sometimes, everyone's stomach grumbled at once, but today their stomachs were quiet.

It was not far. They had all heard the word. Chaim had etched it on the wood in the hall, and each of the boys had taken a turn to see: *Treblinka*. The day before, Madam Stefa had made sure they were each washed in the big cauldron—what if the tub smelled a little foul from all the children before, and there was no soap, no soap for months, so they were cleaned behind their ears with dishwater and lye?

The guards were giving out bread and jelly, and Jaryk reached with his fingers, his lips, his toes, but there were so many wanting, so many pushing, that his feet went ahead of themselves and he fell into the cattle car. In the shadows he thought he saw Old Dog, the mastiff, its large eyes sniffing the world.

One cattle car. So many bodies, worming. One murmured. "My hat," the voice said. "I left it behind."

The doors squeezed shut made the dark so tight not a sound was left unheard.

"What was it like, your hat?" Was it Mordechai speaking?

"Felt, soft, perfect shape of my head."

Not a wheel moved. For a while not a wheel. Then when the train started they covered their ears, so shrill was the sound. He thought it was like an animal who'd awoken from the core of the earth.

With the third whistle, a guard opened the door a crack, pressed his body to the entrance. The light coming through left a shadow the shape of his leg. Still, it illumined. Jaryk swallowed.

Once the train started moving, Madam Stefa began to sew. Six gathered around to watch. He was there when Hanna said, "What is it?"

Madam Stefa turned her face up. This was the incredible thing: she winked. Where had he seen her wink like that? He couldn't remember, but it had something to do with a mischief only the two of them knew about. Was it soup? Spilled soup, that was it.

Hanna tugged at Stefa's dress. "Show me, please."

There was nothing to show: she had raised her needle so many times, but there wasn't a stitch on the white cloth. He stared as her wrist rose and fell again, but every time he thought she would leave a mark she would instead double back and undo the thread. It made him so happy, the blankness—he could see anything he wanted to in that cloth: his life before the orphans, Old Dog, the mastiff, stopping by a stream, with a squirrel kicking in his mouth.

"Children, gather around," Pan Doktor said.

Where was there to move? Some nudged. He tried to square a look at Pan Doktor's face, but the older boys were standing so he couldn't. All he had was the sound of the old man's voice.

"I have a story to tell."

He was relieved to hear their teacher sounded the same. When you listened to Pan Doktor, you weren't sure if he was about to give you something serious, because the way he spoke, he might also be about to tell you a good joke, so you always had to be prepared for either a frown or a laugh.

"Can you all hear me?" Pan Doktor said.

"Yes," they said. The black boot by the door turned his neck, looked outside.

"You have to close your eyes," Pan Doktor said. "This is a meditation. Have you all closed your eyes? Pinhas, I see you with your eyes open.

"Now, children, imagine you are in a bright white room. There's nothing in the room but you. It's a wide white room. You are walking to the edge, where you think there is a door. It's a wide white room, and you walk. You walk awhile, and you begin to hear pleasant music, the kind your mothers sang when you couldn't sleep, and because you like this music, you keep walking. Then you see a boy, waiting there for you."

"Who is it, Pan Doktor?"

"It's Amal from the play. He's been waiting, and he wants you to put all your worries into a little bag—do you see the bag that just came into your hands? So, one by one, take a worry you have, put it in this bag, and when it's full, pass it to Amal."

"What will he do with the bag?"

"Ah, Mordechai, what will he do with the bag? He'll keep it, of course, and, from time to time, he'll dump out the worries from heaven, which will make—"

"Thunder!"

"Lightning!"

"Yes," Pan Doktor said. "Lots of rain."

From the next car, they began to hear the weeping of men. The last time he had heard a grown person cry was the holy afternoon of Yom Kippur, when he'd seen a man in a fine wool suit beat his chest in the middle of Grzybowski Square, saying over and over, "We have stolen, and we have taken."

A passerby had laughed. "What have you taken?"

The man opened his eyes. He said, "The sun, of course."

It was true. That day it was only the clouds.

The train hummed an efficient rhythm. Perhaps fifty of them in that one car alone. The older ones stood, the younger ones sat on laps. Not a breeze, only the smell of sweat and piss, the floor slick with it. A few boys climbed on top of each other to look out a window that was covered by two rusty bars.

"Pan Doktor," Jaryk said, pushing his way to his teacher. "Where is Misha?"

"I sent him off on a little errand. There was a rumor of an apple tree. I sent him to find this apple tree, to collect and bring back apples from the apple tree. The goal is to make a pie."

"An apple tree, in our Warsaw?"

"Of course. There is still an apple tree somewhere in our city, and if anyone can find it, it's our Misha."

"Maybe it's a small tree?"

"Tiny," Pan Doktor said.

He imagined Misha combing the alleyways on his belly, turning up rubble and leaf to look for the smallest tree in the world, searching for the husks, the cores, the stem, and the fruit.

One and two jerks, Chaim rolled onto his lap—kicked—then the train stopped again.

"Here?" someone shouted.

He knew—they knew—they were far from reaching *there*, so no one bothered to answer. The talk had shortened. Only the necessary sounds now. Whatever kept the spit in throat, so thirsty on the bridge between. To swallow was the most important.

He looked over at Pan Doktor. Ever since he'd come back from Pawiak Prison, arrested for the crime of failing to wear an armband with the Star of David, the old man walked slower, talked slower. Everyone had made room so Pan Doktor could stretch out his knee. The old man caught Jaryk's eye and grinned. Then he stood up, took off his armband and tossed it out the window.

"Good riddance," Pan Doktor said. Jewish Star, unannounced, caught the wind blowing through the eaves and fell through the car cracks and into who knew what town, what field, to settle on the legs of, who knew, maybe a moo cow, just as the milking man came to knock the new grass down.

....

There were two windows on that train. One was covered by two bars, and the other, next to Madam Stefa, was open. They were both just big enough for a cat to crawl through, so it didn't matter that one had been left bared.

....

Sometime between living and dying the train again stopped. It was the moment Jaryk remembered more than any other. Thirty years, he hadn't grown himself another version. Some memories were like that, bolted and nailed to the mind's eye. You could try to change them, shape them into something they weren't, but you would always be the boy with trousers that reached his ankles, the boy with a tweed cap found by Misha and given special; and the train was stopped now, who knows whether for a moment or for a longer time, and the guards were shouting now, because, he thought, someone ahead had jumped. He was holding Chaim's hand—who he knew didn't have the heart to move an inch—and the heat had already burned and he had already cried and Pan Doktor could do nothing because he was just breathing.

He thought, *Jump*, but the rifles had colored the air outside with smoke. Still, he could see it: the window was big enough not only for a cat but also for him, if only he jumped and squeezed through. Except the train had started to move again; the screams had died down. The soldiers had stopped firing. He looked at Pan Doktor, and Pan Doktor winked the way he did whenever a mischief had been made but no one was going to be told, because love was that kind of secret-keeping.

The train had started moving again, but he saw the sun through the window that was big enough just for him, and what spirit launched his body, what ghost slid him forward, because it was not his nine-year-old bones that did. Still, it happened. He jumped on Chaim's shoulders. He pulled himself up. He went headfirst, and someone—he'd never know who—pushed his body through the gap.

He landed so softly on the sloping hill and rolled so quietly down the field filled with sharp rocks, holding his pain, that no soldier heard. For a while, he watched the train pass, expecting others to have followed, but no one else did. Not another soul had jumped on another boy's shoulders and been pushed into the fields. Was he simply the skinniest, the fastest, or just the most daring of them in that car—the one most willing to leave the others?

Now he was alone again in the field of damp and moss. He heard water nearby, and he thought of Pan Doktor's face. So much hope. His knees bloody with it. His left wrist bruised dark. So much hope in the wet grass under his palms that when the train gnarled away, the old trees called and he crawled his way from the light of the sun into the light of the trees.

....

Sometime between living and dying the train stopped. It was the moment he remembered more than any other. Thirty years, he hadn't grown himself another version. He heard the first gunshot, saw the two officers turn away, rushed to Pan Doktor's side, who was breathing so heavily his whole chest heaved with the effort.

Jaryk pointed to the window, whispered, "We can squeeze through that."

Pan Doktor said, "Not all of us can."

He looked again. Not the darkness but the light of the waiting. He couldn't tell if Pan Doktor would be afraid. Still, it happened. With one held breath, he jumped on Chaim's shoulders and squeezed through. He landed so softly on the sloping hill and rolled so quietly down the field filled with sharp rocks, holding his pain, that no one heard.

....

Sometime between living and dying. It was the moment. Thirty years, he hadn't grown himself another. Some memories were like that, as stiff as Madam Stefa, who refused to sit the whole time. She stood; she guarded the window. On the back of the first gunshot, he bolted, but her legs were like a guillotine—how could he pass through? "If we all don't go, you don't go," she said, as if he should've known.

He remained by her knees. To love your brother. But he had not stolen. He had not thieved.

....

Sometime between living dying it was the moment thirty years he hadn't when Pan Doktor removed his spectacles and lolled, "Not all of us can, but you can." Pan Doktor was the one who lifted him up, and Jaryk squeezed through the back of the first gunshot crawled his way from the light of the sun into the light of the trees his knees bloody with the memory of his old teacher with no spectacles winking at that too-bright light. For he had been chosen—he had been reborn.

The Broken Train

NEW YORK—1971

Lucy Gardner spent her days listening to stories. When she'd first started at the city employment agency, she thought she was meant to match qualified candidates with good jobs, but there were never enough jobs to go around—the few that showed up disappeared from the register so quickly she began to think of them as brief points of light that did little but float false hope for the growing line of the newly unemployed and the regularly unemployed, to whom she attributed that particular listless walk, the casual shuffle that said *"I don't care"* and the lowered head that said otherwise. In the end, her work came down to deep listening, and for this she was willing and suited, so much so that she earned a small following.

The regulars made a habit of it. After a few weeks of searching for a job without luck, they would tell her their best life story and their next-best. They were mostly men. It became her duty to see them through the day, the week, the whole New York winter. *"You have a friend in me,"* she'd say, and off they'd go, one confession after another.

Her coworker Miles Norton kept a plaque at his desk that said *"A Decade of Honest Service,"* signed by Mayor Lindsay himself. He gave folks a sober dose, rehearsed and polished over the years. He pruned down the dreams of the new ones and flattened the regulars whenever he said, "Sir, you need a reality pill." Miles, who liked to flaunt his Ivy League degree, had complained to their supervisor more than once that Lucy spent too long with her clients, delivering her "touchy-feely Down South wisdom."

Miles did not care for the heart-to-heart, and that was the way of this whole city, she supposed. She had come from a town with a weekly dance, which was held in the old church and always over by nine. She was mostly certain about God, and a year and nine months of New York hadn't taken this from her, though sometimes, after a long day at the agency, she would feel her heart hardening—there were so many stories and so few cures. When she felt this way, she would climb up five flights of stairs and practice the Hula-Hoop on the roof. It was something Mama had taught her when she was thirteen and mad at the world. "Do it for ten minutes, and I guarantee it'll clear your head." Mama had been right. Staring at the skyline while she did the hula not only cleared her head, it gave her a way to shed the bruisings of the day to make room for the new.

This wasn't at all what she'd imagined of the big city. When Mama passed after high school, Lucy had job-hopped from waitressing to working at Jeannie's Pastry Shop. *"The years of kneading dough and counting change,"* she called that time. But the idea had caught on inside her, allowed her to make it every day for the five a.m. at the Country Diner, for she'd do what Mama hadn't: she'd make a musician out of herself. It meant saving every penny, not even buying an extra pair of socks, taking on night shifts at her dad's taxi dispatch.

When she was twenty-five, she applied to every conservatory in New York and was accepted by just one, and a good one at that, the Manhattan School of Music. They gave her a scholarship for about half the tuition. Still, it was too much to balance classes and practice time with the job that was paying the other half of the bills, and after eighteen months of living in the residence hall, skipping meals, and practicing Mendelssohn in the middle of the night, falling asleep twice in a row during her eight a.m. theory class, she quit. There was no one to hold her to account. Mama wasn't around to call or send her little notes of encouragement. Back before Lucy was even an idea, her mother had tried to leave Mebane, and she'd succeeded to a degree, enrolling in a conservatory in Atlanta, but eventually she'd married and come back to North Carolina. It was never easy to leave the vortex of your life.

So far Lucy had succeeded. She'd failed to make it as a pianist but had stuck to New York, though her father, from time to time, would chide her about coming home. She wasn't sure what held her away other than the fear of going home with half a degree and the waning hope that someday she'd save enough money to study music full-time.

She met Jaryk Smith soon after she'd quit the conservatory. It happened on one of those last humid days of August when she'd head to the recorded music archives at the New York Public Library at Lincoln Center to escape the heat. The third floor of the library was air-conditioned, and for hours she could listen to rare recordings of her favorite composers. Out in the streets everyone was listening to the the Rolling Stones or the Jackson 5, but in her cubicle she was transported into the orchestral works she'd learned to love.

The last few times she'd come to the archives she'd noticed a tall man who'd sit in the corner, and when he'd listen to music it'd be with his eyes closed, as if he were trying to memorize each note. She couldn't help spying; he was handsome in a way that made her think of frontiersmen: broad shouldered, square jawed, and deeply brown-eyed, with long lashes.

One Wednesday evening, she left the archives as he did and followed him to the Columbus Circle station. Down by the tracks, she felt safer sidling close to him as if they knew each other. The trains were running slow, and all the ills of the city were out on display. Astronauts had walked on the moon, but it hadn't helped New York much. A man with thickly gelled hair and glassy eyes was carrying around a jar of some dark liquid, yelling a refrain she couldn't understand. A panhandling saxophonist was trying to drown him out by playing some of John Coltrane's *A Love Supreme*. Coltrane—go figure! It wasn't so bad a rendition.

"What kind of music do you listen to?" was how she'd introduced herself. She had the feeling that if she hadn't gone first, he would've stood by and said nothing. At first she wasn't sure if he'd even recognize her, but when he spoke there was an intimacy there, maybe earned from all their hours together listening a few feet apart.

"I like the Romantics," he said. "Tchaikovsky, Dvořák, Brahms. I found this little orchestra who used to play in the fifties. They were based in Iowa, so I doubt many people would know them. I ask for their recordings most nights."

When he said that, he stopped being a stranger. "There's this intermezzo Brahms wrote when he was around sixty, in E-flat minor. They called that part of his life *autumnal*. When I play it, I can see the November storm that's coming up from the fields. Maybe I'll play it for you sometime. If only I knew your name?" She didn't know why she'd said all that; she'd no idea if she'd ever see him again.

"My name is Jaryk. It's spelled a little like *Jared* but the *j* is pronounced like a *y*. Most people get it wrong."

"Nice to meet you, Jaryk with a *y*."

They got on the downtown D and sat next to each other. En route to Broadway-Lafayette, the train jerked to a stop. Still uneasy with this subterranean world of transportation, Lucy said a prayer under her breath. Jaryk sat next to her, unperturbed. His long legs were curled into his body, as if he were afraid of taking up more than his share of space, and when the train started up again, only to crawl a few feet until it sputtered back to a stop, leaving several passengers springing forward, he sighed, but softly, and for some strange reason—perhaps because sadness comforted her—this eased her anxiety and she began, again, to breathe.

But the train did not move. A minute turned into two, and when she saw the panhandler, who the stop before had been upping the ante—"*a dime, a nickel, two pennies, I just got back from your war, so give me anythin' you got*"—peer through the windows nervously, she too became worried. She turned to Jaryk, his dependable face. "Do you know what's happening?"

"Might be traffic," he said. "Too many trains for too little space."

She heard a hint of a foreign accent in his voice, but it was a few layers below the surface and if someone had asked her where this man was from, she wouldn't have known what to say, other than "*Not here, I guess.*"

She kept going because she felt lighter when she talked. He said he lived on the Lower East Side, a walkup at Orchard and Broome.

"I have some nice neighbors," he said, "and there's the sunset every night, right from my fire escape."

She'd come up against a lot of sarcasm in the city—because she supposed people liked to live in their shells and give only when they felt absolutely sure a stranger wasn't strange—but his voice didn't have the first note of irony and he wasn't unkind. "I'm on First Avenue and Seventh Street," she said. The address made her a real and true New Yorker, but there wasn't much to say after that. They sat quietly and waited for the train to move.

The usually garbled announcement came out clear a few minutes later, when everyone was sweating, because the air-conditioning had stopped blowing air. "Ladies and gentlemen, there has been an incident. This train has got a problem. We're going to be handling this car by car. Please be patient."

Her father had warned her about the city. "It's going to explode any moment," he had said. "All that sin can't keep going on." A small piece of her had always suspected he was right, and now that piece grew bigger, large enough that she had trouble breathing. With no AC in the compartment, all the covered smells were uncovered, heightened, with the odors of a homeless man's shoe and expensive French perfume and fresh Gristedes fish competing for space in her nostrils. "I have to get out of here," she said. She turned to him and said it again, "I want out," as if he controlled the doors.

He nodded. "I understand," he said. "I want out too."

He laid his hand on hers. His was a pleasing mix of soft and firm; what's more, she liked his smell and found herself shifting closer to him, to his scent of old books, which helped mitigate the other fumes around her, so that when the workers came to evacuate their car, she stood awfully close to him. When an MTA man pried open the doors, she followed Jaryk onto the tracks.

The dark of the tracks was a mystery she didn't care for. Jaryk shuffled forward and she followed. At one point, she asked him, "What about the third rail?" He said he didn't know, but he didn't think it was their destiny to die here.

They walked a hundred paces and into the sallow light of the Broadway-Lafayette station, where men with large bellies in beige suits hoisted them up. She supposed they were the managers and not the angels of this place. Several of the passengers were taken to the station superintendent's office and told the power had gone out from the rails and wouldn't be restored till morning. They were offered little pins that read *"MTA Works!"*

Afterwards, Jaryk and Lucy walked to the nearest diner, and he paid for a couple of cherry Cokes. She was still shaken up and was talking too fast about her father's time at Fort Worth as an army mechanic when he took his last sip. "But I'm only halfway through mine," she said, as he rose to leave. It was nearly midnight.

"I'm sorry," he said. "If I don't get home now, I won't make it in time for work. Maybe I could get your number? Maybe I could ring you, sometime?"

There it was again, that hint of a faraway accent. "Where are you from? Paris?"

"Far east of Paris," he said.

She gave him her number. She'd never dated a guy who wasn't from North Carolina. Far east of Paris was about as exotic as it could come.

·············

Their first date was at Coney Island. She was late, so she rushed to the intersection of Stillwell and Surf Avenues to find him waiting on the other side of the street, overdressed in a beige blazer, perfectly ironed pants, and a plaid cap that looked like it belonged to an older man. Watching him, she became conscious of her sundress; it was a pretty hand-me-down from Mama, but she'd felt herself sweating through the cotton as soon as she stepped off the train. She figured she would have a cigarette to compose herself, when he noticed her and waved shyly.

"You look handsome," she yelled, across the street.

He took off his cap and waited to cross till the light turned red. He walked like someone who knew his body, from the muscles to the bones: languid, but full of a deeper confidence. She forgave his sense of fashion. That could be changed.

They did everything she'd wanted to do at Coney Island, and then some. They rode the carousel, even though he complained that he was the only man riding; on the beach, they watched Russian ladies in impossibly tight stockings barbecue scallops on a clay pot grill; they helped a boy wearing a Superman cape find his mother, who was at the Nathan's stand just a few feet away, ordering a tray of hot dogs, of which she offered two to Jaryk and Lucy; they shot at toy targets and, with a sharpshooter's aim, Jaryk won a giant stuffed moose; they got prints from the photo booth, chins and noses wonderfully out of proportion; they walked to the sideshows and shook hands with the alligator man and left a quarter for the three-legged girl, who seemed lonely with her condition. They watched old men crab in the sea, schools of horseshoes rising up in their nets.

She looked at him gazing into the water. Oh, the old soul was there, but she could also imagine the little boy with a bowl of dark hair falling over his eyes. She didn't know him well enough, but the vision came anyway, an unexpected tenderness.

As sunset was coming around, they got on the slow side of the Wonder Wheel. When they reached the apex, Lucy could see the whole of the New York shoreline, and beyond, she could see into the dark mass of water, where the last of the seagulls dove with the hope of dinner. The Wonder Wheel was a soothing rise and circle, and for the first time that day, she didn't feel like talking. She'd already told him about Mebane and a couple of anecdotes about Mama. He seemed to hang on her every word, and she loved this about him, how deeply he listened. It made her feel beautiful.

Afterwards, when they were sitting on the beach, he said, "Lucy Gardner, I like you."

She blushed, but there was only a slice of moon, so he couldn't see. "That's a relief."

He reached out to hold her hand. "But I have to be honest with you. I haven't dated much. I've tried and gotten set up a few times, but it never goes anywhere."

"Oh," she said. He'd told her he was thirty-nine, but he could've been younger. He had one of those faces that held together neatly, but in all that time, he hadn't been in a serious relationship? Back in Mebane, she'd loved her high-school sweetheart and stuck it out with a few others after that ended.

"Let me try again," Jaryk said. "What I want is to find someone real. Misha told me to. He said, 'Go out more.' Misha's my brother. I mean, he's *like* my brother. Lately, he's been pushing me to look for someone. I am. I did go out with a few girls before you, but none of them worked. One date, that was all. But you—the way we met, that was special. Something there. Do you feel it?"

She did feel something. *Butterflies* was what people said. But it could simply have been nervousness, a strange man sitting next to her on a strange beach. Still, when he leaned forward, she allowed him a kiss on the cheek.

On the train ride home, she said, "Funny, I think I talked too much. We didn't get to talk about you. I don't even know what you do. All I know," she said, gesturing toward the giant stuffed moose he was holding, "is you've got really good aim."

"I'm a boring guy," he said. "Books and records at a synagogue. Hey, what about football? You were going to teach me about American football."

"How long have you been in this country?"

"Thirty years, give or take."

"Oh, Lord." She didn't understand how a man could live in this country and not know the rules of football. Where she came from, pigskin was king. You went to games, whether you played or cheered. Still, there was something sweet about his ignorance, so she explained the nature of the four downs, noting, as she did so, how he looked relieved not to be talking about himself. Books and records at a synagogue, she told herself—that didn't sound so bad.

When his stop came, he said, "Could I see you again?"

"Maybe," she said, but she flashed him a *yes* smile. She liked how he turned to look at her again after he'd walked off the train just as the doors were closing.

Their second date was at Veselka in the East Village. This time, he was late, and she smoked alone at the bar and got chatted up by a sailor named Manny with two missing front teeth. When Jaryk rushed in after fifteen minutes, she was happy to see how he dwarfed Manny, how he towered over everyone in the restaurant. "Sorry," he said. "It took me a while to get the best ones." He produced a bouquet of pansies from behind his back.

Veselka was his choice, hearty Ukrainian food. He ordered three kinds of pierogi to share, and borscht for himself. The first spoon of soup he took in with his eyes closed, and when he was done, it was like the bowl had been licked clean. She immediately loved this about him.

When she went to light up her third smoke of the evening, he frowned. "I wish you wouldn't," he said. "It's not my place, I know, but I read so many bad things about that."

"You don't really believe," she said, taking a good pull and blowing smoke rings his way, "any of that talk! That's to scare people."

"I do believe. That's why I'm worried."

He seemed so serious it struck her as childish. Still, he was earnest about it, and it made her feel guilty enough to put the cigarette out. Later, when he was walking her home, he stopped to help an old lady cross the street. This woman had to be ninety plus. Jaryk helped her along, all the while speaking to her in some foreign language. When they were alone again, she said, "Seriously, you help old ladies cross the street? Who are you, and what was that you were speaking?"

"It's the language of the Old Country—half Polish and half Yiddish," he said. "I was telling her she reminded me of someone I once knew."

She guessed he didn't want to say more. When it came to his past, she'd noticed his jaw would tense and he would get quiet or change the subject. She didn't push it. The Old Country. It had a ring to it. It was the kind of place, she imagined, where old ladies were taken care of and men showed up with bunches of pansies.

By their fourth date, she had found out that he had no parents—or at least none that he could remember well. The closest he still had to family was this Misha. Sometimes he would talk about Misha like she already knew him.

She would listen, eager for his every word. Often she hoped he would fold more of his life into hers and reveal things, as she had. Their balance of information was terrible. She had already shared how Connor, the first great love of her life, would curse in his sleep, and she'd told him about Connor's moods—how he'd swing from joy to despair and back again and how she'd somehow felt as if it were her fault. Jaryk didn't say much, but he knew how to hold her grief without judgment, accept her story as if it were his own.

That was the night he gave her a book of poems. It was from Rabindranath Tagore, and he'd copied out the pages by hand into a leather-bound journal, his own copy being a tattered mess and new editions hard to find. She'd never been gifted a book of poems. For years, she'd remember a few lines from Tagore's *The Gardener*, wondering whether it was for her sake or his that Jaryk had circled them in the text:

Trust love even if it brings sorrow. Do not close up your heart . . .
The heart is only for giving away . . .

....

After they'd been seeing each other for a few weeks, they went to his apartment. It wasn't much of a place. An antique bookshelf with room for more books, a table that straddled the slope of the floor, a bunch of wilting pansies in a plastic vase, and by the fire escape a thankfully soft bed. They sat on the frame and looked out into the night, the business and beauty of the city, and then they looked at nothing, because, where they were, the power went out. Then it was just the darkness and the swelter. It was just the two of them on the bed. She reached out and grazed his neck, and when he accepted this and touched the slow curve of her spine, she felt a gladness in the core of her belly. She liked the way she stuck to him, the rhythm of his breath on hers. He didn't talk when they made love, and he was patient, removing her underclothes slowly, as if they were the most valuable artifacts, but his delicacy didn't surprise her, though she also experienced the opposite feeling the first time they'd touched hands, that he could break her in his grasp.

Afterwards, she didn't think about Connor's face—Connor, whom she'd loved with the certainty of becoming his wife—she thought instead of the little girl in her who'd climbed trees and collected sap in glass bowls.

It went on like that for some time: a few more walks in the park, a few more nights in his studio. Except for their lovemaking, when she felt he was pouring into her an old, sad story, he managed to keep his guard. At first, she'd understood. She'd understood some men had a hard time talking—after all, she'd grown up around army colonels and sergeants—but three months into their relationship, she took matters into her own hands.

She told herself it had to do with his last name. He'd said he was from Poland, and could someone from that part of the world really have a last name like *Smith*? It was the smallest thing she could ascribe her doubt to. One night, after they'd made love and he'd fallen asleep, she went through his wallet. His ID confirmed his name. He hadn't made *Smith* up after all. She kept going, though, looking for clues to his deeper history. In the billfold was a faded black-and-white photo of a matronly lady and a bespectacled, sharp-featured gentleman—whom she assumed were aunt and uncle, since he'd told her he had no parents (or did he mean he had no parents alive?), but certainly these were folks from the Old Country—and behind the picture, there was a business card that read, "*Jaryk Smith, Associate of Records, Temple Beth Israel, 72nd Street and Amsterdam . . .*" About his job he'd said with that shake of his head she'd come to know so well, "Oh, it's just books and numbers. I'm a record keeper, that's all." So that part was true. She'd never suspected him of being a liar, just a coverer of secrets, and it was what he was covering that so drew her attention.

At dinner at Sarge's Deli earlier that night, she'd asked him, "Why don't you tell me more about your life?"

Between bites of his pastrami sandwich he said, "What more do you want to know?"

"Oh, how you came to this country, what your childhood was like, who raised you, what you do every day at work. All we do when we see each other is eat and—" she lowered her voice—"fuck."

"Lucille!" he said. He liked to use this version of her name when she was cross.

"We can't have a relationship until you agree to share some things," she said.

"What we have means a lot to me, but I'm not one for talking about my past. Can't we have a relationship in the now? Like what that guy says, *Be Here Now*."

"Ram Dass? Seriously, Jaryk? You told me you thought hippies were lazy people."

"Doesn't mean they're all wrong. *Be here now*, Lucille."

She rolled her eyes at him, but they had a nice time after dinner, heading to the flea market at Stuyvesant Town. The market had spilled out onto the Avenue C Loop, and though it was nearly sunset, most of the vendors were still selling their wares. They saw artifacts from all over the world: tattered muslin from Persia, kilts from Ireland, woks from central Asia, and little dolls from Russia. She bought the dolls and unscrewed one from another to reveal the little bodies waiting inside.

It was the beginning of November, and the breeze had turned cool. Jaryk wrapped his arm around her shoulders, and they walked back to her apartment. They were good together because their silences were good together. They knew how to keep quiet and still be in love, and perhaps for an earlier version of Lucy, that would have been enough. But she wanted more. She wanted to go deeper into Jaryk, and maybe that was where things began to break.

....

The next Friday, she donned dark glasses and a picnic hat and headed to Temple Beth Israel on the Upper West Side, where a small crowd milled around the gates of the synagogue. She didn't expect to see Jaryk. From what he'd said he kept the books, but when it came time for services he was nowhere to be found. Still, she scanned the crowd nervously. Aside from the men's head coverings and the faint melodies coming from inside the synagogue, it wasn't so different a feel from a Sunday outside the Mebane First Baptist.

She went into the synagogue and sat in the back. There was no cross, no Jesus anywhere, but there was a beautiful chandelier with only a single light that worked. Months later, when she'd return to the synagogue, Jaryk would show her his good work, with all the bulbs restored—saying, *"This is for you"*—but now almost all the light came from ugly steel lamps that had been placed by the pews, which made the place seem more modern than it was. The mahogany finish, the old scrolls, the gilded candle holders, and nearly everything else seemed from a distant era, as if it'd been rescued from another century.

She wasn't sure what she was hoping to find, but whatever

it was, her gut told her it would be here. Her gut said so, even though Jaryk had said he didn't have a religious bone in his body. She didn't believe him: everyone kept a place for God. Everyone, whether they did or didn't believe in Moses or Jesus or whomever, had room for the divine. Besides, why else would he work at a synagogue if God didn't touch or tempt him, at least a little?

She studied the crowd. Next to her there was a young woman whose hair was done in an immaculate bob. She was balancing her toddler on her knee while skimming a prayer book. Catching Lucy's stare, the lady smiled. "Are you new here?" she asked.

"Yes," Lucy said. She felt conscious of her hat, its wayward droopiness. Her dress, also, was a shade of rose, while nearly everyone else was wearing white.

"Don't worry," the woman said. "You'll love it. The cantor is amazing. The way they do the Dvar Torah here—pure joy."

"Oh, that's good," Lucy said. She didn't have a clue about what the lady was telling her. Back home, Jews had been a foreign country: you didn't go, and they didn't visit. Here in New York, she supposed, they were everywhere, aligned with the backbone of the city. She couldn't help being curious.

When the cantor came out, the room grew quiet. Somewhere in the second song, her heart opened to his sad melody without words; it took her into a place of low-moving nimbus clouds, and she sank into her seat and let the music gather inside her. This was the part she'd loved about church in Mebane—when Mama would play the organ and nearly everyone would sing along with her. It was when she heard or played music that she could feel God rise up in her like a benediction.

Afterwards, the service wasn't unpleasant, but she left when the rabbi started to speak. He was hunched with age. When he began his sermon—if that was what it was called—she felt as if he were directing his words to her alone. "Let the truth be said, even between lovers, especially between those we love," he had said, just before she'd snuck out the door.

The next time she and Jaryk met was on their lunch break. Jaryk had trekked down to City Hall Park. He brought her an arrangement of tulips and lilies that looked as if they'd been sent from a faraway country. She took them and said, "You don't have to do that, you know. We've been dating for two and a half months."

He looked confused. "So flowers are for beginning couples?"

"No, it's sweet. *You're* sweet. What I mean is, we haven't gotten past flowers."

"Gotten past?"

"First, you give flowers," she said. "Then you share something about your life."

"Why are Americans always in a rush? Why do they put so much into talking, talking, talking?"

"Because that's how we get to know each other, Jaryk." And there was another reason for the rush. Lucy had been receiving a steady stream of wedding invitations from her school friends for the past few years. She wanted to start her own family. If this Jaryk Smith wasn't up to snuff, if he stayed inside his fortress, she couldn't afford being with him. The walls had to come down, and soon.

She said, "I went to your synagogue."

She wanted to look into his eyes, but he was staring at his hands and wouldn't meet her gaze. She went on, even though she felt she was punishing him in some way. "It was a beautiful Friday service. The cantor's got some voice. He made me cry. I was bawling, actually, and I didn't even know what he said. Then he sang a melody without words. All those sad songs."

"They're niguns," he said.

"What?"

"The wordless melodies the cantor sings, they're called niguns, and he was welcoming the Shechinah, the feminine presence of God."

"Well," she said, "for someone who doesn't have a religious bone in his body, you seem to know a thing or two."

"Just a thing or two. I told you I grew up without much God. We did the High Holidays, but that was it. Why didn't you tell me you were going?"

"Jaryk, it's nothing bad. I just wanted to see another side of you. That's all."

"Fine, I'll show you," he said. "But you might not like what you find."

She understood that he was cautioning her, that maybe they were on the brink of something breakable, but he was earnest all the same. There were men you could go to war with, and men who would squeeze the sidelines all their lives. In that moment, she thought she knew which kind Jaryk was, and she imagined the two of them growing old together. They would sit by a fireplace in the open country drinking coffee with a little bourbon. Every Friday night, he would sing her those old wordless melodies.

....

It was the twentieth of December and the last night of Chanukah when Lucy visited the house of Misha Waszynski. As she stepped off the train at Brighton Beach, she got a whiff of sea air mixed with the smell of burning trash; all around, she could feel the tide of a neighborhood falling into decay: every other shop was boarded up, and gutted cars had been left on the street. Coney Island was one of the few places you could get a good tattoo, and a couple of men outside of a parlor looked at her in a way that made her wrap her coat closer around her body, and she thought back to her first date here—how safe she'd felt in Jaryk's company.

Underneath her old coat, she was wearing the same velvet blue dress she'd worn to her conservatory audition; her lipstick was a modest red; her long, wavy hair had been rehearsed into a bun, which showed off the fine curve of her neck; her nails had been manicured and polished to the color of Minnesota frost. Because this evening felt like a meet-the-parents. She had been so patient, and this evening was a serious step. She checked her makeup again before she knocked on the door. She waited a minute, but no one answered, so she knocked again.

Whenever Lucy had felt nervous as a little girl, her mother told her to imagine the people she saw as animals, and that's what she did now, turning the street of ogling men into anteaters and skittish zebras. It calmed her nerves until Misha Waszynski finally came down to open the door. She named him then: *Woolly Mammoth*. He had an unkempt beard with patches of gray, and there was a mass of hair sloping over his forehead and covering his right eye. His forearms were thick and full of complex tattoos. There was one on his neck that she'd always remember when she thought of him—of a marlin breathing fire. A dragon fish.

Misha squeezed her in a hug. "It's nice to finally meet you, Mr. Waszynski," she said, deep inside his embrace. "Jaryk's told me so much about you."

"Misha. Call me Misha."

Jaryk was upstairs in the kitchen. All around him lay the implements for an enormous meal: two heads of cauliflower, sliced portobellos, onions and rosemary, a thick chunk of pig—Jaryk's beloved country food. A little electric menorah had been placed by the kitchen window.

Misha clapped him on the shoulder, and they exchanged something in Polish, a ribald joke, judging by the rhythm of the syllables, and soon the three of them were sitting around Misha's kitchen table, drinking a sweet vodka that tickled Lucy's throat as it went down. When they were out together, Jaryk hardly raised his voice, but in Misha's presence, he let his head roll back when he laughed, which he did a lot, and he drank a lot, too. Over the evening, all three of them ate and drank generously. They talked, too, but mostly it was Misha telling anecdotes about his work as a freight loader at Fulton Fish Market, where he handled the nautical treasures of the world. "Big responsibility," he said. "Little fish, big fish, and even bigger fish."

"What's that?" she asked, noticing a statue in the center of the table, next to the salt and pepper. It was of a boy riding an elephant, carved from a single piece of wood, small enough to be tucked into her purse. The apartment had few decorations, so she immediately felt this one carried meaning for Misha, though it wasn't ostentatious.

"Ah, that's a gift I made for Jaryk when he was nine years old. I made sure to take it back when he moved out on me."

"Well, I was the one who managed to smuggle it all the way from Poland to America," Jaryk said.

"Can you believe I've known this beanpole thirty-plus years?"

"You were a beanpole back then, too, you know," Jaryk said.

"Thirty years, huh? Tell me how you met this handsome man," Lucy said to Jaryk.

Jaryk poked the pierogi on his plate. His eyes were swimming in a murky happiness that made her feel afraid. "Misha's a better storyteller," he said.

"It was before the war," Misha said. He was smiling. Then he wasn't. "It was before the war that we met."

Misha had large hands covered with sun spots, warning signs from his liver, and he did the same thing Jaryk did when he didn't want to go on—he looked into his palms as if he were a fortune-teller—but she felt with him a more porous boundary; plus, she was here, in his house, and she wasn't willing to let go. "Please, tell me about that time," she said.

"Well, it was Korczak's orphanage, you know," Misha began. "Korczak was a good soul. We called him *Pan* Doktor. He was our people's heart. He had a way, and he took little Jaryk in. How old were you when Korczak found you?"

"Seven," Jaryk said.

"Seven years old," Misha said with a low, dry whistle. "Seven years old and Janusz Korczak takes him in. Believe it? You must believe it. Child wandering the streets of Warsaw in the September of '39, right as Germans storm in, and what does Korczak do? He takes another boy to add to his one hundred and ninety-one children. I worked for Korczak, you know? I was the junior carpenter of the house, and of course I kept my little brother Jaryk out of trouble. As long as I could, that is. As much as I could."

"What do you mean? What happened?" she said.

"What do I mean?" Misha said a little too loudly, but not unkindly. "We are the only souls left of that story. Everything, everyone else, burned."

"But you and Jaryk," she said, feeling free to speak as much as she dared, "the two of you—how did you make it?"

"Me and him?" Misha said. He poured a shot of vodka into his cup, then took a swig straight from the bottle and chased the motion with a fit of coughing. "Me, I won the lottery. Had a job outside the ghetto. When I came back, nobody. Didn't see this one—" he poked Jaryk in the ribs—"till the DP camp. Two years after. Was a scarecrow when I found him."

"DP camp?" Lucy asked.

"Displaced Persons," Misha said.

All the noise of the street gone. The three of them, the leftovers on the table, the drink in her hands. She felt a murmuring by her ear, shook her head to clear the feeling. She tried to poke Jaryk in the ribs the way Misha had. "And you," she said. "How did *you* escape?"

For a long time, he didn't answer, and she noticed that he was moving his fingers underneath the table, as if he were tallying a large sum.

She repeated her question. He shifted his jaw left to right, right to left. She could hear Misha breathing: an old grizzly waking up to roam.

"I'll tell you," Jaryk said. "If you tell me one thing. What were you doing on the sixth of August, 1942? What were you doing when the Germans came?"

She tried to connect the date with a memory, even if it was carried over from her parents, but nothing came to mind. "I wasn't even born," she said.

"Then please," Jaryk said. "Don't talk about what you don't know."

"Jaryk," Misha said.

Misha put his hand on Lucy's, but she still felt the hot white light of shame on her face. With Jaryk, there was a line, and she had been pressing and egging him to go beyond it, when all he wanted was to forget. She left the table and started washing the dishes in the kitchen.

....

Afterwards, she went back to her own place. She knew what had been said couldn't be unsaid. Their relationship had begun in the bliss of an America she understood, but all along there'd been this other story she'd been scratching at. As the vodka began to wear off, she thought about a boy from kindergarten who'd joined in the middle half of the year and, like Jaryk, had a lonesome way to him.

They'd all given him his distance, even the teachers. Lucy's parents had told her to stay away: *"He's suffered."* At first, like all the other kids, she left him alone, as he played on the swings and the jungle gym, grunting each time he peaked in the air; but then, after a while, she began to approach him. At first, he would hide in the sandbox when he saw her coming, but then he loosened up, or maybe she grew on him. Either way, they became friends, and one day he showed her something.

They were by the elms at the edge of the schoolyard. All the other kids had headed inside with the first rain, but not them. "Come," he said. He had a funny way of talking, like he was underwater. She did, she came closer. Overhead, there was a skirmish of geese. She glanced up to see the commotion, and when she looked at him again she saw that he'd stretched his tongue out of his mouth. In the middle of his tongue there was a coin-sized gap. Beads of rain ran through it.

She was repulsed, but she was also curious to see more. It was the first time in her short life those two feelings had traveled through her body at the same moment, and her spine tingled with the energy of it. They were getting soaked. Soon, the teachers would be out looking. He put his tongue back in his mouth and she said, "How did it happen?"

He shrugged and turned back toward school.

That's the way it worked in one version of her memory: her asking him the question. In another, he stretched his tongue toward her, and she stuck her little finger in the hole, and she felt the pulse of his mouth, the work of his heart. She felt the whole memory of him. He'd slept in a shed and had gone half his life without a good meal. Just two towns over, she'd later discover, a boy left to fend for himself.

....

The week after they had dinner at Misha's, Jaryk and Lucy didn't see each other. Partly, with the new year around the corner she assumed Jaryk would be busy at work, but there was something else: she felt she'd opened a door into his suffering. Her mother had once chastised her, "Leave the dead for the dead." What she meant was that Lucy shouldn't dwell on other people's woes—she should stick to her own—but it was an unfair accusation. All her life, her mother had been the same way: making friends with the homeless man who hung around Hoffman Pond, mending his old clothes and giving him fresh pairs of socks, inviting him for dinner three nights in a row, until her father complained and ended things.

Her father. He had been calling since Thanksgiving, hinting that it was time for her to visit—they had not seen each other for nearly a year. She'd lied and said that recent layoffs meant that it would be impossible for her to leave the office for long, but she agreed to come for three days. He accepted that, though it was clear he'd hoped for longer.

She boarded a bus at Port Authority at eight o'clock at night and crossed into the Carolinas the next morning. The bus's lights were dimmed until dawn broke over stretches of farmland. She saw leaves of tobacco and ears of corn that had withstood the first frost. Well-fed cows peered at her through wooden fences, and she spotted in their midst a baby calf. The closer to home they headed, the more churches and roadside diners retook their place of prominence. The Lord's name was on the highway billboards, above the flashing marquees of racetracks and next to the room rates that announced *Vacancy.*

At the station, she took time to freshen up, though she knew her father would be waiting impatiently for her. She smoothed the wrinkles out of her dress and pulled her hair tightly into a bun. Her face in the mirror struck her as more urbane. She had visited the year before for the holidays, when New York was still terrifying to her, and the trip home felt like a respite from the city. She'd spent the better part of her vacation waking up late, strolling to Jeannie's pastry shop, then walking to the Haw River alone, then back to the house again to make dinner for her father, who asked her detailed questions about the geography of New York. But she'd never been good at the directions of things, and the questioning left her feeling she should've paid more attention to the relationship of the Hudson River to the Long Island Sound, or exactly how many blocks Central Park spanned. This year, she'd felt more prepared, having ridden the trains in four out of the five boroughs, and she'd even been out kayaking on the Hudson. It had been a lazy Sunday, and Jaryk had done all the paddling, keeping them away from the wake of passing barges.

She found her father in the waiting area talking to a station employee. He'd kept his head of jet-black hair, shaped into what her mother had called the "military marquee," but his posture was less than its usual perfect. As he asked the station employee a question, he was hunched over, seemingly deferential.

She tapped him on the shoulder. "Daddy," she said. "Remind me to take the train next time."

"You too good for the bus now?" he said with a grin. She thought about hugging him like she used to as a little girl, but they settled for a handshake. His grip was as ironclad as she remembered it.

Their house was well away from the road. They owned enough of the surrounding land that they would never have to worry about neighbors peeking in. That had been one of her father's retorts when Mama wanted to pursue music in New York or finish her training back in Atlanta. They wouldn't have their space, he'd said. Everyone would be looking in on them. Not that there was anything of note to look in on; he just loved his own land.

She left him to walk the grounds and didn't return to the house till she knew he'd left for his job. Her father was in charge of the regional taxi dispatch and would be coordinating operations until dinnertime.

She found that the living room had been meticulously maintained. Mama hadn't been a good housekeep, but her father believed in the orderliness of things. Soon after Mama passed, he'd created a system of cleaning each part of the house, one day at a time. Perhaps there were a few more copies of *Field & Stream* on the mantel, but otherwise the house had kept its harmony. For the final eight years they were married (the culminating event of which was not divorce but death and bereavement), Carol and Jim had slept in separate rooms. They still walked to church together, still threw dinner parties for their small group of friends, but once it was just family, they wouldn't bother to strike up a conversation with each other unless the need was severe.

Lucy had always been pulled between her father's and her mother's affections, but everyone concerned knew that she had to make a choice. Mom or Dad, Carol or Jim. Not both. That she chose her mother was no surprise. They had always bonded more deeply. It was in her mother's room that she could delight in chaos. The sheets on the bed were perennially rumpled. Folders of sheet music covered half the floor, so that she had to tiptoe to the bed. The ashtray on top of the upright piano was ever full.

When she'd visited the year before, she found the disorder of her mother's room beautifully maintained, but this time she saw that her father had reclaimed the space. The bedcovers were the same silk her mother had ordered from a catalog, but now the bed was properly made, the stray sheets of music had been collected into piles, and the floor had been sanded and treated. What struck her the most was the framed picture on the dresser: the three of them at the Grand Canyon in the summer of 1955. It had been a time of extraordinary, unrecoverable happiness, when Mama had been fully theirs—not worrying about that other life she could've had as a musician but waking up early with the family, making each day bloom with her imagination.

That portrait made Lucy worry. Her father had never been one to dote on the past; he believed nostalgia was a manageable side effect of growing older. Perhaps he did need her to visit more now. She settled down to the piano and played from the sheet music lying atop it. Bach, her mother's favorite. She had had hopes of Lucy doing better than she had, becoming a concert pianist, and Lucy had tried. Now, she thought she ought to have paid more attention to Mama's lessons. She missed the feel of her hands on the piano, all the quiet it brought out in that room.

Her father was busy most of Christmas Eve at the dispatch, and when he came home he seemed too exhausted to do anything but help himself to her reheated steak and potatoes. Christmas morning, they walked to her mother's grave to lay flowers. She brushed snow off the gravestone where it said, *"With a Voice Divine."*

Afterwards, her father left to check on his drivers, and she headed to Jeannie's pastry shop, which this year had to stay open on Christmas on account of the backlog. She'd worked at Jeannie's when she was saving money for college, and now she worked herself into a sweat kneading and carrying dough into the ovens. Jeannie pretended to be mortified by her helping on such a short trip, but Lucy knew she was happy to have the extra hand.

Back at her father's house, they had Christmas dinner with

Richard, her maternal uncle, and his four sons and their families. Her oldest cousin was her age but already had three boys under five. Noah, the middle child, followed her around the kitchen and held on to the hem of her dress. After dinner, they sipped brandy from mugs her uncle had fired in his kiln. It was that hour when the children summoned the last of their energy for one more run around the tree. The evening ended after Noah scraped his forehead on the mantel. Lucy held him close, sang him a lullaby, and reminded him how wonderful his presents were. Soon he was smiling again.

When everyone had left, Lucy sat on an arm of the sofa, leaned against her father's shoulder. The fire burned with a soporific glaze. Neil Diamond's *Just for You* played for the fifth time.

"Daddy," she said. "I'm seeing someone." It was news she would have told her mother, saving it from her father till she was ready and sure. Now he was the only one left to tell.

"How long's this been?"

"Six months."

"Well, I'll be darned."

"Now what do you mean by that?"

He ran his hands through the thick mane of his hair. "I just figured that after you quit music school you'd come back home. But now you're seeing someone, and you're setting up roots. It's not the story I expected for my old age. You see that chair?"

She looked over at the rocking chair in the corner, which always had seemed too wobbly to support anyone. "What about it?"

"It's fixed now," her father said. "I've been cleaning up around here, but I could use your arm with the roof. I'm not sure I can get up there by myself anymore."

She paused. There was a pine tree in their yard that had been there since before she was born and looked just the same now as it had when she first could remember it. That was how she thought of her father: unchanging through the seasons. She gave him another look: maybe more gray around the temples, a few more wrinkles. Otherwise, he seemed like the same man who'd built her wooden play set from scratch.

"Daddy, I don't believe that. You've got the heart of a teenager. You'll climb that roof when you're a hundred and two. Aren't you happy for me?"

Her father stoked the fire into a renewed vigor. When it was good and bright, he made his way up the stairs without another word.

Alone, she put Bill Withers on the stereo, cleaned the dishes, and dried them with Mama's monogrammed towels. For once she'd shared something meaningful, but her father had been thinking about himself.

The next morning, Lucy made a point of taking a walk before breakfast. Her bus wasn't till the evening, and with a few hours to kill, she hiked to Timothy Norwood's house. Timothy was their family's oldest friend, though he was a generation older than her parents. For as long as she'd known him, he'd lived opposite the Haw River in his two-room log house that seemed too flimsy to withstand even a single winter; but with Timothy's patchwork skills, it had survived every storm the Carolina winds had carried.

Her last semester of high school, when life without Connor seemed unbearable, she'd visited Timothy almost every day. He would lead her out to his garden and put her to work: "*Prune this*" or "*Lift that one up*," he'd say. He seemed to know how the sunlight would fall before it did, which of his beloved marigolds or goldenrod or hyacinths would make it into the heart of summer. Those ones he knew weren't likely to survive were the ones he gave the most attention, bending at the hips to spray water at their roots, whispering some secret language into their shriveling cores.

The night they found Connor in the ditch, the medics had cleaned as much of his remains from the car as possible; only then had they called the family. Connor's father had been the one to tell Lucy. He had begun the conversation by saying, "*I thought you should know . . .*"

They all gathered by the side of the road: Connor's parents, an uncle, three siblings, and Lucy, all in their pajamas by the turnoff to Hoffman Road. Nobody had bothered to change into anything more formal, so there they stood, deep into the other side of midnight, the emergency lights illuminating their flannel. Connor's uncle, who was a lapsed pastor, said a few words in the direction of the mauled Ford. Nobody talked about how blue Connor had been the last few months, how his moods had begun to shift like a pendulum in an earthquake. They prayed over the dead, though the body had been removed; they prayed toward whatever remained of the boy they'd loved.

Lucy knew better than anyone else that Connor was suffering—decades later, she'd come to think of it clinically with a word, *bipolar*—but for years she'd blame herself for not doing more, his ghost rising up in her bed to haunt her. It was only with Jaryk that she'd felt absolved. When she'd told him about that night by the ditch and all the months before, the signs she thought she should've seen, he'd listened to her as if his life depended on the telling.

"You loved him. You let him experience joy. For that, I believe he is grateful," Jaryk said.

He is. Jaryk pointed to the sky, to the dark beyond the roof of his apartment, where they were, the cosmos over the bend, and said, "I believe he loves you still."

It was strange to think she'd fallen deeper in love with a man as he'd said her old boyfriend was looking down at them from the ether, but already she knew Jaryk Smith would be no ordinary encounter.

Timothy had helped her live through that time by giving her work that took her mind off her troubles, but it was only time and the deep attention of a new lover that let her see Connor in a new light. She could not have saved him—she never had the power.

Timothy hadn't known Connor or asked about him; that wasn't his way. She found him now by the fire, reading a leather-bound book.

"Well, look at you," he said, rising gingerly from his chair.

When he held her hand, she could feel a slight tremor. Even he had aged and brittled. "I came to see Daddy," she said.

"I know," he said. "He talks about you more than he talks about any one thing."

She thought he was joking. How could her father spend more time talking about her than about his beloved baseball cards or the deplorable state of the North Carolina roadways? She'd known him to talk about everything *but* her life.

Timothy continued, "He tells me about your job. All those people who come to you for advice. That's a lot of responsibility. And he talks about when you were a little girl, when you climbed up trees looking for honeycomb."

She tried to seem unsurprised. In New York love and work had hurried her along so that she spent less and less time dwelling on home. But it seemed her father had assumed the familial role of guarding her in his thoughts.

"You need any help around the house?" she asked. "I got my daddy's arm, you know."

Timothy asked her to haul in firewood. She took a sled out onto his property to salvage tinder by the armful. He stood with her in the cold in his flannel shirt as she worked up a sweat.

When Timothy was resupplied with enough firewood for the rest of winter, she made him tea. "What about his health, my old man?"

"He's complaining more, but he's all right," was what Timothy said. It was an enormous relief to hear it from him.

All those afternoons she'd visited in her senior year of high school, Timothy never asked her why she came. He was too patient to force anything out of her, but when spring blazed into summer, the daffodils at the edge of his garden having acquired the look of preening ballerinas, sun-washed and proud and full of hope, he said, "Lucy, look at those nails on you. When did you last trim them?"

She said she hadn't trimmed her fingernails in a while, even though they'd started to bother her when she played the piano. He sat her down at the river's edge, where bream were swimming up to the shallows, and from his pocket he withdrew an ancient nail clipper. It was gold rimmed and monogrammed *J.N.*, which were his father's initials. Then he put his hands over hers. She felt the places in his palm the sun had kissed.

"Why don't you call your papa to pick you up?" Timothy asked her now, after they had finished their tea. "Bet he likes to chauffeur you fancy city people around."

When her father came to get her, Lucy made every effort to be kinder, through the rest of the afternoon and into the evening of her departure. He seemed more fragile, more in need of Mama's grace, which now, truth be told, was Lucy's to give. She hugged him hard and was grateful when he reciprocated, albeit awkwardly, in the station full of strangers.

"You call more often now," her father chided, gently.

"Yes, sir," she said. She hugged him once more, then boarded the bus to the life she'd learned to love.

....

She was back in the city and at work the day of New Year's Eve. There were hardly any clients, so she spent the day thinking about Jaryk but not calling him. When it was time to wrap up, her coworkers invited her dancing, and later that evening she met them at a dimly lit club in Spanish Harlem, where the band started out playing soul. Soon the claves, congas, and trombones came out, and frenetic rhythms born of another continent pressed against her. It no longer mattered that it was below freezing outside and the club poorly heated as she danced and sweated through her dress. At the stroke of midnight, she found herself in the arms of a capable dancer, who spoke only Spanish and taught her steps she didn't think her body could muster. She got home at three in the morning, feeling alive with the city that had taken her back.

The next week she saw Jaryk again. He visited her at her office (she had resolved to let him call her, not the other way around) and approached her desk shyly with a handful of pansies.

They went out for lunch, talking about everything but Misha and that night at his apartment, as if the conversation about the orphanage in Warsaw had never happened. They began seeing each other again, but this time it was a harder love: she was into him so solidly she couldn't see how deep the fall was. She made a little home in his apartment, bringing in shelves of her own books and her makeup and three or four of her dresses. They cooked together, giant meals that welcomed winter: squash, buttered corn, stews thick with spice and love. They lived through each other, through the frost and the chill, and when he held her in his arms, she thought of the possibility of children, of the something deeper and lifelong she hoped would soon come.

One evening, after a dinner of herbed chicken, to which Lucy had added dollops of butter and heavy cream, he told her about his earliest years. "I grew up a country boy, so this is the food we dreamed of," Jaryk said, addressing the leftover chicken on her plate. He'd been raised by his aunt, alongside her four sons, and as soon as he'd turned five had worked on the family farm. There was no memory of a mother, who'd died shortly after he was born, or of a father, who'd left not long after he was conceived, but Jaryk said he remembered the many hours of work. The contented mornings waking with the cattle, carrying his pail to their stalls to collect fresh milk. He said he remembered the soreness of his muscles and how that made even the simplest food taste wonderful.

Lucy asked why he'd left for the city, how he'd ended up in an orphanage, and Jaryk shrugged. "When the Germans came, I was one mouth too many to feed. If you've ever seen a house with five young boys, then you'll know how much they can scarf down. So, my aunt packed me off with warm clothes. She'd heard about this doctor in the city, who was taking children from the villages and who had food to go around."

Lucy was an only child; she didn't know the first thing about fighting for your portion. Still, looking at the remnants of their meal—Jaryk's plate without a crumb but hers with half a chicken breast in its cream sauce—she felt grateful for these comforts. Surreptitiously and also a little guiltily, she took a few more bites, but Jaryk didn't seem to notice. She knew he was thankful for her felicity in the kitchen, the way she'd saved him from a life of street food and takeout. After he did the dishes, Jaryk kissed her for a long minute, his hands smelling of the lavender detergent she'd introduced to his apartment.

That weekend, Jaryk said he was going to surprise her with a special date and that she should dress up nice. She picked out a blue chiffon dress she rarely had occasion to wear and met him at the Lincoln Center fountain, where she found him waiting in a suit and tie, a little pomade in his hair. He took her by the hand and led her into the gilded premises of the Metropolitan Opera House for a production of *La Bohème*.

"What an idea," she whispered.

They were seated in the balcony, and he'd brought along a pair of binoculars for her to see. She knew he didn't need them; he could make out faces a football field away.

"What can I say, I've been branching out," Jaryk said.

At the end of the third act, she found him weeping. She kissed him under his eyes, knowing he'd allowed himself to be unguarded in her presence. He was a man who could be moved by music, which was important for her. That night he was tender. He kissed her a hundred times on her ankles, as if she were a princess, which she often felt she was in his presence, or at least someone of value, someone worthy of his deep and singular attention.

At work, even Miles Norton couldn't take away her happiness. That was a testament to the life she and Jaryk had made together. During the early part of March and into April, as the first tendrils of spring settled on the city and Central Park was full again with strollers, panhandlers, musicians, and the two of them, they went to the waterfront to watch the construction of what would become the tallest towers in the world. In the evenings, they grilled meat on Jaryk's fire escape.

They made a date of getting their passports. "Just in case," he'd said to her, but this opened up possibilities in her mind: a life of travel, a little vagabonding abroad with the man she loved.

Then came the eighteenth of May. She had bought a white dress that came down to the middle of her thighs, and she was going to surprise him with it, and with a new pair of shoes she'd bought from a store on Madison. She was going to cook him a nice meal, and maybe they were going to see the new Redford movie.

She tried her key on his door, but the lock was bolted from the inside. "Jaryk," she called through the door, "you home early?"

She got that funny feeling in her belly even before his voice came back. "Go away."

"Go away," he said again. This time, she heard the sound of bottles and the shifting of furniture.

"Jaryk, it's me, Lucy," she said. But there was only silence.

She pounded on the door until her knuckles ached. The pain was good—at least, it lessened the worry.

Jaryk's Ukrainian landlord lived next door. She could hear the old woman washing her laundry in the bathtub, the pounding of the sheets aligning with the rhythm of Lucy's own body, with the memory of her own furious knocking. She smoothed her dress and rang the doorbell.

"Yah?" The old woman appraised her from shoes to hair.

"I need to use your fire escape," Lucy said.

"You are the girlfriend."

"Something's wrong with Jaryk," Lucy said. "I need to get in."

The landlady shrugged. Perhaps she had once loved with all the curiosities of her soul funneled into another being. Perhaps she had been on the verge of loss. "You go ahead," the landlady said.

The fire escape jutted five floors above the city, and three feet away was the entrance to Jaryk's apartment. The landlady had used half of the space to host geraniums and forget-me-nots. By the far corner, there was a grill and Lucy climbed atop it, balancing with her hands on the railing. The wind blew up her dress and she heard pockets of noise from the street. The buildings huddled together in the Lower East Side, and she could imagine their history as tenement dwellings, all the misspent promises of those who'd come to the country for riches only to end up living in filth.

From down on the street came the catcalls of the street preacher, who loved to spread the word of God as much as he loved his women; Lucy heard, too, the trilling of a domestic argument in rapid Spanish, and she heard the voice of the Ukrainian landlady, who was standing at the balcony door. "If you are to do, do it," she said.

She did it. She jumped and landed on Jaryk's fire escape. It was full of rust and going a little uneven, but it held her weight. "Thank you," she yelled to the landlady, a little breathless and terribly alive. She crossed herself, crawled through the open window, and there he was. Passed out on the couch. A little dribble on his five o'clock shadow. The smell of liquor surrounding him like a wet blanket.

"Jaryk," she said. "What in heaven's . . . ?"

It took a little bit of shoving, but he came to. Vile breath. He smelled of everything the future father of her children shouldn't. His first words were "I don't want any." His hair was caked with sweat; he raised his head to say, "Misha's dead."

She felt a piece of his heart lift away. It was gone with the sound of the name. *Misha*. Two syllables and a whole past. Misha was the man who'd lifted the veil to reveal an orphanage in the Old Country and Jaryk as a boy. Misha had watched over him before everything fell apart. "Misha. Oh, God—how?"

"Dead because I wasn't there for him."

She took a wet cloth to Jaryk's forehead and brushed the hair from his eyes. Then she made a stone soup with the few things in the fridge: carrots, a bunch of parsley, leftover strips of chicken, and a beef broth. Eventually, he sat up and ate, but he refused to look at her the whole night. He was willing to be cared for, but only to a degree. She could tell he was in his own world, and he wasn't ready to make room.

....

Lucy was working her caseload, coaching a middle-aged woman on how to rejoin the workforce, when Miles walked into her office to tell her she had a phone call.

"It's about a funeral," Miles said, trying his best, she knew, to come across as caring, though it did not come naturally to him. "I transferred it into Albert's room."

Albert was a caseworker who'd retired last year but left his office decorations intact, as if he were only gone on holiday. His room was filled with family photos, and some days during her break she would sneak in, just to stare at the children and grandchildren he'd had with a succession of three wives.

"Lucy," Jaryk said. "I'm outside your office."

"Stay put, I'll be right there," she said.

She found him a block away, wearing a black fedora and faded jeans, standing near the pay phone. When he saw her, he seemed relieved.

"Sorry," he said. "I tried to find you in there, but there was no receptionist. It was awfully confusing."

She imagined him entering the labyrinth that was the unemployment office, thinking which of the hallways would lead to her. She knew he hadn't asked anyone for help, had likely wandered for minutes until he tracked his way to the pay phone. That was Jaryk. Until he knew you, he'd never ask for a good word.

They walked to City Hall Park and from a distance watched a lady in a wide skirt Hula-Hoop.

"There's a tradition to invite people to funerals in person," he said finally. "A lot easier when you live in a village." He told her it was to be held tomorrow morning at Green-Wood Cemetery in Brooklyn. "We're going to have vodka in Misha's memory," he said.

The lady with the Hula-Hoop had tired herself out, her skirt tracing a snow angel in the parched grass. Lucy wasn't sure what she could ask Jaryk. Not *"How are you?,"* which forced folks to make politeness out of misery. Nothing could undo the grief of a beloved friend, a brother, departed. She led him onto the grass, and she lay down—what did it matter if she soiled her work clothes?—and he beside her, the two of them staring into the midday sun.

....

When Jaryk had said "morning," apparently he had meant the earliest part of the morning. Lucy got to Green-Wood Cemetery at seven o'clock and by that time the men from the fish market were already assembled in a line by the gravesite. Ten men, each of whom Jaryk had personally invited. Each one rose to eulogize their departed colleague. Earl Minton's was the one she'd remember through the years.

"He was a king amongst us," Earl began. "He didn't care if you were Jewish or Irish or whatever. He'd fight for you whoever you were. That was Misha's way."

Jaryk didn't take a turn. He had worn an oversized black coat for the occasion, and after each man finished his speech, he fidgeted with his collar and poured a shot of vodka.

"L'chaim," said the men who were Jewish. "Sláinte," said Earl and Misha's Irish friends.

She walked into the circle and saw there was no casket, no hole in the ground. Only *"Misha Waszynski"* carved on a gravestone that barely fit the letters. Had she missed that—the viewing of the body, the lowering into the earth? Jaryk wasn't meeting her eye. The men from the docks circled closer, and she had to worm her way to him. She whispered into his ear that she would cook dinner for them tonight, if he wanted to be with her—if he didn't, she understood that, too.

He looked at her and nodded what could've been either *yes* or *no*. Someone tapped her on the shoulder, and she retreated from Jaryk and the circle, feeling that her entry had upset some ritual of brotherhood.

....

That night she made his kind of comfort food. Ribs, mashed potatoes, alongside a decent red wine. She waited until nine o'clock, then called his apartment, but there was no answer. He was out mulling things over, she figured. She fell asleep to the rhythm of a welcome rain. Finally, there would be respite from the heat, which had come quick and overstayed its welcome.

Jaryk came over the next night. From the circles under his eyes, she could tell he hadn't slept much.

"Misha's ghost keeps me up," he said, by way of a hello. "I go all the way down to the river. It doesn't help. I feel his whiskey breath on my neck all the same."

She reheated the ribs and mashed potatoes, which he consumed without a pause—not a piece of meat left on the bone.

"I've been walking these streets, thinking that if I get tired, it will help me fall asleep. Except, Misha and me used to walk everywhere when we first came to this country, so it reminds me of him, you know. The tenement houses on Orchard and Ludlow. The old synagogue on Elizabeth that's so small you'd think it was for little people. We went in there once, and Misha couldn't fit in the seats. We had a good laugh.

"Hold on a minute," he said. Her table was a little askew, or maybe it was her prewar floor. Either way, he left his seat, used his napkin to support the offending leg, then sat back down, leaning forward, hands on lap. "Have you ever in your life just wanted to get away?"

"Yes, I have," she said. "That's how I came here. That's how I met you. Do you want to take a trip upstate? Go to the Catskills?"

"That won't cure what I have." He went to the sink and began washing the dishes she'd neglected all week. Unlike her, he was careful to scrub away each spot of grease, an attention to detail she'd always appreciated.

"Ribs," he said, drying the plates and placing them back in her cupboards. "With your famous barbecue sauce. I ate so quickly I didn't even say thank you."

She laid her hand on the small of his back, told him it was not a one-time event, that such simple joys could be had again. They walked to the foot of her bed, but he stopped and gripped her arm.

"There's something I've kept from you, Lucy," Jaryk said. "Misha didn't die here. He died far away. He died in India."

He'd paused for her reaction, but she was more confused than anything else. What had India to do with Misha?

"He met a professor from India, who offered him a free trip if he'd just come and help stage a play. I was supposed to go, too. They bought me a ticket, but I never got on the plane. Misha went alone, and a week into his trip he died of a heart attack."

All this time she'd thought they were finally sharing their lives with mutual trust, but she'd been wrong. He'd kept things from her. There was Misha and India and whatever else he wasn't talking about. "So this explains the hole in the ground without a casket," she said. She paused to think over the last few days. "Why is this the first time I'm hearing about this?"

"Because it was one more of Misha's crazy dreams. Because I didn't think it was going to come to pass."

"You should've called the day it happened, Jaryk. I don't know how, but I could've helped you."

"There's one more thing. They had to cremate him. Misha would've wanted to be buried, but the professor in India told me they didn't have any other options in his village. I have to go there to bring back his remains."

"Oh, no you don't. They can put those ashes on a plane."

"I'm sorry, I can't stay here, Lucy."

She was trying not to take it personally, his insistence that he could not stay. Surely he didn't mean *here* as in this moment, the breath between them, the rain arriving on the windowsill. She was trying not to take what he was saying as a long goodbye, but she felt distant from him, the walls thick.

"Are you breaking up with me?"

"No, of course not," he said.

"Look me in the eye and say it."

"I have not a single reason in the world to break up with you," he said slowly, as if he were selling her an insurance policy.

"*Not a single reason*—there's a compliment! So, if you go, when would you go?"

"Rather soon."

"For how long?"

"The professor called it 'a semester-long trip,' which I took to mean several months. He wants me to help finish what Misha started."

"A semester—are you serious? Promise you'll talk this over with me again before you do anything stupid."

"Sure, Lucy."

He was keeping all of his regret and fear to himself, and she didn't know how to break him out of it. It felt like a piece of glass in her stomach, sitting there, waiting to scrape her into a deeper misery. She wanted to punch him out of his brood, but when he sat on the bed next to her, she didn't have the heart. Instead, she found herself weeping. She felt ashamed at breaking down in front of him, for not being as hard as the city demanded, and for not being able to hold the grief that was turning him away. She thought of Mama, who'd died in her own bed surrounded by everyone she'd loved, but Misha hadn't had the comfort of family. He'd outlived a war only to die in a foreign land.

The tears softened him. He cradled his body around her, and that was a message she could understand.

Between sleeping and waking, they made love; entangled in the sheets, their bodies fused into shapes the nimbleness of night allowed. When she opened her eyes, the sun was shining through her window, and his body was fierce with light. She sensed he was going to leave her, knew his escape from all that ailed him was imminent. What she didn't know was whether she would follow, whether they would see each other again. "*A semester-long trip,*" he'd said. "*Maybe longer,*" she'd heard.

....

Later that day she called him, but he didn't answer. She tried a few more times, but no luck. Come the weekend she walked to his apartment on Orchard. She knew Roger Garcia, the building super and a veteran of the Korean War. Roger always wore a Mets cap, and once he'd shown her that it was to hide a scar that traced across the back of his skull. Sometimes he'd have flowers for Lucy. When she was in a rhythm visiting Jaryk, he'd always let her know how happy he was to see her, offering her a rose, trying, maybe, to make Jaryk a little jealous.

This morning he didn't give her his usual smile and wink.

"Why the sad face? Did you find another girl, Roger?"

"You're still my girl, Lucy. Hold on just one second."

He returned from the storeroom with a letter in his hands. "Jaryk left you this," he said.

"He's not been around?"

"You could take a look yourself."

She went up to the fifth floor and opened his apartment door to find the place empty. Not empty, exactly—there were a few left-behinds: a floor mat, a broom and dustpan, the bamboo plant she'd bought him when she'd first started spending time in his apartment, but otherwise it was as if he'd never lived there at all. For a moment, she thought she'd mistaken his apartment, but no, this was 5B, so simple to remember. That was the bamboo plant she'd watered so he'd have at least one other living thing. No, he'd simply gone. She'd figured they'd have weeks together before he made any decision, but it seemed he'd already made up his mind.

She tore open his letter.

Dearest Lucy, Jaryk had written,

You gave me a beautiful life. I thought the way we were would go on forever.

Then Misha died. Everywhere I walk in this city I see his face. Somewhere in India they've got his ashes, and maybe holding his remains will bring me relief.

I told you about the professor who bought Misha's ticket and asked us to stage a play, but I didn't tell you how much the play meant to us. We performed it when we were children living in Janusz Korczak's orphanage, and it shaped our days. It gave me a purpose.

You have your life in the city, so this is crazy to even ask: will you come to India and be with me?

I know that you'll read this and think I'm a coward. I wish I had the courage to ask you in person.

I've included the information for Professor Bose if you want to get in touch.

I love you, always and everywhere

—J

She surveyed the empty space of the studio. So many hours spent here and out on the fire escape. All of it like lost time. But what nerve he had, to leave without saying goodbye! Now he expected her to halt her life, follow him to India of all places. She picked up the bamboo plant and threw it against the wall. The pot shattered into pieces. It was a while before she'd calmed down enough to clean up the mess. On the way out his door, she saw the sign she'd missed: *Apartment for Rent.*

She didn't write to him at the Indian address. She understood the grief of losing someone as close as Misha had been to Jaryk, but she wouldn't be at his beck and call. She buried his letter underneath her mattress, where she kept all things she couldn't throw away but was otherwise displeased by. That evening, she walked alone over the Brooklyn Bridge, smelling the air from the river, marveling at the construction that had kept the bridge standing for a hundred years, and, despite her anger, she wished Jaryk were with her to see the sight of gulls giving chase to the schooners docking at the pier. She missed his smell, the feel of his hand on the small of her back.

....

A week turned into two—the sun made the field at Tompkins Square Park barren with a northeasterly dust. One evening, Lucy unburied Jaryk's letter and reread the part that described his task—*to help stage a play he and Misha once performed in Janusz Korczak's orphanage.*

She was still upset but also curious about Korczak and about Jaryk's childhood in Poland. A coworker tipped her off to a place called YIVO where she might find some clues. She went to their archives and read the few translations that were available of Janusz Korczak's life. There were only the barest facts: Janusz Korczak, or to those who loved him, Pan Doktor, a native of Warsaw, Poland, a literary personality, a pioneer in children's education, and the head of his own orphanage. During the German occupation of Poland, Korczak had remained with his children, though his influential friends outside of the ghetto's walls had on multiple occasions offered him ways out of the country. The last that was heard of him and his orphans was on the sixth of August, 1942. On that day, the 192 children in the compound, along with ten staff members and Korczak himself, were taken to the embarkation point, loaded into cattle cars, and driven to Treblinka and their deaths. It was a story without any loose threads. *There were no known survivors.* All the children shot or gassed or starved to death. That was the way of a death camp. But Misha had survived. So had Jaryk. Between them, there had to be a story that lay outside the books.

....

When July came, it had been four weeks since Jaryk had left for India. At the office, they finally had hired a replacement for Albert. His name was Jonas and he'd moved up from Monroe, Louisiana. Really, he was a musician, he told Lucy, but he'd studied social work so he could make his way to the big city. He had an accent that made hers seem more urbane, and when he said *"big city"* there was a note of wonder in his voice. She offered to take him out after his first day of work, but when five o'clock rolled around, she began to feel nauseous and out of breath. She blamed the chow mein she'd had for lunch.

He'd seemed so excited to discover the city, it broke her heart a little to cancel on him. "Rain check?" she said.

"Anytime," he answered.

He was handsome and, like her, had lifted his life away from a small town, searching for a dream he hadn't entirely defined.

That night, she lay on her side, a cold towel on her forehead. Nausea came and went. It was difficult even to read, so she thought of Jaryk, tried to imagine what he was up to in the land of holy cows. She turned her face toward the one fan in the room, and images came to her: Jaryk posing next to a Bengal tiger, Jaryk on a boat floating down a river as wide as an ocean.

....

The next morning, she awoke feeling lighter and went to work with lipstick on. Knowing that Jonas would be there made her want to shine. He was so well presented, with his blue blazer and his silver cuff links, as if he meant to make a good impression no matter what.

Her first client was an old regular, who just came to talk, so they got on about the grandkids and fishing off the Long Island Sound, but halfway through she started to feel an ache in her belly, but it wasn't bad enough for her to leave her desk. She grinned through it, then saw Glenn Adkins, whom she'd been counseling every week for the better part of a year. Glenn used to manage a dozen men at a textile mill that moved south, and since then he had failed to hold a steady job. At forty-six, he was too old for either deskwork or manual labor, he'd claimed, but really she knew he missed bossing people around. So he crashed from one odd job to the next, hoping to regain what he'd once had. His latest gig, which she'd helped him find, was working security at the Met on the night shift. A month on and his eyes were sandbagged; he had a hard time holding his head up.

"What am I working for?" Glenn started. "My wife left me. My kids are grown, and anyway they don't want to talk to Pop. So who cares?"

"Honey," Lucy said, grinding her teeth to keep the nausea at bay, "*I* give a damn even if you don't."

"Listen, will you come see me play jazz? I'm going to take a night off, do a real show."

"I wouldn't miss it," said Lucy. She had to excuse herself to the ladies' room, where she deposited the morning's cereal.

An elderly coworker from the retirement bureau helped her clean up. "You need to take care of yourself," the woman said. "This early on, before you're showing, nobody understands."

"Oh, it's just a stomach bug from street food," Lucy said, turning away thoughts of any other possibility.

Miles told her to go straightaway to the doctor, but going to the doctor had never been her family's custom. Her father had steeled her against going in for the small worries, preferring to administer to cuts and bruises himself, and stomach upset wasn't worth bothering anyone about, so she felt a little ashamed when she had to let Jonas call her a taxi.

Back home, she threw up once more, an expulsion so violent it left her feeling peaceful. That's when she noticed a blue jay chirping at her window. What a marvel that the bird had come, sallow city streets and all, its plume dusty, but still . . . When she made to get a closer look, he was gone in a final glimpse of blue. She tried to count the weeks since her last period, and the effort helped her fall asleep.

Sometime in the late afternoon, the phone rang. She'd resolved not to take any calls until she felt like herself, which at that moment seemed would be never again, but the phone kept ringing, and finally she got up to answer it.

"Hello," she croaked. At first it was like hearing the ocean through a conch shell, and she imagined it was Jaryk on the line. He'd finally thought to call her, thought to tell her he was okay, and she felt a great yearning for him, for what they'd built together.

But it was Jonas. "I'm just calling to check up on you," he said. "You seen the doctor yet?"

"Who are you, my father?" Lucy said, though she was flattered that he'd called.

"Don't be tough. I know how you people from Carolina can be. By the way, Miles was asking about you. Should I say you'll be back tomorrow?"

"Yes," she said, "I'll be in fighting spirits."

She looked up the closest clinic in the yellow pages and headed there straightaway, hoping to get a pill that could set her stomach at ease. Miles asking made her uncomfortable. She had a feeling he was out to get her. He was always bringing up his degree from Columbia, and she didn't have any more than a community college certificate. If it hadn't been for Albert taking a liking to her, she wouldn't have gotten the job. Some girl from Carolina with a good smile but little experience in the field—it took a stroke of magic, she knew.

At the clinic, she waited alongside folks who reminded her of people who came to the Municipal Building. Anxious like her, and a little bored, a little desperate with all that waiting, that smell of sickness and disinfectant hovering around them.

It was two hours before an elderly Indian doctor, whose last name was so long that he went by Dr. C, saw her. Dr C listened to her story of the street food and the ensuing bouts of stomach sickness, how it was the worst of times for her to miss work, their case load being heaviest in the summers. He felt around her stomach— too gently, she thought. "Are you sexually active?" he asked.

"Yes," she said, "but every time we used protection. Me and my boyfriend, that is. Right now, he's in India." Bringing up India with an Indian doctor helped to ease her anxiety. "Do you know Calcutta? He's going to a village near there."

Dr. C raised his eyebrows, which, Lucy ventured to guess, had never been trimmed and were the only hair on his face without a streak of gray. "Miss Gardner," he said, "it may be best for you to undergo a small test. As you may know, protection is not one hundred percent. There is always a small chance of the unexpected thing."

The unexpected thing. The news settled on her even before the nurse drew blood. While she waited for the results, she thought of all her girlfriends from Mebane who, over the last few years before she left, had had babies and so, entering a new part of their lives, had grown distant from her. She had babysat for them to keep up the veneer of friendship, but it wasn't permeable land—her solitude, their blossoming families.

The nurse who came to tell her didn't bother to take her back into the doctor's office. "It's good news," she whispered in Lucy's ear, and Lucy clutched her hand for dear life.

....

She walked with the news, feeling changed already by the knowledge, a different person who stepped out onto Houston than the woman who'd entered. At first, elation lifted her spirit and left her feeling cool, though the sidewalks were hot enough to grill meat on. Soon that elation gave way to terror. How would she raise this child—*alone*—and in this city of all places?

"What's up, Mama?" someone catcalled.

She walked along Broadway, then Bleecker, turning onto Mulberry to pass by the Basilica of St. Patrick's Old Cathedral. Her feet had begun to ache, but there was comfort in the ache—it held back her fear. She began to feel as if she had entered a mysterious chapter of adulthood, thus far forbidden to her, forbidden those early years with Connor, when a child was out of the question.

Six weeks was what the nurse had said, which meant that it had been just before Misha's death, when they'd been in the sweetest place.

The being inside her: could it already hear her voice? Could it—could *she* (a girl, she wanted a girl)—feel her heart's rhythm? The last few years, she'd noticed herself studying babies on the street. Once, she'd even stopped a mother to ask about her stroller, pretending she was expecting. In Mebane, as she'd cuddled her girlfriends' newborns, she began to feel the cousin of what could only be called jealousy. Now, as she walked up Houston then watched a couple herd their children into the stop at Broadway-Lafayette, because she had no desire to go home, she followed them into the station.

The parents were probably her age, maybe younger, and the children, a boy and a girl, were maybe both preschoolers. The way the mother pointed out the platform graffiti announced that they were from out of town. When they boarded the uptown D train, they searched for a map, but the car had been stripped. They wanted their children quiet, but the boy and the girl refused to sit still, playing jungle gym on the poles, smiling at a homeless man who winked back at them.

Right before Rockefeller Center, when the mother had had enough, she yelled, "Both of you, sit—or else!" The father studied her dubiously, then cradled both children into his lap.

Witnessing that embrace, Lucy felt fearful of parenthood, its enormous challenges, and what would it be like for her, with the father of the child living on another continent, gone for who knows how long? Jeannie, who ran the pastry shop in Mebane, had raised two daughters alone, and when Lucy had come by to work her part-time shift, she'd seen the struggle of single parenting.

From Texas all the way to the Supreme Court they were debating whether a woman could have an abortion, though in this town the act had been legal for two years. Even knowing about that possibility, or that she could give the child away, Lucy knew she wouldn't do either. Maybe it was her upbringing or just the bonds of the flesh, the love of an unknown sentience forming inside her. She didn't know how Jaryk would receive the news. He was a man of rituals—an everyday job, sonatas in the hallway, a call to Lucy at exactly the same time of day—and yet he was made of unknowns: who could say what Jaryk would do?

The family got off at the next stop, and Lucy was left alone to simmer. The compartment felt too small, and every time the train veered hard, she felt it in her body, worried about her unborn being jostled. Of course, that was silly. It was deep inside her, protected, and safe for the moment. She wished for that same kind of cocoon for herself, somewhere she could retreat to until she figured things out with Jaryk. She didn't even have a phone number for him, she realized.

When she got off the subway, she was on the Upper West Side, and the first wave of office workers were returning home.

She thought about what her mother would have done. Her mother, who could navigate her way out of storms by ear alone. When the world hadn't made sense to Lucy as a girl, her mother had said, *"Go talk to the pastor—but really listen,"* and she had, which was all right, because Pastor Hoffman loved her like his own daughter and would talk to her for hours, explaining in his clumsy way the difference between wrong and right.

Now, in the deep of a good muddle, she went to Jaryk's rabbi. She knocked on his office door at Temple Beth Israel, and he answered by saying, "Not at this hour, Yehoshua." She didn't know what this meant, so she persisted, knocking again. "Hello?" she said. "This is Lucy."

"Lucy?" he said, from across the door. "Is that you?"

"It's me," she said, mostly because she wasn't sure what else to say, partly because she thought it would open the door.

It opened the door. On the other side stood an enormously old man, who seemed disappointed to see her, as if he'd been expecting a divine apparition, but she parlayed his reaction with, "I'm Lucy, Jaryk's friend."

"So you are," he said, maybe for a moment imagining that other Lucy whom he'd supposed her to be. In his prime, the rabbi might have been the tallest man in any room, but now he was so stooped he was level with her. His long gray beard had curled around his belly, which, like his fingers and his forearms, was a size too large. He had thin wire-rim glasses, which shook a little as he spoke, because he had the habit of jittering his head as he projected his words into the air. "Jaryk is an old soul," he said.

She expected him to go on, but he stopped there and appraised her. His eyes welled up. His whole form became the sadness his words missed.

"He's gone away," she said. "And I thought maybe you could help me in my figuring?"

"*Figuring*," the rabbi said. He chewed on the word before he led her out of his office and through a dimly lit corridor into a padlocked room marked Books and Other. He flipped through a set of keys he had chained to his belt and opened the door only after considerable searching.

It was a high-ceilinged room true to its name—Books and Other—with books and voluminous folders and parchments stacked floor to ceiling, rising in places to tower above the unfinished woodwork. Each row of stacks led to another artery of the room. The rabbi mumbled under his breath. Several times he inspected a book from the middle of a heap without upsetting the delicate geometry.

Finally, the rabbi stopped in front of a particularly disheveled pile and gave one manuscript particular attention. "There's a story from the midrash," he said. "It's about an orphan who lived in the Second Temple, before it was destroyed. This boy worked as an assistant to the priests in the inner chamber, and whenever a priest opened the door, he would think, *Here is my father, here my father comes.* But no, it was never his father. He had to be content, therefore, to live as the other boys, except without the regular allowance of love. For this reason, he did not see the beauty of the chamber, where the ark was stored. He did not value in his heart the immeasurable love of God. For this reason, he waited for his own shadow, and his shadow neither came nor left his person. When he was old and gray, he had lived a life of worry and waiting. Is this a way to live?"

"No," Lucy said, because she supposed that was the right answer, but then, she'd never been good with stories where the moral was unclear. She needed the rabbi to speak directly. "Do you know why Jaryk left?"

The rabbi tapped his nose. "Perhaps," he said. He led her through several more rows of books and into one of the dim corners of the room. He combed his way through a pile of newspapers and file clippings and held up an article. It had a photograph with another bearded man, who looked like a soothsayer. "Rabindranath Tagore," the rabbi said. "The article is in Polish, but you may have it. Tagore wrote a play, Lucy, and I believe Jaryk may have felt some affinity to it. At least, he spoke about the man's philosophy. The last time we saw each other, he confessed he was taking a journey."

Lucy remembered the book of Tagore poems Jaryk had given her early in their relationship. Sometimes she'd stroke the leather cover, imagine the feel of his hands.

"Now let me ask you something," the rabbi continued. "What is our Jaryk to you?"

It was the first time he had met her gaze. The whole time they'd been together—was it a minute, half an hour, a half day, browsing those layers of manuscripts?—he'd avoided her eyes, but now she saw they were the color of icy blue water and from them spread a deep curiosity: *What was Jaryk to her?* She had spent nights at the library reading about his Warsaw before and after the war. She had even become familiar with the history of Grzybowski Street, the thoroughfares and the alleyways that would have made his world, but what was he? A year of being together and what did it come to? She saw him in her mind: the chiseled angles of his face, the graceful bend of his neck, the way his hand knew the small of her back, the furrows along his temples carved from living in a world she couldn't see. *What was Jaryk to her?* Sometimes you had to cross over oceans to answer a question.

PART 2

An Orphanage

(The nine-year-old sits by the upstairs window. All week he's wanted to roam the streets, but Pan Doktor has said in his stern voice that it is not safe. All afternoon Esterka, his beloved teacher, has watched him from afar. She knows his moods and so, approaching the window, can feel that he is full of surliness and suspicion.)

ESTERKA: Strangest thing, we're looking for someone to be the hero of the play and I come up here and I see the handsomest boy standing by the window. I just wish he would join us for auditions. What do you suppose?

(The boy continues to stare out the window.)

ESTERKA: Hanna is auditioning for the part of the Flower Girl and Mordechai wants to be the Village Headman and Misha the Uncle. Even Pan Doktor will play a part. Better to play or better to be left out?

(The street is quiet. Not even a donkey walks its furrows. Esterka touches the boy's shoulder.)

ESTERKA: One other thing—the hero of this play, he was like you in many ways. Would you like to hear about him?

(The boy nods faintly.)

ESTERKA: Like you, he wanted very much to leave his house, but he could not. All day he looked at the mountains and wanted to bathe in waterfalls, but his guardian said he couldn't do any of that.

BOY: So . . . what did he do?

ESTERKA: He learned to see the world in his mind. The mountains, the clear water pools, all of the King's road.

BOY: Why can't I be by the window?

(Enter a thinly bespectacled, respectably balding, noticeably limping man. He possesses an ease around the boy earned from a lifetime of stewardship.)

PAN DOKTOR: Because you have a cold and by the window there is a draft and if you catch more of the draft you might catch more of a cold.

BOY: Let me see who's there. Lift me up and I'll see.

(Pan Doktor raises the boy to the window. The street is empty. A cold sun falls through the glass.)

BOY: I see a man with raspberries on his head and a donkey with two tails I see Hanna skipping rope on a roof I see Misha carrying the biggest cake I ever seen.

ESTERKA: Will you come down with us now? Will you take part with the others?

(The boy smiles his gap-toothed smile, leaves with Esterka.
Pan Doktor keeps by the window, observes the patrol of a soldier in uniform. The soldier strolls from the apple tree to the gate of the house.
Pan Doktor watches a man dressed like an inspector nod to the soldier and pass the gate. The man is blue-eyed; full-bellied; long-stepped.
On the bottom-most floor, he passes slow-moving children who are making a stage: a frayed green mat that is to mean grass, a hollowed

door hung by twine that is to mean window. Up the stairs rumbles
this man dressed like an inspector; blue-eyed; full-bellied; long-stepped.
The man meets Pan Doktor by the upstairs window.)

IGOR NEWERLY: I've heard the news and rushed back for you,
   Pan Doktor. I've brought a note that will take you past the
   Wall. Close this orphanage. If you do, some may still escape.
   Upon my God, *you* will escape. Let me hold your hand, sir.
   You are so thin. Please, come with me, Pan Doktor. This
   cannot be your end.
PAN DOKTOR: Come with you? Why, dear sir?
NEWERLY: They will take you all. The Ukrainians and the
   Latvians are here. There has been talk. You know what
   will happen. You know that crossing the Wall is no longer
   simple, even for me. I may not be able to return, though I
   wish to give you a thousand chances. Do not waste this life.
   Presently come!
PAN DOKTOR: Ah, but I cannot leave unless two hundred
   children can fit under my coat and pass through the Wall
   unscratched, but two hundred children cannot fit under my
   coat and so I cannot pass the Wall unscratched. Excuse me,
   dear Igor, but I must make arrangements for the play.
NEWERLY: A play? Good Doctor, are you gone mad? What for?
PAN DOKTOR: Dear Igor, a play for the end of the world, of
   course.

Misha's Calcutta Diary

I don't know where else to begin but around my last days. I mean I've been told with not so much doubt that I am good as dead. They wanted to make a surgery of me, start with a pacemaker and end with no heart at all. I saved them the trouble, all the nurses who'd fuss, the doctors who'd speak in that voice serious enough to make believe they cared when they didn't one way or the other way.

I am thankful the heart attack came on the second of the month because it is on the second of every month that Gladys visits my apartment to collect the rent. Long time ago when I forgot to pay on the first instead of making explosion she baked me a cake—it was an upside-down orange cake (and who knew cakes could taste so good upside down?) though over the years she has baked everything in her collection: lemon meringue, double chocolate, key lime pie, carrot cake (my favorite)—and so I have come to expect her each evening of the second of every month, making a pot of tea to have with a slice or two or three of her offering.

She came in because she heard my teakettle sounding a perfect note and no one to open the door or to answer the tea. I am telling you that Gladys is a good woman, and were she not married to a decent man perhaps there would have been something between us. In any case, she opened the door with her landlady key and found me clutching my heart.

Later, when I woke up in the hospital, she'd say, "You were listening to some old Yiddish croon. That's what did you in."

I did not think so. I have Yiddish music on the turntable at all times—songs sad enough for my beard to get wet—but that was the first heart attack of my life. I am fifty years old, too young to have the heart stop working as it did. Anyway, I checked *No* on the boxes that asked if I would do this procedure or that one, or if I would change my eating ways (double No on that). I keep little love for doctors, have not seen one since I got a fishhook stuck in my hand, and that was only for the stitches.

So, I didn't tell Jaryk about the heart attack or the diagnosis, *congestive heart failure,* or all the ways I could now stretch my life a little longer. I hardly saw him after coming back from the hospital and before going to India. Gladys had her eye on me, and Jaryk was with Lucy. I didn't want to get in the middle of that. I had Gladys promise that she wouldn't tell Jaryk neither. I wanted him to be able to fall in love without a dying old man getting in the way.

Besides Gladys, the one person who did know was the professor. I felt it was only right to explain why I wanted a one-way ticket. It was a long shot that Jaryk would come along. I knew that from the beginning. The professor looked at me and said, "It is a good place to die."

That is what he said, no squeamishness at all about my going. He wants me there to help the village people. I know that, and I know he wants his own name in the papers. It's the first time in my life I can help poor people with my hands and history. It is the first time that something from my life can be used for the sake of others. I cannot go back and become what Pan Doktor was to Jaryk and me. I have not lived that life, not at all.

But I remember what that play did for us. It made our days bearable, all that ghetto heat, all that feeling that reminded us just how unloved we were any time we stepped a foot from Pan Doktor's house. We knew we were meant for death. Even the littlest ones knew. Especially Jaryk. Not once in my days in America did I meet a nine-year-old boy who seemed to know something about dying, but so many of our orphans did. So many of them knew exactly what it was. We had that play to make believe death was something honorable and exotic like a vacation to somewhere with cliffs and gentle currents. I don't know now if that is true, or really anymore what death is—though surely I will soon enough— but I think in my heart that it is better for children to believe the kinder story.

This boy Neel who will play the boy Jaryk played is wise beyond himself. They took his daddy from him, and now his mama is armed with a rifle.

I will stand in this village long as I can. I will protect them, for I have a fight or two left in me. That day they came to harass they yelled at me, confused I'd come, and I yelled right back. I laughed in their face, and the gang turned back around. I don't know how long I can do this, but I will till they put me in the earth.

If I ever see Jaryk again, I want him to know that there is still time for us to help others as Pan Doktor and Madam Stefa did. They could've run, but they did not leave us. I could go back and die in Gladys's apartment, but where's the joy in that?

Anyway, Neel knows me now. His mother knows me, and there is something fetching in her eye whenever she tries to pronounce my full name. At least we have settled on *Misha* and I have found hers, which is like a song into itself, *Hema*, which means gold, the professor says, like the lines she draws along her palms, which shine in the afternoon sun. If I were not an old man set for death and if she were not in mourning and if there were not between us a language and the distance of many countries, there might've come something special for us—something maybe a little sweet, like Gladys's upside-down cake.

The Village

When night came, the constables outfitted Jaryk's room with a radio. The gift felt like an act of mercy—an insomniac's best ally. It was a proper Marconi with metal dials greased with oil and an antenna, which at its full wingspan nearly touched the low ceiling. He shuffled through to settle on what seemed like theater. Dramatic whispers, muffled shouts. The actors were speaking so close to the microphone he could imagine he was listening to them in the studio. Musical interludes filled the spaces between one soliloquy and the next; the music was sad but tolerably so, as if what the melodies conjured were a familiar guest, recently diseased.

Misha would never have approved of such music. He was a man who loved the big bands. They'd searched the city for the brass troupes that came touring from New Orleans. Elaborately suited men in pompadours playing through the other side of night. Misha's beard shaking to Louisiana rhythms.

Listening to Calcutta radio, Jaryk didn't understand the words, but he thought the melody was Lucy's kind of melody (she had, after all, been enamored of his cantor the one time she'd slipped into his synagogue), and as he fought for sleep, he tried to imagine her life in New York. Maybe she would be out with her girlfriend Renée. Maybe she would be arguing with her dad in Mebane. Or maybe she would be reading a book with the warm air coming in through an open window, the nail polish drying on her toes.

He'd wanted to keep the possibility of India away from her. He didn't think the trip would ever happen; even in May, after Misha arrived at his apartment with a set of passport pictures, he hadn't believed he would end up *here*. So, he didn't involve Lucy, out of expediency, he first thought, though it was likely there was more, a liminal fear he did not wish to address.

It was a question of who could know the whole truth. If he told Lucy about the play, she'd want to know more, how he'd been able to survive the deportations when all the other orphans hadn't. This was what he wouldn't reveal to anyone in the world. It made life with Misha a brotherhood. A shared history. A refuge where there was nothing and no one to impugn.

Though even with Misha, he hadn't offered the whole truth. He hadn't told Misha what he'd done that day to escape. Instead, what Misha knew of their last day in Warsaw, when Misha was working on the other side of the ghetto's walls, was what Jaryk believed to be a reasonable version of the truth: that in the chaos of the deportations, he'd gotten lost from the others, that he'd then wandered and made it to the countryside, where he'd taught himself to survive until the war ended. At first when they'd met in the DP camp, Misha had pressed to know more, but Jaryk had kept the truth to himself; he hadn't dared explain that last day with Pan Doktor and Madam Stefa—how he'd jumped the train and left them to survive on his own in the woods. Now there was no one left to tell.

When the attendant came to deliver his breakfast, the radio was murmuring slow morning songs. He'd hardly slept, but he still wanted to see the sun. The deputy had informed him he was free to go as soon as he secured "proper transportation," but he still felt like a prisoner. He asked the morning watch if he could venture outside, and in a somber procession, they led him to the prison hospital grounds.

It was a fragrant, humid morning. Along the length of a foot-ball field protected by sentries and high concrete walls, dozens of unwell convicts milled in loose groups. They were all dressed in white; some were shackled at the wrists but could still loiter around; a few, he noticed, were escorted at all times by guards. They looked so young. College boys with bandages on their foreheads, or eye patches barely covering a swelling bruise.

His presence triggered a fierce whispering among the prisoners, and soon the field was hushed. They were all watching him: the constables, the prisoners—even the washerwoman hanging uniforms on a clothesline had paused her work.

"What?" he said. "What's the problem?" What could he do for them? What had Misha planned to do for all the poor souls here? It wasn't his war. It wasn't his fight to take on.

The last time Jaryk had seen Misha was at the Brighton Beach apartment, a couple of days before they were supposed to fly to India. Misha had set his traveling clothes out on his bed.

"Will I look funny in these?" Misha had asked, holding up a pair of beige shorts.

Jaryk couldn't remember Misha ever wearing anything but long, dark pants, even from their time in Poland. "You will absolutely look and feel funny in those," Jaryk said.

"Bah!" Misha spat. "Live a little, will you?"

Afterwards, Misha had shared what he'd gathered from his research. They were taking youths from the city, lads who'd rather be studying economics or writing poetry, or the ones they'd corralled from the villages, who had no money to their name, who fashioned bows and arrows from the wood of their ancestral trees. The problem was familiar: they wanted to live in a world where everyone—even the refugees from Bangladesh—had their share of workable land, but wealth belonged to the old guard.

Now he didn't return to his holding room, though that would have relieved him of the attention. Instead, he closed his eyes and allowed the morning sun to bathe him in its light.

When he looked up again, the prisoners had resumed their shuffling. Even the constables who'd brought him down had returned to their own pursuits; they were passing around snuff and dealing a deck of cards. He felt the soft, trilling sounds of Bengali create a veil of anonymity that rested above him, a layer beneath the rising heat of the day, so that, his eyes closed, he could imagine Misha in his largeness, in his perpetual busyness.

It was Misha who'd taught him to wear a watch. On the eve of his beginning work at the synagogue, they'd headed to Chinatown with a mission. Misha believed that wearing a watch helped turn a boy into a man. So, they combed the street vendors and the basement shops along Canal until at last, on Mulberry Street, they found the perfect one: its original scrawl of *Montefiore* half-erased by wear, with a silver band and a gold-tipped windup pin, and when Jaryk put it on, Misha said, "Now you are free to go."

The next day, Misha took off work to accompany him to the Upper West Side. Too nervous to simply walk inside, Jaryk asked that they first get a feel for the neighborhood, so they circled Temple Beth Israel, sniffing the place out like detectives. At the time, his bookkeeping experience seemed questionable; while he'd been noticed at the docks for his ability to quickly add and subtract the prices of cuts and subsequently been promoted to working Fridays in the office, coordinating delivery routes and schedules, he didn't know if this work was a bookkeeper's work. He doubted his experience and doubted himself, but Misha told him, the moment before he walked into the dim hall of the synagogue, "If you pretend you know bookkeeping, then you know bookkeeping." Misha meant that he should seem confident—be a model of sturdiness and resolve—but Jaryk could also smell Misha's anxiety, and it was this pinch of failure from a man who wasn't afraid of much at all that pushed him to knock on the rabbi's door.

On the prison grounds, as he wound up his well-worn *Montefiore* watch, Jaryk found himself weeping. He turned his body away from the groups of shuffling men, so there was no one to see.

The news about Misha's death came from Professor Bose, who'd called him at Rabbi Samuel's office and repeated the facts half a dozen times before Jaryk accepted the situation for what it was. Now he could put the story together for himself. On the sixth day of his India visit, after Misha had found his way to Professor's Bose's estate, his heart had stopped, or perhaps it had not simply stopped but sputtered its way to a final exhaustion; he liked to believe that it had not been a struggle, that whatever pain had come had diminished quickly. On this point the professor had agreed, "He died in his sleep, probably no pain at all."

The professor had said he'd kept the guest room intact with Misha's things. Jaryk wanted to collect Misha's possessions, sleep in the bed where Misha took his last breath. He didn't sit shiva when he got the news that morning, or at any time the whole afternoon as he made arrangements for the funeral; but in the evening, he lay on his couch and flipped through Misha's picture album. Of the album's two hundred pages, only about a dozen were filled: there were a few pictures of Misha with his coworkers at the docks and a few pictures of Jaryk, a younger version, on their early trips to the far reaches of the boroughs, but otherwise the album was empty.

Those empty pages began to haunt him. He forced himself to remember moments of joy—from the early days at the docks; earlier, at the orphanage, before the war began in earnest—but even those moments came unmoored from their bliss.

It was the beat of his Ukrainian landlady's towel washing, the violence with which she pummeled the towels against the bathtub, that finally roused him.

The traffic Sunday-subdued and the washing finished, there was almost silence. Except for the hum of his answering machine, which had been calling to him all this time. He pressed Play with his big toe. Five messages, all Lucy. The last one: *"Jaryk, honey, I'm coming over. I'm coming over, whether you like it or not. I'm bringing beer, and we'll watch Here's Lucy on TV."*

It seemed to him the greatest missive of love, frightening in its boldness, impossible to claim.

························

Later that morning, through the bars of his cell, he saw a young man dressed in a paisley shirt and dark slacks brought into the room next to his. Two guards he'd seen before were leading him by the elbows. For a moment, they locked eyes. The man called out, "Hello, you there—can you help me?"

The guards pushed their charge into the cell next to his. "Don't mind," one said to Jaryk.

When the door to the adjacent cell was shut, he heard the rapping of a baton against steel. A rapid conversation in Bengali. "They have imprisoned me wrongly!" cried the man.

Then baton struck flesh, the dull thud of bone. It had been years, but Jaryk knew that sound from the work of the black boots. Instinctively, he started to yell. At first the sounds that came out seemed closer to country Polish, and he had to focus to enunciate in English, "Stop, stop right now!"

More whispered Bengali. The panting of the youth through the walls began to ease. One of the guards came to Jaryk's cell and smiled. "No worry, sir. That one is Naxalite. He was found making bombs. Many apologies for disturbance."

Jaryk gripped the bars of his cell, tried to peer into the next one. He couldn't hear the young man anymore. "I thought this was a military hospital, not a prison. I need to make a call. I need to get out of here."

"Certainly, sir. Use of phone is permitted. Let me get deputy."

Almost an hour passed before the deputy came to retrieve Jaryk. Now, there was no one in the cell next to his, only a spot of blood by the latrine. "What happened to the man you brought? Where did he go?"

"I am not knowing, sir," the deputy said. "So many pass through, it is hard to remember each."

He tried to call the professor that morning, but the professor was out, his butler said. The incident with the accused bomb maker had unsettled Jaryk. He was being lied to, treated as if he were a child. Still, his purpose was to retrieve Misha's remains; he didn't want to become entangled in a guerrilla war. He tried the professor again. Again, the butler chided him, "No professor. Call later, maybe."

Aside from the Bose estate, the only other number he had was the Pals'. He reached them on his fourth attempt that morning. Mrs. Pal answered the phone in a voice deeper, more sonorous than he remembered it.

"This is Jaryk, your houseguest," he said, terrified that she'd forgotten him, though their encounter was only a day removed. Perhaps his endeavors to contact them amounted to no more than a foreigner's foolishness.

When she answered, "How is your sunburn?" he felt grateful for the goodness of strangers. The poultice Mrs. Pal's children had spread on his arms had helped mitigate the painful spots of red into manageable rings of suntan. "Much improved," he said. "But I'm calling because I need your help, your husband's help, with an urgent matter."

"I'm afraid he's out at the moment, ferrying guests. Why don't you tell me what you need?"

He explained his predicament in a way he hoped didn't sound desperate. A minor cut above the eye, he said, earned from a hasty move at an intersection. He shared the fact that his bicycle had been removed from him and that he was now in a state of virtual custody, a crimeless prisoner. "They are saying it's to protect me from the troublemakers, but I know nothing about that.

"I need your help to get to Shantiniketan. You're the only people I know here."

There was a pause before Mrs. Pal answered, perhaps even a susurration on the line, during which he feared he would be left alone, the sequence of his days in India spent winnowing from the holding room to the switchboard to the grounds, becoming over time no different than the other prisoners; but Mrs. Pal said at last, "You know, as a child I traveled to Shantiniketan. We would learn about the flora and fauna.

"Stay put. We shall come to get you." Then, continuing in her agreeable tone, "For West Bengal touring, my husband charges forty-five rupees a day."

He was relieved, not only that they had agreed to save him from his sequester. but that he would reciprocate in a familiar way.

....

At three o'clock that afternoon, Mr. Pal arrived, wearing a three-piece suit. Jaryk found the outfit to be poorly chosen for the weather and ill-fitting to boot—Mr. Pal's belly testing the vest buttons and his slim forearms poking out from the sleeves—but the garment seemed to confer importance: constables saluted, tea was ordered, and a tour of the premises readily offered.

"Not presently," Mr. Pal said. He spoke to the constables in English and to the ranking officers in Bengali. There was a mélange of forms to fill, all the more, it seemed, because the deputy and his deputy were away for tea and proper authorizations were required for Jaryk's transfer into the free world. This was all handled by Mr. Pal, who balanced his teacup on the flat of his palm and spoke about his time traveling the north of England. Afterwards, a group of deferential policemen led them back to his cell.

"You were pretending to be someone," Jaryk said, as he collected his things.

"Only the chief inspector of military hospitals," Mr. Pal said. "And a childhood friend of the venerable Mrs. Gandhi. Nowadays, some of these institutions have been converted into prisons. I'm pleased you received care for your wound, though not so pleased you got that care here."

A few blocks from the hospital, they came upon Mr. Pal's white Ambassador, where in the backseat Avik and Priya were fanning their mother. Jaryk hadn't been expecting the entire family and was unprepared for Avik running from the car and into his arms for a sizable hug, but he responded as casually as he knew how; he patted Avik's head lightly and extended his hand to Mrs. Pal.

"Avik and Priya have never been to Shantiniketan," Mrs. Pal said, as if it were for their benefit that he'd solicited their services and chosen the remotest of towns.

....

On the road, Jaryk soon found that all four of the Pals were great debaters; even the youngest one, Avik, had no problems taking arguments apart. The taxi had just gotten out of the city and onto a country path when the conversation turned fiery. One moment, Priya was explaining how she'd learned about the invention of the zero—a discovery of the Indus Valley, she said—when her father clucked his tongue and praised the Egyptians for the same numerological feat. "But Papa," Priya said, "zero is ours." She had the limitless confidence of an eight-year-old raised in a house of love. Even though her brother, two years younger, was chorusing her father's words, she fought back with the rhetoric of her teacher. Jaryk smiled, a little perplexed at the zeal, and caught Mrs. Pal's eye in the side mirror—she was looking at him with intent, weighing him as if he were one of the prized bluefins Misha would show at the docks. "So, what about this Tagore play?" she asked him. "Why such an interest for you?"

"So many stories are about how you should live your life," Jaryk said. "But this one is about how you should die."

"Oh, that is morbid," said Mrs. Pal.

"Not at all, Aditi," countered Mr. Pal. "On the contrary, thinking about your own death can feel like a spring shower, a little enlivening, actually."

"Don't go on, Mr. Pal, not in front of the children."

They let the matter drop. On both sides of the road villages emerged: women balanced enormous bales of hay on their heads, saris brightened in shales of sunlight, hips moved along with the sway of the rice crop, men prodded the bullocks, and the great beasts, the engines of toil, sniffed the humid air and rejoined their work. Since he had settled in New York, Jaryk had rarely seen the countryside. Here it was—plainspoken, untendered.

"The problem with India is its traffic system," Mr. Pal said. Beyond the bend a shepherd was leading his thirty or forty sheep, and though Mr. Pal honked, neither the shepherd nor his sheep moved off the road. Mr. Pal eased the car close to the shepherd, and the two men spoke as the taxi rolled along.

"Is it always like this?" Jaryk asked Mrs. Pal.

"They feel they own the countryside," she said. "But shouldn't they?"

"The shepherd informs that it can't be helped," Mr. Pal said. "All the roads are filled with the protesters, this one included. Even if I pass him, in one kilometer I'll run into a line of angry youth."

Angry youth. Were these the ones Misha had championed, the ones who wanted to reclaim land from the rich—to make something their own? Perhaps these protesters included the family of the man who'd ended up in the cell next to his.

"Some of them land in that fancy military hospital you found yourself in," said Mr. Pal, as if following his thoughts. "But know that our protests are as numerous as our collections of poetry. The shepherd says this particular is one of the last throes of the Red Army. In the last few years not only did communism become religion in the villages, we also had people fleeing across the border. Because the two Pakistans had a war, we now have a new country that both despises and adores us. Now all Bangladeshi Hindus want to come and live here. Like the Commies, they want land. They want equal treatment. But who says they get what they want?"

"We are all immigrants," Mrs. Pal said. "So don't be a bigot."

"Be that as it may, there is also the Indira factor," Mr. Pal said. "We are all tragically in love with her."

Indira Gandhi, Mrs. Pal went on to explain, had won the national elections with convincing force. She had supported the creation of Bangladesh, and in so doing had opposed not only the arch-enemy Pakistan but also its main ally, the United States.

"Your commander in chief, Mr. Nixon, was so gracious to send the USS *Enterprise* to the Bay of Bengal. Just so the sailors on the ship could get some sun, one supposes." But Indira Gandhi wasn't deterred, Mrs. Pal said. She called Nixon's bluff and sent Indian troops deep into the heart of East Pakistan, and when they returned home, the land they'd fought for was hailed as Bangladesh. The Iron Lady facing down the greatest nation on Earth. When Mrs. Gandhi was seen in Calcutta with the newly crowned prime minister of the newly minted Bangladesh, the nation and the state of West Bengal cheered.

"Anyway, Indira's predecessors mostly ousted the Naxalites," Mrs. Pal said. "The left-wing peoples who stirred up a great deal of trouble. For the last few years, every day two or three college-educated young men were making political parties."

"And making bombs," Mr. Pal added. "Thank your gods that part has been restrained."

Mr. Pal slipped the car into neutral to roll down a hill, so close to the sheep that Jaryk inhaled their grassy smell. He noticed that a couple of them had coats with burn marks and that one of them had a thickened scar where an ear should've been. He pointed this out to Mr. Pal, who said the shepherd had already explained.

"The flock lived close to a gang of graduates who made bombs in a shed. Bombs they intended to use in the city proper. Against the police and the government. One went off accidentally and took that poor fellow's ear."

The earless sheep, as if knowing it was being observed, trotted off the road, and the shepherd, cursing his luck, followed. Everywhere, unhappy young men were breaking things. Even in America, the old regime was in trouble. The trick, wherever you were, was to keep your head low to the ground, to listen, but then to move on. It wasn't always enough, though. Sometimes the black boots did their dirty work in front of you. Then, you couldn't look away; you couldn't unsee.

....

They arrived at the Bose estate as the sun was beginning to set. Seeing no one around, Jaryk opened the byzantine gates himself, and the Pals' Ambassador rolled in. There was a grand foyer from which, he imagined, countless guests had been whisked into the thick of the mansion's many soirées, for it was a house that was meant to host lavish colonial engagements, evidenced by the gargoyles carved into the gates and the wide verandas that looked onto fields of wheat. Now a piece of the veranda had crumbled, and one of the long-toothed gargoyles was a little less of tooth. The new masters weren't so keen on appearances as the old. The professor had told Jaryk a little of his inheritance at Seven and a Half Dimes, but it had seemed too theoretical then to absorb the particulars.

As he walked toward the back, he could hear music from the courtyard. Someone all in white was playing a row of bells strung on a large walnut tree as if it were a dulcimer, hammering lightly on the limbs to make music that carried in the wind.

"Hello," Jaryk called, but the man continued playing.

Mr. Pal sidled up beside Jaryk. "Judging by the prayer mark on his forehead, I believe that is the priest who visits this place. Better not to interrupt the fellow."

"I'll look for the professor." Jaryk tried the door to the house from the courtyard and found it open. What first caught his eye was a beautiful piano, which even in a room of dusty effects remained well polished, consuming its own light, and he thought of Lucy, her hands that knew Bach and Schubert by heart. Would she ever take up the instrument again, or would the city consume her with its busyness—its belief that there was always something more important to work for, just around the corner?

He saw then that a man in an indigo blue shirt was sleeping under that grand piano, his snores covering the song the priest made on the bells. Hoping he'd have a clue to the professor's whereabouts, Jaryk shook the man awake.

"Thief!" the man cried, followed by a long stream of Bengali.

Mr. Pal wobbled into the room, followed by his two sleepy children and his wide-eyed wife. "What in the heavens?"

"Thief!" the man repeated.

Mr. Pal calmed the man down, who it turned out—despite the lack of uniform—was the butler, gone down in his favorite spot for a late siesta. They weren't expecting Jaryk or the Pals, but the professor, the butler informed them, was practicing music upstairs. If Rudra Bose would have them, the butler said, hands on hips, then they would need to arrange their own dinners. "He says he is a butler, not a cook," Mrs. Pal offered, finishing the translation.

"No problem," Jaryk said. "I can go without dinner."

"We'll see about that," Mrs. Pal said.

Jaryk took a spiral staircase up to the third floor, following the sound of a flute. The melody stopped as soon as he entered the professor's study, where he found Rudra Bose behind a large mahogany desk, every square inch of which was covered by books and clippings.

"Welcome, Mr. Smith," he said, setting his flute down on the mess of his desk. "I am so glad you have found us, even if it is under the most difficult of circumstances." When they'd met in Manhattan, Rudra Bose had been attired in a stiff suit, his golden cufflinks catching the dim light of Seven and a Half Dimes, his nervous energy attracting the bartender's scorn. Now he was in an Indian shirt, his hair oiled back, but his fingernails, chewed to their ends, betrayed a hidden fluster.

"Thank you for arranging my travel," Jaryk said.

"Of course. My deepest condolences for your loss," said the professor. "You know, Misha and I met almost every week when I was teaching at Columbia. We became friends. He talked about you all the time. Even when he arrived here, he'd tell me tales from your childhood in the orphanage. He was convinced you were on your way, on the next plane here. In the end, I suppose he was right."

How strange that this man and his oldest friend had broken bread together, Jaryk thought. How strange that while he'd been falling in love Misha had found a new companion: a bookmonger with oily hair and long, womanish lashes. He probably had soft hands, too, which Misha definitely did not. But Misha had loved to learn about the world. Once for his birthday he had bought Jaryk an engraved copy of *One Thousand and One Nights*, which he'd only skimmed, and which Lucy ultimately took back to her own apartment.

"I'd like to see how he spent his days here. I'd like to see his things," Jaryk said. "Anything he left behind."

"Tomorrow, I'll show you how he spent his days. But now follow me, and you'll see where he kept his things." The professor led Jaryk down to the second floor. They passed several rooms where all the furniture was draped in sheets, evidence of a larger life now covered away.

"This was his," said the professor, stopping at a room with a bay window that faced west, the sunset laying its colors on the plain blue sheets of Misha's last bed.

"He was cremated in the village, but I brought his ashes back," said the professor pointing to a brass urn. Jaryk tested its weight and imagined for a moment that the heft came not from the metal but from whatever Misha had left of his body in this world. He would never have wanted cremation for his friend. The ignominy of it still bothered him. "At least he passed in his sleep," Jaryk said.

"Not an hour of suffering for your dear friend. I packed all his things back into his suitcase, if you wish to look."

The twin to his own suitcase lay in the corner, just as pristine and an ugly shade of green. He touched the handle gingerly, conscious of the professor's stare. "I need a moment alone," he said.

The professor left the room, and he sat down on Misha's bed, bringing the suitcase onto his lap. Misha had bought the luggage years ago at a yard sale, but they hardly traveled, Misha having made a few trips to Florida, twice scouring Naples for retirement condos but never having the money to sign.

Inside the suitcase there was a set of Hawaiian shirts and the linen pants that Misha had proclaimed were suitable for tropical weather. He tried to find Misha's smell in those clothes, the vodka and the pomade he massaged into his beard. Maybe there was a trace, but it was mostly the mothballs he noticed, which had kept the suitcase insect-free. Besides the clothes, there was Misha's India guidebook. Misha had marked through Jaryk's copy but mostly spared his own. He'd circled a few pages like *"Important Numbers to Call in West Bengal"* and *"Basic Bengali Words,"* but mostly the book had been left unblemished, though in the middle there were newspaper clippings about a village called Gopalpur and a piece about the professor himself, whom the article described as *"debonair"* and *"cunning,"* words that Jaryk had never heard spoken about an academic. Searching the inside pocket, he found something encased in bubble wrap. It was the little wooden statue of an elephant with a boy astride it that Misha had made him after they'd returned from Little Rose, the farm he and the other orphans would retreat to in the summers.

He remembered the night at Little Rose when a storm had passed through, bringing lightning but no rain. A lilac bush burned, and the smell reached the children, who were huddled by the door of their dorm. Perfume and sulfur—but no rain. They were too scared of the storm to sleep, so Pan Doktor told stories, holding up a candle, making shapes with his fingers. Wild horses, a duck wobbling in stormy water, an old elephant standing on two feet like a man.

When they returned to the orphanage, they found the SS everywhere, the black boots marching up and down Krochmalna Street. Jaryk had cried for Little Rose, those days in sun, the light on the cornstalks. He shuffled around the rooms believing it was he who'd led the black boots into Poland, that some spilled milk from long ago—the reason why he'd been given to the orphanage by his own aunt, proof of his tainted birth—was why they'd come. It was Misha who saved him.

"It wasn't you," Misha said. "It wasn't me, it wasn't Pan Doktor or anyone else. They're just evil, and evil comes when it comes."

Misha made him something to quell the tears: an elephant with a little boy that was to mean: *There is a faraway land where boys ride elephants to school.* "Someday, we'll go there," Misha said.

For months, Jaryk had kept the carving under his pillow. He'd hidden it underneath his shirt when they marched to the cattle cars for Treblinka, had hidden it all the way to the displaced persons camp, and had even sewn it into his military blanket on the relief barge headed to America. When Misha found them their first apartment in Brighton Beach, Jaryk had crowned their mantel with the carving, where it stood for a while as their sole ornament. He'd thought he lost the piece when he moved into his own place years later, but Misha had saved it. Here it was in this country they'd once imagined through the stories of Pan Doktor.

Jaryk ran his fingers along the frame of Misha's bed, along the pillow, along the plain blue sheets. One by one he refolded Misha's clothes into his suitcase, but the statue he took with him, as if it were a trophy.

....

Downstairs, Mrs. Pal was coordinating a feast, ordering the butler to carry vats of food to the dining-room table. "You must be famished," she called.

"I could eat," Jaryk said, finding a place, though he wasn't hungry.

The professor looked on bemused as Mrs. Pal had the butler set food on the table, prepare the cutlery, and fold napkins onto Jaryk's place mat. It was a meal indeed. There was one bucket for a yellow lentil mash, another for steaming basmati rice, and a third with a soupy vegetable concoction that smelled like aubergine and onion.

"Well, it's cooking without proper ingredients or proper time," Mrs. Pal said. "But for tonight it must do."

"Just for tonight, yes?" the professor asked.

"Oh, we'll be off early morning tomorrow," said Mrs. Pal coldly.

The butler joined them. After wiping the sweat from his face with his lacy napkin, he was the first one to dig in.

"I keep an egalitarian table," announced the professor. "In any case, Rohan and I have known each other a long time. We are each other's company in this town."

Jaryk didn't mind, though Mrs. Pal seemed offended. Still, the butler's loud chewing soon became eclipsed by the collective sounds of the table. Even though the Pals had been snacking the whole car ride, they ate ravenously, shirt cuffs rolled, sari ends held back to achieve graceful motions from bucket to banana-leaf plate to mouth that struck him as being oddly athletic. Still clumsy at the art of making a ball of rice in his hands, Jaryk ate carefully, wondering, as he managed a bite, how Misha could've weathered such food, all his life a man of meat, cabbage, and liquor.

"Misha ate at the village every day," the professor said, as if guessing Jaryk's question. "He said he loved the home food."

"Which village?" Mr. Pal asked.

"Gopalpur," said the professor.

"Oh, Gopalpur," said Mrs. Pal, as if she were speaking of a maligned uncle.

"For that week he was here, Misha went every day. He started to form a bond with the children. That's where we're performing the play, you know," he said to Jaryk. "Misha said that you'd change your mind and eventually co-direct the production."

"I'm not sure I can. Let's take this one day at a time," Jaryk said.

"Why isn't your friend here?" Avik asked.

"Well," Jaryk said. "Misha didn't take care of himself too well. He didn't eat good food like you do, and it was a long journey to come here. One day he fell asleep and didn't wake up. I'm here to get his things." He looked to Mrs. Pal for help.

"Priya, Avik, this is adult conversation," Mrs. Pal offered.

"We had no choice but to cremate," the professor said to Jaryk, as if the children weren't there at all. "There are no funeral parlors within a hundred kilometers. The deed was done at Gopalpur. I can take you there tomorrow, so you can see the place for yourself."

Jaryk looked around the table with its unfamiliar foods, at the butler who ate with his mouth open. He was slow to trust, but the Pals he thought he knew. At least the children acted like children. The professor was a different matter; something in his story had lured Misha here.

"I'll go to the village tomorrow," Jaryk said. "But only if the Pals come along. They are my friends. I see you have all these rooms. No one staying in them."

The professor folded his hands on the table. He pulled at the ends of his mustache, surveying the children who might make a mess of the place. "There are many rooms here," he finally said. "We were a big family once, and now I'm the only one who's left. Anyway, we'll all go to the village tomorrow. Just know it's not a tourist trip. There'll be work to do for everyone who comes."

"No worries, I have muscles," Avik said, showing off his biceps.

At the head of the table, the butler groaned. Jaryk wasn't sure how much he'd understood of the conversation, but he thought Rohan sensed the old ways had been interrupted. Now he'd again have work to do.

....

That night Jaryk slept in Misha's bed. He dreamed he was walking on a road with a hanging moon. The moon was the size of his arm; the road led to a room with a river running through it. On one side of this room, Jaryk and the few possessions he'd had when he first arrived at the orphanage: a pocket light, a small bottle of hair oil, half empty, and a needlework he believed to have been his mother's. On the other side Madam Stefa and the children from the school. Stefa was in a high mood, and for once, she wasn't afraid to let it show. She pulled Hanna's ear and joked with Chaim about his pant cuffs being too long, but it was all for love.

There was no way to cross the water between them, so he watched as Stefa comforted his brothers and sisters. She fed them soup from a giant vat, and she let them pinch her cheeks, she was in such a mood. He waited his turn patiently, but the river swelled; who would cross such water? He waited some more. He was still a boy, but he knew the first and last thing about waiting.

The universe rewards those who wait for their destiny, then pounce accordingly. Who said that? On the other side of the river, the boys and girls were dressed like brigands, wanderers, and musicians; soon, the time would come for them.

Misha worked across the Wall and would teach them German. *Umschlagplatz.*

Once they'd gotten to ride on a carousel. It'd been for show, though they didn't know it at the time. The chairman was there, as were high-ranking officers of the SS. The carousel had been worked by the arms of starving men, he now understood, but back then he and Chaim and Hanna had loved the feeling of being launched into the air, only to fall again toward the earth.

"It's just a dirty carousel," was all Misha had said.

Those were the days the Vistula swelled with the dead.

Once, Stefa led them too close to the path of the black boots, and an officer had interrogated her in German. He still remembered how that fear felt in his belly, but during that interrogation, neither he nor his friends had screamed. They'd hardly fidgeted until the officer had let them be on their way.

"What changes is not the world but you," Madam Stefa had told them afterwards. "Even those terrible men were once beautiful children."

....

That morning the professor was nowhere to be found.

"Busy man," Rohan said with a shrug, when Jaryk had asked about Bose's whereabouts.

He was annoyed, but there was nothing to do but wait. The Pals joined him for a cup of tea. All morning they chatted. Long, winding conversations from which Jaryk learned more about Mr. Pal's profession. His guide had aspired to be a lecturer at Presidency College in Calcutta but had done poorly in his exams. "The tour-guide business came after a great deal of lost prestige," Mr. Pal said. "No one in our family had done such work. There were foreigners and their desires to see a different India."

"That is old news, Mr. Pal, and not very interesting to our friend," said Mrs. Pal.

Mr. Pal moved on to a tale about their honeymoon in the south of India, when their bus had broken down and Mr. Pal had to devise its repair with little more than a pen and a wrench. Their stories hung in the air like a lazy summer sunset, and he felt nourished by their company. By asking for their help back at the hospital, it was as he'd done in his childhood with Pan Doktor and Stefa—turned strangers into allies. If there was anything he'd been blessed with, it was this gift. He thanked the Pals for having interrupted their lives for him. The money Mr. Pal had asked for but hadn't yet collected felt insufficient to repay their kindness. Being in a house with an unfinished roof and reminders of Mr. Pal's failures as a businessman didn't help, so Mrs. Pal had agreed, he'd suspected, to give the family a change of scenery they could afford. In so doing, they'd become accidental friends. "I'm lucky to have run into you," he said.

"We feel the same," said Mrs. Pal.

When they'd first asked him about why he'd come to India, he'd skirted around the truth. Now, he said that it was for Misha; his friend's death had pulled him here.

"What was he like, your Misha? I feel he is all around us," Mrs. Pal asked.

"Well, we're not related, but he was the only family I've ever had. We lived in the same New York. I mean, we went to all the same places. It was hard to be in the city and to know he was gone for good."

"So this is your pilgrimage," said Mrs. Pal.

"Something like that," he said.

The children met them at the breakfast table and challenged him to a game called *kabaddi*, which, they explained, involving running around obstacles and tossing stones. A few minutes of running after Avik and Priya in the courtyard and Jaryk lost his wind.

"I'm not as fast as I once was," he announced.

At Pan Doktor's orphanage, he'd been the fastest boy. He remembered the August of 1940, when after a request from Pan Doktor reached Chairman Czerniaków, who in turn asked the commandant, through some blessing—or maybe a clerical error—the whole orphanage had been allowed outside the city.

It was the summer Jaryk had discovered a gift for whistling tunes he'd heard just once on the radio. His cheeks were still pudgy, but he was big for a seven-year-old and had begun to take advantage of his size, elbowing smaller boys for the choicest piece of egg-glazed bread, taunting Hanna when she struggled to skip rope, pushing Mordechai into a blackberry bush.

Misha was ten years older and had helped restore the summer camp. For weeks he'd been ferrying supplies from Warsaw. He'd repaired the woodwork inside the dorms; he'd made peace with the wary farmer, whose fields were a stone's throw away. When Jaryk and the other orphans arrived, they would have no idea the Germans had scavenged through the place.

In the late afternoons, Misha took Jaryk into the woods. Misha knew a great deal about which fruits you could eat and which ones would give your stomach an ache or worse. He told Jaryk about the differences in color between poison and life, the differences in texture between berries that would taste tart but fill you up and the sweet ones that would leave you retching for hours. Later those lessons would help Jaryk live on the land like a bison, digging through the frost for sustenance.

Every Friday before the Sabbath began, the boys would be broken up by age to hold races, with prizes for the winners: scarves woven by Madam Stefa, a promise of a trip to the carousels with Miss Esterka. After the races they would bring in the divine presence of the Sabbath, the feminine glory and power of rest, by singing wordless songs at the top of their lungs. They would sleep, nearly atop each other, two boys or two girls to a single bunk.

Jaryk never asked why he was the one who was taken under Misha's wing, but that was how it happened. On Thursdays, Misha would take Jaryk to the cornfield, and he would make him run, back and forth, between the sides of the golden stalks, until Jaryk's heart was ready to burst. Then they would rest and share an apple, while Misha talked about form, about how a boy should run. *"Hold your arms like this,"* Misha would say, *"so that you are moving with the air and not against it. Let your feet fall heel-first, then just let the toe land, and you'll be the fastest boy."* And by the third week, he *was* the fastest of them all. He won the right to Madam Stefa's coffee cake and a promise by Pan Doktor to see the castle of the kings at Kraków. After the races, he would go to Misha, coming in third, then second, then finally a decisive first, and he would say, *"How did I do?,"* to which Misha would respond, *"Do better,"* *"Better,"* and *"This time you did good, Jaryk."*

......

The next morning someone woke Jaryk by shining a flashlight in his face. It was still dark, even more so without the night's lidless moon. Maybe the sun was rising on the other side of the house, but he wouldn't wager it.

The flashlight clicked off, and he could see the professor's hands shaking from what he imagined were the effects of an entire pot of coffee. "It's time to go," said Rudra Bose, wearing what looked to be the same blue shirt the butler had worn days before.

"Go where?"

"The village. Meet me in the courtyard in five minutes."

In the courtyard, the sun was rising slowly, grazing the lower branches of the walnut tree. The professor had passed through a gate in the back and was beckoning him to follow through a path in the rice fields that looked more like mud than road. The wind still felt cool at this hour. He had to jog to keep up with the professor's lengthening shadow, thinking he was indeed out of shape—the years of tending synagogue catching up—when the professor stopped and pointed to something in the ground.

There were snakes swimming in the paddy, congregating where the professor's flashlight hit the water. The largest snake was an arm's length, and smaller ones circled around. Beside the professor's feet, there was a pile of shed snakeskin, which in that light looked like a stretch of rope made from indigo and silver.

"Don't worry," the professor said. "They're barely poisonous." He uncoiled one of the shed skins for Jaryk.

It was cooler than the muck Priya had massaged onto his face to calm his sunburn. He traced along the blue veins.

"I will wager that you don't see this in your New York," the professor said.

He could imagine the professor showing this same patch of paddy to Misha, the same family of serpents stretching their tongues toward the silt. Misha would've laughed. Afraid of snakes, he still would've laughed his way out of the awkwardness, out of the fear.

"I wanted to show you something about our country that you'd only see if you looked closely, if you spent the time, as I do, walking along this field every morning."

Jaryk could look closely. Ever since he'd been a little boy, he'd cataloged his life as if he were making a map of its details—the brand of the pepper grinder, the exact way the rabbi tilted his hat on a Saturday morning—for it was by noting the details that he could sense the suffering that lay ahead. Those years Pan Doktor and Madam Stefa had pretended they'd had more food stored away, he'd suspected the truth. He'd seen the blood on the old doctor's thumb from slicing the meat thin so they'd all have a piece. No one else had seen, but he had.

"Come," said the professor. "My jeep is parked on the other side."

Again he had to jog to keep up. "Why don't you park by your house?" he asked, as they entered the professor's jeep, camouflaged by trees at the end of a rice paddy.

"The government tracks my whereabouts," the professor said. "So, I like to make things difficult for them. They hate the youthful bomb makers, they hate the villagers, and they definitely hate me."

He didn't have a chance to probe as the jeep turned onto a dirt road. They were heading due east, the sun coming through the treetops. A mile or more in they came onto a paved path, and the professor drove faster. Jaryk clutched the door to keep from being jostled each time they hit a pothole.

"Almost there!" the professor yelled through the wind.

Eventually the jeep swerved onto another turnoff, which led to a hilly road. The professor leaned on the gearshift so hard that it seemed like it was his own force of will, and not the crank of the engine, that was moving them forward. In a little valley surrounded by small hills stood rows of huts and a field of goldenrod.

"This is Gopalpur," the professor said. "This is where they will perform your play."

This time Jaryk didn't bother to correct the professor that it wasn't *his* play. He was looking at the goats tethered to a barn, at a lonely cow that grazed the field. Next to the huts there were rows of gardens. In the center was a well; a boy drew water, the squeak of the pulley against the hinge like a long-lost melody.

"That one knew Misha," the professor said. "The people here were so curious. They'd never seen a pale giant before, and now they will have seen two."

But Jaryk hadn't been thinking about Misha. He'd been imagining what it'd be like to live in the country again, rise before dawn, more crickets than cars. All that good work, the purpose of the day, crowned in the gardens with the goats. He'd once tried to explain it to Lucy. "Just imagine," he'd said, "what it would be like to live like that." She'd laughed, though she came from a small town herself. For a moment, he tried to imagine her here with him, making a hut of their own.

"Come on," the professor called, handing him a flask of what he'd come to regard as the bitterest, darkest coffee—the taste reminiscent, years later, of those mornings in the mud. "There's much to be done and so little time."

He watched the boy struggle with his bucket of water all the way back to his hut. A woman came out to bring him back inside, and Jaryk saw—though it was nearly concealed in her sari—that she was carrying a rifle in her left hand; with her right, she waved to the professor.

"The people here are good people," the professor said, waving in return. "Quite friendly."

Years later, he would remember the moment when the woman with the rifle held her son's hand—the glint of light that revealed the steel she kept balanced against hip—and he would wonder, time and again, why he hadn't at that moment commandeered the jeep, turned it around, headed back to the airport. But he had not. He had stayed to learn of Misha's end.

The Blessing Circle

Most days of his life Pan Doktor believed in the goodness of the world, but this morning, the air felt dense with the evil of man. The Great Deportation had begun, and soon he knew it would be their turn. Still, he removed himself from bed. That was the hardest part, *the first step*. With the second, his body reminded him of how old it was, how hungry, how bruised and harmed; there was fluid in his lungs, and soon the heart would go, if the liver didn't go first.

Through the light of a single window, he observed his attic room. The orphanage had overflowed with too many children. There was never enough space, so a few had begun to sleep in the attic with him, arranged so beautifully on top of a single mattress that he nearly wept with delight. The world had betrayed them, but these ones still slept like children. In the early dawn light, he watched as dream after dream traveled over their brows, and he tried, with the full force of his intellect—by pressing his thumbs deep into his temples—to remember his own dream.

What was left of the dream now, the first he'd had in weeks, was mostly rubble and ghosts, but he could remember the shape, the voice, the look of a particular man, a gray-bearded mystic who had visited the orphanage. As soon as the mystic had spoken, Pan Doktor knew it was the myriad-minded man, the perennial artist, the one from far away. They had walked together into an English garden with hedges that rose leagues above their heads; sheltered by orchids and bougainvillea, Pan Doktor explained that they had been chosen for resettlement to the east. Many thousands had already gone, but Pan Doktor suspected there was no resettling to be done: the only way forward was death. The mystic listened with a bowed head, with his open palms held toward the sky, and then he said, in his quiet singsong voice, "Old friend, you must bless the world. You must bless the world before you die."

This morning what Pan Doktor remembered most was the mystic's face as he had said those words: between the wrinkles, some mixture of compassion and brotherhood and mercy but also shame. It was difficult to bless the world with an empty belly, but Pan Doktor tried his best: he sat cross-legged on the pocked wood and breathed the attic's stale air until his heart slowed. Several summers ago, he had learned of meditation, and now he channeled what he knew, taking breath and giving it away, again and again.

It was difficult to keep the eyes shut. He peeked to see the sleeping children. There was Mordechai, who told jokes to passersby on the mouth of Pawia Street. Sometimes people stopped to listen; sometimes they even laughed until their bellies hurt. In the evenings, Pan Doktor would sit Mordechai down and pluck the lice from his head. Then there was Hanna. She had lost the most weight, though the more she became skin and bone, the less she cried. She was ten years old, but she had begun to think like the elderly. Yesterday, he had found her staring at a column of ants climbing the walls for the whole of playtime hour. He didn't say a word to stop her—what could he have said? Finally, there was the youngest one, Jaryk, a nine-year-old who had come to him from the countryside, whose skin was covered by a layer of the ghetto's oily dust, some mixture of dirt, shit, and blood. Pan Doktor cleaned the sleeping boy's face with his handkerchief.

Again he closed his eyes. Again he tried. But the meditation would not come: you couldn't bless the world if you no longer believed in its goodness. His knees had tired from the sitting, but no, it didn't come, because hope was still on the other side of the sea, where the mystic was, where the gardens were as wide as the squares of Kraków. Pan Doktor surveyed his room. He had carted his books and journals into the attic, using what little space remained between the children to make piles. *The Little Review* newspaper, the books he'd written for children, medical tomes, and his favorites, *the dream journals.*

He had taught children in the orphanage to capture their dreams and to write to him or to Stefa. Stefa saw *the dream journals* as books of grammar instruction, so she would mark along the pages so thoroughly it was sometimes difficult to read the child's handwriting. But for him *the dream journals* had been a window into each child's psyche, all the unbearable fears and joys. So he would write back, as honestly as he knew how.

He shuffled through the pile underneath his cot and found Jaryk's. They never learned how the boy had discovered the orphanage. He seemed to have walked an enormous distance, and his little legs had trouble carrying him up the stairs. At first, *the dream journals* were the only way he would make his feelings known.

September 1939—Dear Pan Doktor,
    Here I begin. A moocow I see. A moocow I see jump moo moon. On the other side the swift horse big hooves. He runs from field to house my field my house. He has a wet carrot in his big brown mouth.
    This is the dream I like to have.

Pan Doktor had written back, careful when beginning the dialogue with newcomers:

Dear Jaryk,
    Thank you for sharing this beautiful dream. I will not easily forget this cow who jumps so high he crosses the moon.
    Have you settled in with your fellows? Do not be shy. If there is something you want to share with me but are afraid to with others around, this is the place. Speak your mind and do not fear.

Dear Pan Doktor,

Today Hanna lost her tooth but is funny I found it. I found it by the tree Miss Esterka reads. I said to Miss Esterka do you know where a tooth goes?

I said Hanna lost it.

She said no but she helps me dig. We push the dirt.

Then long time pass we find the head of Old Dog. One Old Dog with holes for eyes. I say to Miss Esterka don't be afraid.

Then I open Old Dog's mouth and find inside Hanna's tooth. I take this tooth and Hanna says she take it to Pan Doktor because Pan Doktor will give lozenges.

I say what about me? I want lozenges also.

Dear Jaryk,

Thank you for finding Hanna's tooth. When she'd learned she lost it, she was indeed distressed. I understand she lost it by our courtyard maple—it is a wonder of wonders how many prized possessions that one tree has kept for us.

Many years ago, there was a tree I myself would go to. It was an apple tree that produced especially sweet apples, up until the first snowfall. I never saw a dog by this tree, but I did see the face of the pet canary I once had to bury. This was when I was your age, and it was the first time I experienced life leaving this world. I would see the canary, who had sung for us, who had greeted all the guests faithfully from his position in the living room—I would see his sweet face anytime I went near that tree, anytime an apple fell.

This Old Dog—were you friends with him? Madam Stefa and I know so little about your life before the orphanage. Was the dog an unhappy memory from your life before?

Now as for candies. As you may know, I give lozenges to our children on special occasions, but I believe your finding Hanna's tooth merits its own reward. Come see me after your class with Miss Esterka.

If they lived beyond resettlement, Pan Doktor believed, he would look for a pet. A queenly bird, who behaved with only the right strangers. From the street, he heard a donkey bray; he peeked from his window to see it rise on two legs and protest its master's whip. He turned back to his journal. The pages smelled faintly of sulfur. There were stains above the margin. He would not burn these pages for kindling, though he'd often considered how wasteful it was to covet such luxuries. But the lozenges, which many a child believed could cure all the world's ills—those were long gone.

Dear Jaryk,

So, you are not speaking to me. I can accept this, but will you keep writing? Will you keep sharing your dreams?

Dear Jaryk,

I know you were in a fight today. I know the Council of Children reprimanded you with extra-time-in-room. I do not object to their decision, because we all must accept the consequences of our actions. After you have been here for six months, you may yourself run for the Council, at which time you may try and pass your own laws, but at this time, the best option is to accept extra-time-in-room.

However, to ease your mind, I have requested one of my best juniors to keep you company. Almost ten years ago, he came to this orphanage, just like you, from a farm outside Warsaw. When he first came, he knew no one. He was so afraid he barely spoke. Now he is nearly a man. He is someone I look to.

His name is Misha. Make sure you call him Sir. I'm not much for titles, but he seems to like that from the younger children.

Dear Pan Doktor,

Misha is good I push him he push me.

When Misha was my size he had moo cow too.

If you speak to cows before the sun they give milk. My aunt said once say your prayers in a cow's ear if you do this the moon will listen too.

I am a little sorry I hit Mordechai not a lot just a little.

If a dog has no food it dies even Old Dog with no food so I see his face all the time.

Last night Madam Stefa comb my hair one hundred times before bed I dream white corn the Old Dog.

Do you think Pan Doktor Old Dog will come back?

Dear Jaryk,

I am glad to hear you feel repentance about what happened with Mordechai; we all fight, once in a while, even with those we love, but the key is to see the goodness after the dust.

Regarding Old Dog: well, it is not an easy question. The best way I can answer your question—even begin to answer your question—is by telling you a story. It's an old Indian story with a prince named Nachiketas, who's sacrificed by his father and goes to the underworld. There he meets Yama, the God of the Afterlife. Yama teaches this boy many things he would not have known had he lived his life as a prince. Later, when Nachiketas passes through the world of death and back into life, he is a little wiser, a little more aware of the darkness and the light.

Perhaps Old Dog is speaking with Yama now. Perhaps they are having a fine conversation about the apples in the trees. Perhaps Old Dog is learning about the force that makes the seeds that grow the apples. When he comes back to this earth, he will know that much more about the soil and the love of God.

PART 3

Bee Hides

INDIA—AUGUST 1972

Over the years Lucy's father had accumulated a series of nonsensical expressions. He'd arrive home from work and use them as if they'd always been part of his vocabulary. Her mother found the expansion of his speech maddening—*"mice keep"* (referring to disorderliness), *"tomato catcher"* (for someone stuck in a bad job), or *"curly-toed Susan about town"* (whenever Lucy was late).

If Lucy had called her father to explain that she was flying to India to meet her boyfriend, who had disappeared on her and whose child she was carrying, he would have likely said, *"Is your brain full of bee hides?"* He'd asked her that question whenever she'd been on the precipice of doing something dumb or bold, depending on her perspective at the time, and she didn't have the courage now to ask for his blessing.

Instead, she called Timothy to explain and not explain. She would be away, she said. Away for a week. India, she said. For the man she'd told him about. But not only that. There was more but she couldn't talk long.

Timothy was too polite to press her for the details. "Well, if that's the way it is," he said, "I know you'll tell me more when it's time."

"You don't have to worry," she repeated, before she said her goodbyes.

Her plane ticket was sold on the cheap (a bucket seat with two stopovers in the Middle East, she was duly informed), but when she landed in Calcutta, after a day of nearly missed connections, the spell of fearlessness dissipated.

Now, she was terrified of the officer with the handlebar mustache, who palmed her passport with his greasy hands and said, *"You find transport out there"*; terrified by the maul and lurch of the seemingly hundred thousand orphans who came to greet her; terrified by the cow with a nose ring who walked into the middle of the road (expecting what exactly, she wanted to ask the animal), though as soon as she stumbled into the courtyard of the Park Hotel, which was the fanciest hotel she'd found (and fancy, she figured, was what she would need walking onto foreign soil), she felt herself slow down.

Her gut told her being here was the right thing to do, but in this first trimester of her pregnancy she also knew it to be an ill-advised trip. Being from India himself, her doctor had warned her about the "hordes of infectious diseases, rampant and running around." But she wanted to tell Jaryk the news herself. She wanted to tell him in person, not over the phone and not by letter.

The Park Hotel sheets were softer than any she'd ever slept on, and the staff treated her as if she were the queen of England. On her bed was a single pink rose, and on the nightstand was the steaming glass of milk she'd asked for. She scraped off the top layer of milk fat before she drank. This was her first time leaving America, though she'd once planned a budget trip around Europe with Connor so thoroughly she imagined she'd already been there. But there was no substitute for experiences like the taxi ride, which had been filed now into Lucy's lexicon of inconceivable adventures. She drank her milk, then slept uninterrupted for eighteen hours.

When she awoke, a few errant bands of sunlight had made their way through her window; she followed the pale-orange streaks and raised a window slat to find evidence of morning. She was on the eighth floor of the hotel, but even from that height and even at that early hour, she could tell Calcutta was a city of multitudes. Men in loincloths hurried rickshaws past girls dressed for convent. Barbers shaved their customers right on the street. A decrepit trolley overflowed with the rush-hour traffic, or was it merely the early-morning traffic? She had no way to be sure. She tried to imagine Jaryk wading through this city, but she couldn't. How had he known where to go? What had he eaten? Who had helped him along? He could be prideful, but she hoped he'd allowed someone to show him the ropes.

She was content to remain in the Park Hotel until the plan to reach Shantiniketan firmed up. Before getting her passport, she'd reached Professor Rudra Bose on the phone, but the connection was poor: she'd heard her every word echoed back—*"Should I bring anything? . . . Are you sure he's going to be there? . . . Who should I call if I can't find you?"*—and the professor had answered each of her questions patiently, in his fine British-Indian accent.

"If Jaryk Smith is not here, our production cannot happen," the professor had said.

Now, down in the hotel lobby, she called him again from one of the plush cubby booths where hotel guests had private conversations. Each booth was sectioned off from the others by means of a velvet curtain, and the soft lighting inside suggested the conversations that happened here were more personal than political.

She got through to Bose's office on the fifth ring. The professor didn't sound as happy to hear from her as he had before. Maybe that was only his lack of morning manners, but he gave her directions anyway, enunciating each of the foreign words as if she were a child.

"Take the train from *How*-rah Station, not *Seal*-dah," he said. It was about three hours, give or take, and would be a pleasant ride, he assured her.

....

Lucy had never been anywhere as crowded as Howrah Station. The concierge at the Park Hotel had gotten her into a sedan with tinted windows, which had taken her, feeling nearly blindfolded, across the city. The car dropped her off next to the main terminal. There were over a dozen tracks, and the loudspeaker that declared the comings and goings of the trains was barely functional; announcements came one atop another, but the words were muffled, indecipherable noise.

Worse, from the moment she'd been dropped off by the driver, bands of poor children had begun to follow her. There were other foreigners around and certainly enough wealthy-looking Indians, but all the beggars seemed to gravitate in her direction. With so many yanking at her sleeve, grasping for her suitcase, she ran into the crowd and the crowd obliged, accepting her into its scores of colors: the bright greens and blues of travel saris; the reds of the turbaned porters, hunched with their weights; the blacks of the habits of nuns, who pushed and shoved as hard as anyone.

She reached her track an hour early and congratulated herself on the accomplishment by lounging atop her suitcase and eating one of the twenty-four granola bars she'd brought to sustain her on the trip.

The child who broke her heart had dirty, knotted hair. She climbed up from the tracks like a ghost, her tiny hands and feet finding the right-sized cracks to make it over the divider. When she saw Lucy, she ran over. She couldn't have been more than four years old.

Stretching out her hand, the child said, "Milk, not money."

At the mouth of the station, the children had asked for rupees, or "*just one Amrikan dollar,*" but this was new. The child repeated again and again, as if it were a chant: "*milk, not money.*" There were strands of red in her hair. She had the strong chin of tomboys everywhere.

"What's your name?" Lucy said.

The girl seemed puzzled by the question, but she responded in her own time.

"Shristi."

It took Lucy a few tries to get it right, but she liked the sound of the name. Shristi led her to the closest vendor's stand, which carried everything from biscuits to *Redbook* magazine, and pointed to the largest bottle of milk in the refrigerator.

"That all for you?"

Shristi nodded. Her teeth were stained the same color as her palms, but her smile prodded Lucy in all the right places. She'd brought along a sketchpad and she thought that Shristi might want to draw with her, but before she had the chance to offer, Shristi was gone, walking back down into the tracks, where a pair of sunning dogs regarded her with territorial contempt, then up onto the other side of the station.

Lucy watched her for as long as she could. After Connor, she'd never found the right man in Mebane. Had she stayed, she would've found someone. That was how the law of attraction worked in small towns: live there long enough and some man would cleave through her defenses and ask for her hand; soon, a family would appear. But she hadn't done that. She'd been a trailblazer of a kind. A woman with a career, her girlfriends back home said. But it didn't mean she hadn't thought of the possibility of a child, of the imagined serenity that would come. Now that was she living it, she didn't feel any calmer. She felt anxious about how Jaryk would view the baby. She imagined him taking her into his arms and returning with her to America on the first flight home, though in her darker moments he was a different man. Full of mistrust, someone who viewed her and the life inside her as strangers. She wasn't sure which she was going to find.

When the train arrived, she was crammed next to a couple of office workers stinking of cologne. They tried to strike up a conversation. She told them about the girl on the tracks who'd asked not for money but for milk, and both men laughed. They tried to absolve her of her charitable notions. The child would probably take the milk and sell it back to someone else, then bring the money to her parents the pimps. So the men claimed, but Lucy wasn't convinced. After all, she hadn't seen any of this herself. For all she knew, the office workers were talking about some other group of children at the station, not Shristi.

"Well, we can agree to disagree," Lucy said to the men, smilingly but firmly.

....

At the sleepy station of Prantik, there was a rickshaw waiting for her, courtesy of Professor Bose. It was no mean feat climbing aboard with her suitcase while managing her dress, but she pulled it off with grace. On her way to Shantiniketan, she passed by rice terraces, sloping fields that spread as far as her eye was willing to see. Here and there were a few cows in the middle of great bounty. Mist curved around the animals' ankles and gave them the appearance of levitation—*holy flying cows*, she thought, which made her laugh.

The guesthouse where she was staying offered none of the amenities of the Park Hotel, but it was close to a deer park and just rustic enough for her tastes. The staff had been waiting all morning for her arrival. They'd prepared a plate of Bengali-style lunch delicacies they presented with such pride that she couldn't refuse, but none of what lay arranged made much sense for an empty stomach, at least for her empty stomach. The morning sickness, which in her case had been an any-hour sickness, still came when it wished. There were certain tricks that helped—sucking on lemons, for instance—but anyway, it wasn't as bad as the first few weeks, when it had seemed she'd been infected with a rare virus.

She bit into the puffed warm pockets of fried bread and it was good and doughy in her mouth, but the various vegetable concoctions were either too bitter or too spicy to eat whole. In the end, she opted for a piece of toast and stuck it in a pot of jelly, but that too was full of spice.

When the waiter came by to ask if she needed anything else, she asked for directions to the university.

"Not far," he said, pinching a straight line with his forefinger and thumb. "Two kilometers east."

The distance shocked her. Two kilometers she could jog in ten minutes, maybe less. And what then?

"Perhaps, madam, you are requiring rest?" the waiter asked.

"No," she said, firmly, and set out toward the town.

As she walked along the side of the road, receiving long stares from passersby, she worried whether she was properly dressed. It seemed innocent enough—a skirt and a sleeveless white top—but maybe the arms were too much on display, or the legs, which were free from the knees down. Then again, the women in saris were sending mixed signals: the garment did cover the legs down to the ankles, but it left open the midriff, and wasn't that worse than a little leg? There was even a woman she'd passed with a cut-off blouse, who was showing just as much arm, who had stopped by the side of the road to fill a clay jug with water from a tube well. "University?" Lucy asked her, and was directed up the road.

It was like no other university she'd seen. Teachers were holding classes under tree shade; younger students in uniform walked alongside elder classmates, who wore brightly colored dresses and shirts; the buildings were gated by gardens with sunflowers and forget-me-nots. When she started asking for Rudra Bose, it seemed everyone from the rickshaw drivers to the security guards knew who he was, though reactions varied: one of the rickshaw drivers gave her an encouraging nod farther east, but the security guards barely hid their disapproval as they showed her to the Language Arts Building, where she found the professor.

Rudra Bose was sitting in a courtyard taking notes with an old-fashioned pen; every few strokes, he would dip it into an inkpot and leave a mark on the edge of his desk. He had unruly hair, graying at the temples, and a long handlebar mustache whose ends he chewed as he scribed. An immense, restless energy emanated from him.

"Professor Bose?" she said. "I'm Lucy Gardner."

When he stood to shake her hand, Lucy noticed that a spot of ink had smudged his white pants. If they'd known each other better, she would've told him about it. She'd expected his grip to be soft, but his hold was exceptionally firm; she could feel the calluses on his palms. His breath smelled of sweetened coffee.

"A great pleasure to meet you," he said, releasing her hand. "Why don't you come into my office?"

Rudra Bose explained that he worked mostly at his outdoor desk to be among people and nature, and used his office only when visitors arrived. "Call it the sign of a sympathizing proletarian," he said. "But fresh air keeps my mind fit."

There was a musicality to his Bengali as he shouted for tea. A boy, maybe ten years old, delivered it, and the professor assumed the role of a mock-stern patriarch, scratching the boy's shaved head as he poured two cups. The boy's lack of hair made his thick, nearly fused eyebrows seem all the more severe. He was doing his best to avoid Lucy's gaze.

"His name is Neel. *Neel* means the color *blue*," the professor said. "He shall be a star performer in our play."

The boy nodded gravely, his gaze still fixed on her feet, but Lucy wouldn't have it. She tickled his ribs and got a laugh out of him. Though he nearly dropped the pot of milk, it was worth the smile he gave her. As he left the room, she noticed his knobby knees. He walked like a lithe dancer.

"You'll excuse me if I don't entirely remember our conversations," Rudra Bose said. "I have been coordinating visitors from multiple countries. Still, I'm not sure how many will come. We've started getting the right kind of press, but the difficulty is that I'm not aligned to any cause. Not to the Congress Party and not to the CPM, or any flavor of *The Communist Manifesto,* for that matter, which means visas are harder to get for everyone involved. But this play, Miss Gardner, is worth all the trouble."

"Tell me more," she said, wanting to know what had kept Jaryk here for a month. "Why do this performance now?"

"Miss Gardner—"

"It's Lucy, if you don't mind."

"Well, Lucy." He seemed discomfited by having to call her by her first name, as he ran his hands through the wild mop of his hair. "Lucy, call me Rudra. I see *The Post Office* firstly as a work of art. When I teach the play, I refer to the composition and the themes and the way emotion is constructed. Like building a house, I say. But lately, I see it as something more than a literary mansion. I suppose it's from my obsession with history.

"When I learned the play was performed in Paris the night the city fell to the Germans, when I discovered that it also had been performed in the Warsaw Ghetto during the time of the Great Deportation, I began to see it as an instrument of change. I suppose it has to do with the fact that it is performed by children. We older people are vaccinated against most strains of emotion, but the works of children occasionally manage to get through our defenses. So I've invoked the spirit of Paris, of Warsaw, of the original intention of Tagore, if it shall make a difference. And art has become academic, hasn't it? Art has been pushed into the ivory tower where only academics may invoke meaning from it.

"But what if you could have a revolution with art? What if instead of machetes and guns and bottle bombs and guerrillas in the night we could stage plays? What if the exploited could stage the plays themselves? What if the ivory tower transformed into a weapon the poor could use to change the world?"

Rudra Bose paused to take a breath; the vein in his temple was pulsing like a trapped snake. "I'm sorry," he said, "I fear I've lost you."

His hair covered an eye. A flush rose over his cheekbones. It was true that she didn't understand his history and wasn't in a position to judge, but his passion was contagious. She'd found herself compelled to listen. There was something in the creases of his face that implored her, asked for her trust. In that moment, she was willing to give it. "You haven't lost me," Lucy said. "But what is the change you're hoping for?"

"Specifically, as it relates to Gopalpur, it's a claim to land. That little boy you met, Neel, and his father walked across Bangladesh into what had been unsettled dirt. During the elections, they were visited by folks who told them who to vote for, and all the villagers showed up and did as they were told. In return, they were promised schools in the village, jobs in the winter. Instead, after the elections, they got nothing.

"Neel's father was one of the protestors. He threatened to go to the papers with the truth of the vote rigging. That's when the village was visited by thugs. That's when Neel's father died. Afterwards, the authorities came and said the land was needed to build a car factory. By the end of the year, all of the villagers have to go. But where? They've fled violence in Bangladesh. They've no money, no friends in high places. In Warsaw, *The Post Office* helped to prepare the children for death, but here it's all about a new life. About resistance! Their performance gives them publicity. It provides safekeeping."

Safekeeping. She was taking it all in. She tried to make a story of it in her head. Once upon a time there was a village in India, or rather there was just land. Into the land came people who were running from something. Or, once upon a time there was a boy who was fleeing with his mother and father. Now he was serving tea to a professor. He was missing his father.

"And Misha? What did he have to do in all this?"

"Ah, Misha," said the professor with a twinkle in his eye. "Misha was here for a short time only, but he fell in love with the village. He was their protector, you could say, much like Jaryk is now."

She flushed at the mention of Jaryk. What had he gotten himself into? "I can feel the importance of this play," she said. "But how long do you think it will take? To get the children ready to stage the production?"

"Well, that depends on a few aspects. Depends, for example, on how quickly we can find our collective vision. A few months, I would think."

It wasn't the answer she was hoping for. She wanted Jaryk to return home with her and, as soon as possible, to begin planning for the baby. A gang of children had gathered by the door and were pointing at her and giggling. She smiled at them, distractedly. It came out of her then, the question she'd been keeping to herself, guarding across interminable stretches of ocean. "So where is he, the man I came all the way here for?" she asked. "You know where I can find Jaryk—don't you?"

"Of course," Rudra Bose said. "A man who does good work is easy to find."

....

She told the professor she needed an hour. Then he would take her to see Jaryk.

The ease of it confused her. She had imagined a series of possibilities, many of which involved her wandering aimlessly in a country she didn't understand. But while her father had tried to inoculate her against upturns of fate (*"There is no such thing as a golden fish,"* he'd told her when she was four) her mother had encouraged her imagination. Her wanting of impossible things.

The man she'd been searching for was on the other side of campus, but she was in her hotel room. Pacing. From bed to table to chair.

She would go to him, and when she saw him, either she would give him a good slap for disappearing on her, or she would kiss his mouth. Or maybe both.

She picked out a dress and steamed it in the bathroom to exorcise the wrinkles. It had been her mother's favorite for the summer—a sweet blue chiffon with a respectably plunging neckline—and of the few things she'd taken from Mama's bedroom after the funeral, this had been one. It fit her perfectly. She studied herself in the mirror, feeling prettier with each turn. Her left breast had begun to waver below the right, and the moles along her calves had become too many to count, but she felt all right in blue chiffon.

....

The professor was sitting in the front seat of his open-top jeep. If he was surprised by her outfit, he didn't let it show. They traveled along the arterial road with such little hesitation that her hair lost its form and became as wild as the country itself, the half-sparse, half-dense forests of *taal* the area was famed for.

The professor had explained that Jaryk had been engaged to direct and supervise the play's production. If it was going to have the feeling of the performance in Warsaw, the professor said, then it should be directed by someone who had taken part in the original; he himself would strive to be nothing more than a facilitator. "It took some time, though, to convince Mr. Smith," Rudra Bose said.

When they reached the village of Gopalpur, they had to leave the car and go by foot through a grove of slender birchlike trees the professor explained had been transplanted to the area. From above the tree line came birdsong: grave, in octaves so somber Lucy at first confused the melody with the sound of water. They passed through a dirt trail, a pair of dragonflies hurrying them along. The professor asked questions, but she barely heard. She was woefully overdressed for the occasion, she realized, and the drumming of her heart kept her from conversation.

Gopalpur was nothing more than a few huts spread across a small valley. Cows grazed freely and sampled grass door to door. A huddle of goats was tethered to a crop barn. Lucy watched a young mother sweep the outside of her house while balancing a baby against her hip. Lucy waved to her but received only a wary nod in return.

"We've set up a small audition area where the football field used to be," the professor explained. "Just watch for the pockets of dung." He directed her through a zigzag of manure she had to lift her dress to navigate. It was hot in chiffon, and she was cursing her choice of clothing when she spotted Jaryk in a field where the grass was just long enough to tickle her ankles.

He was hammering a plank onto the side of a structure whose

purpose she could not immediately guess. His face was tanned darker than she'd ever seen him, and thinner, the cartography of his features more strikingly angular. She didn't know how to introduce herself. Jaryk was far enough away that he hadn't noticed her coming.

There were others helping him. Villagers, she guessed. Men in loincloths and a phalanx of children inspecting the progress. Among the kids, she recognized Neel, the tea bearer from the professor's office.

She yelled, "Hey, you!"

Neel turned around to wave shyly, and Jaryk finally noticed. He set his hammer carefully on the grass. His approach was painfully slow. Every few steps, he paused, inspecting her from a new distance. When he was close enough that Lucy could smell the cinnamon on his breath, she thought he seemed profoundly serious, his expression that of a man taking a long, arduous examination. Did he want her here? she wondered again—before he took her hands in his and squeezed so tightly she was sure it would bruise. He had never believed in public affection. The pressure of his hands began his message of gratitude.

················

"I was stupid to leave you in New York," Jaryk said, on their way back to Shantiniketan. "I'm usually steady as a tree."

She remembered how broken she felt standing alone in his apartment, reading his letter. She wouldn't forgive him so easily, but neither would she deny herself this moment of sweetness. "Yes, you were stupid," she finally said. "And tree, you have a lot of explaining to do."

Jaryk was staying in a single-room carriage house on the professor's property. "We'll have dinner this evening," the professor said, "after the catching up is done."

The walls in Jaryk's room were sky blue. Low ceilings: on tiptoes, he could reach the house's single structural beam. A four-poster bed took up much of the floor space; termites had eaten from one of the sections, but it was nevertheless beautiful, old mahogany. Jaryk pulled down a mosquito net and draped it with a sheet so that the daylight making its way through the half-shut window met only darkness once they settled on the cool bed.

She felt the new calluses on his hands when he touched her. Maybe they had come from building what he'd explained was a stage. But the slope of his arms felt familiar, and so did the bridge of his nose and the way it met hers when they kissed. The hollow purses marking his waist. But above his brow, she could trace a scar. This, too, was new.

"Were you expecting me?" she said.

In their silence, she heard the melody of a cuckoo's call.

"I wasn't expecting you," he said. "I was praying for you to come."

He was hungry for her and she for him. "You've forgotten how to kiss me," she said. She made him slow down. She made him come to her lips, the first time barely grazing, the second time touching only the bottom lip—"*like that,*" she said—and only when he had kissed just her bottom lip half a dozen times did she kiss him back. By then his warmth filled the room. His hands roved her skin awkwardly, hurriedly, but by then, she was beyond the rules of play.

The Dinner Party

He knew the smell of Lucy in sleep. There was the sweetness in the hollow of her neck, in the rub of wrist where she dabbed perfume. Her freshly washed hair was the dream smell of their home. But now there was the dirt slipped underneath her fingernails. How long had she been in this country? To believe the flesh of her, he rubbed his nose along her every meridian. Did they still belong to each other?

Soon, she would want to know why he'd left without a proper goodbye. She'd want to know when he was returning to New York. Questions he didn't have answers for. Not yet, anyway.

He wanted to tell her about his life here, about the Pals, who now felt like family. Professor Bose had arranged for a twice-weekly teaching position for Mr. Pal in the local school, so they remained transplanted indefinitely, just like him. Each night, he ate dinner with the Pals, Rohan the butler, and the professor in the palatial Bose mansion, and every morning he accompanied the professor to the village of Gopalpur.

Lucy knew none of this. In the shuttered cabin, it felt like the darkest part of night, but when he heard the bells from the courtyard, he knew it was only an hour before sunset, the priest so punctual in his comings and goings that Jaryk had begun to synchronize his watch with the calling of the bells.

When he'd first come to Shantiniketan with the Pals, he'd known almost nothing of the professor's plans, or of the sad story of Gopalpur, a story he'd now been inextricably linked with, whose next chapter he himself would act to shape. They were poor people; without the professor's machinations, they'd never be in the papers. Except, they'd become *his* poor people, a month here just long enough for loyalty to grow in him like a desert plant. This was despite the fact that his relationship with the village had begun with a lie.

It was the professor who'd lied. Misha hadn't died in his sleep. He'd died at Gopalpur, taking his last breath on the lap of Neel's mother, who spoke no English at all and who, as she'd first met Jaryk and understood their history, had wailed as if Misha had been one of her own. The professor had shared the information slowly, or rather, Jaryk had discovered the story himself through what the professor let slip, the choice words he used to describe Misha's time in the village. "*A martyr,*" the professor had said that first day, then corrected himself, but by then Jaryk already felt what he'd known of that other war: no one, not even those he loved, would ever tell him the whole truth.

Jaryk had pressed. "Why does everyone have a rifle?" he'd asked. "Why are all the children so skittish? Why did the woman cry when she saw me?"

Rudra Bose had told him that a week before Misha's arrival a gang of mercenaries had come to Gopalpur. Their leader claimed they had no affiliation to the government, yet they were there to reclaim the land. Their clothes bore no official insignia, yet they spoke with purpose. "*Land reclamation for the factory,*" they said. This valley that no one had lived in until refugees arrived now had to be returned to the capitalists.

There had been notices and warnings delivered in batches over the course of several weeks, which the professor and the villagers had duly ignored. That's when the mercenaries were dispatched. A car factory in place of a village, two- and four-wheelers powered by diesel and gasoline. Jobs to be had, if only the people of Gopalpur could find somewhere else to live.

The loudest of the protesters had been Neel's father, or so the professor said, his own understanding a secondhand version of the truth, being that the professor was teaching a course that morning, nowhere near the village when the mercenaries arrived. "*Bang, bang, bang,*" he'd later hear from Neel when they'd play hide-and-seek; and he'd come to believe the boy had witnessed everything: the bullet that pierced his father's skull, the blood that pooled near the well.

"I'll tell you about the rifles," the professor said to Jaryk over dinner that first night while chewing a piece of fried bread. He said it as if Jaryk had just asked the question, but Jaryk had grown quiet over his food, having gotten little out of the professor the whole day. He'd wanted to know about Misha's death, then about the rifles, then about the malaise of the village, which he'd recognized as a kind of fear no one talked about, emanating from deep in the well, mixed into the water that everyone drank, wedged into every conversation as nervous laughter or, worse, as silence.

"My friends in the black market had procured the rifles," Professor Bose said. He winked at Rohan, who seemed uneasy with the conversation. "Now the government knows that they can't send the same ragtag bunch of mercenaries. Every man, woman, and child of a certain age knows how to fire their weapon, but do you know what's more valuable to them than any weapon?

"It's you, of course," the professor said, smiling at Jaryk. "As long as an American is holding fort in the village, no harm will come to them. Now do you understand why we need you here—why the play keeps them alive?"

"Yes," he'd said. He understood all too well how a man with credentials could harbor a whole community. Pan Doktor had done the same, at least for a while.

Yesterday, he and Neel had spent hours in each other's company. He had the day off from Gopalpur, and good thing—the calluses on his palms were on the verge of bleeding. He'd awoken late to find the house mostly deserted, the Pals and the professor off somewhere. Rohan was still asleep, making the den inhospitable with his snoring.

Neel was waiting in the courtyard, a stack of papers held close to his chest. "For Professor," the boy said.

"He's not here," Jaryk said. "Did you come all the way from the village?"

Neel shrugged. Offering up the papers, he retreated to lean against the walnut tree. Jaryk had walked longer distances as a boy, but not so many had. More than the play connected them.

"Why don't I make you breakfast?" Jaryk asked. "I'm hungry myself."

"Fine, but how tall are you?" Neel asked.

"A hundred and ninety-two centimeters."

"Good, you are the tallest person I have ever met," Neel said. "Taller even than Misha."

What did the boy remember of Misha? In time Jaryk would discover more. Now he set about to make breakfast for them. There were no refrigerators in the house. Food was kept atop cabinets balanced on bowls of water to discourage the ants. Whatever wasn't used in a day or two would need to be thrown out. Jaryk didn't recognize half of the vegetables, but Neel did. Each misshapen green Neel took from Jaryk's hands and said either *This one"* or *"Not now."* In this way they mapped out a meal.

Neel gave precise instructions: "Add this one now . . . stir . . . step back . . . add spice . . . stir . . . step back . . . now taste."

"How old are you again?"

"Almost twelve," the boy said.

"Who taught you all this?"

"Mostly I teach myself. After Baba passed, Ma was too sad to cook. I listened to her long time before, so it was no problem. I learn fast."

"Baba passed"—that's how he'd been taught to talk about the killing. He knew enough about loss to know that when it was referenced, it was often in the simplest rituals.

After they'd had their first course, Neel asked, "May I teach how to make roti? I would like to teach at least one person."

"I'd like to learn," Jaryk said.

Neel found a rolling pin and a cutting board. From a ball of dough, he showed Jaryk how to make a perfect oval, which in a single motion could be tossed right on the burner, fifteen seconds to let the center rise.

"Because you have big arms," Neel said. "Your rotis will come out better than ours."

Jaryk got into a rhythm working the dough. Neel scarfed down each roti as if it were candy.

"We don't waste any food," Neel said.

"I know," Jaryk had said. "Neither do I."

The rest of the morning Neel watched Jaryk as if he were conducting a science experiment, following a few feet behind while Jaryk made the bed and rolled up the mosquito net, as he sat by the walnut tree and stared at nothing in particular. "Come on," Jaryk finally said. "Let *me* teach *you* something."

He knew countless ways of passing an afternoon from the orphanage: games involving running, or holding one's breath, or climbing trees, or memorizing the most words. During the next few hours, he entertained the boy as best as he knew how, which was good enough, it seemed, Neel coming close to him after the last run around the walnut tree, looking for a good hug—the boy's sweet coconut smell surprising him into a deeper embrace. At the end of the day, he even showed him Misha's carving and watched with pride as Neel inspected it.

This was what belonging to a place meant. It was a courtship, a slow dance with the land and the people who lived on it. He didn't know how he'd explain all of this to Lucy. The story of Gopalpur felt as if it'd spun out of his childhood, and he feared it was a world away from anything she'd understand. Still, when she awoke, he would try to tell her about the woes of the village, then about his old life. That world couldn't be saved, but maybe something here could be redeemed.

Lucy turned in her sleep. She had a habit of clutching the sheets as she sank deeper into dreams, snoring a little between the tides. He would let her rest. When she was ready, he would explain everything. Now, he dressed quietly. Once in the courtyard, he kept his eye on the cabin door. He knew she'd want to see him when she awoke.

Inside the house, what he'd first thought was an ordinary piano was playing a waltz. It still seemed strange to see an instrument playing itself, but the pianola could do this perfectly. The professor would feed a roll into the device and out would come Chopin, the keys pressing themselves in time. Few locals knew how to play the piano, Professor Bose had explained, but this was close enough.

Tonight's composition seemed more festive, danceable even. At first, Jaryk thought that it was his own mind celebrating Lucy's arrival, but no, through the windows of the mansion he could see the hurriedness of many feet. Men in gray tunics were carrying cutlery from the hall to the kitchen. Rudra Bose was carrying a giant bowl and barking orders. When he saw Jaryk, the professor called, "Help, please!"

It was hard to say no. Whenever the professor smiled, as he did often, his mustache curled impishly, which made Jaryk feel like he was in on some harmless scheme. He took the clay pot the professor was carrying and muscled it into the kitchen, where he found the butler ordering the gang of men in gray tunics.

"What's all the fuss?" Jaryk asked.

"A dinner party is all!" the professor exclaimed, a little spot of grease smeared on his chin. It was with that same look of relentless industry that the professor had asked him to help with the building of the amphitheater at Gopalpur. From the first week, the two of them had begun to attach sections of the stage, carrying planks of wood into the center of the field. Everyday Jaryk would return with mud in his hair and his nails, and when the professor came along, he'd get equally sullied; it was strange to now see the professor in fine attire.

"But what's the occasion?" Jaryk asked.

"The occasion is you," the professor said. "And, of course, our young cast from the village. Plus, I've invited the foreign guests to get early input on our direction. Half of the art is in the making, is it not? Now, won't you help get something down? You are much taller than us."

Directed by the professor, he brought down large earthenware pots from the top kitchen shelf and carried the containers into the courtyard, where a man in gray washed each one with increasing disdain. Jaryk kept looking back at the cabin, worrying Lucy might wake up alone. He refused to risk it.

....

Lucy awoke with Jaryk beside her. The cabin door had been left ajar and a streak of light came through, illuminating the lines on his face. She thought he'd been watching her sleep, which felt oddly comforting.

"I could use a good coffee," she said.

"I make no promises, but let me see what I can do," he said.

Wrapped in a bedsheet, as Jaryk left to search for coffee, Lucy peered outside. Sunset was unfolding in the professor's courtyard, lighting the tops of the mango trees in a thickening flame. Workers were laying a trail of candles from the grand walnut tree to the door of the house. One of them spotted her and yelled a "*Hullo*"; in no mood for conversation, she retreated behind the cabin door.

A minute later, the same worker came by with a set of Indian clothes. "Madam," he said, "Dr. Bose sends finery for dinner, presently."

"Presently?" Lucy said. The worker only smirked in response. She wrapped her sheet tighter and bade him goodbye.

When Jaryk returned with a overly sweetened coffee, Lucy was trying to understand the complexities of a sari. She'd seen a few different arrangements: the body entirely covered with the sari as a kind of shawl, or the midriff entirely exposed, or the shawl hung on either the left or the right shoulder; and from a few of the village women, she'd even seen the garment worn without a blouse.

She didn't know which style she was going for; really, anything would do, except that the geometry of the problem confused her. Long spools of green silk lay by Jaryk's feet.

"You listen, buddy, no way am I wearing this," she said.

"Makes two of us," Jaryk said.

Lucy was wearing just the sari's undergarment, what he'd learned was called a petticoat. He stepped forward and moved to touch her neck before drawing back, feeling her breath on his. Sometimes after they'd made love he'd think about the frames of their movement, the way she stretched her body toward him or the way he squeezed her thigh and felt the heat in his core. He moved his hand up the curve of her spine, slowly, until he took a chance and gripped the hair at the nape of her neck the way he knew she liked.

Lucy drew in a sharp breath. "Oh, no you don't," she said. "Not till you give me a full report." They'd been apart a month and a half. She had so much to tell him, and surely he had as much to tell her. The comfort by which he navigated this place made her think he wasn't just a foreigner anymore.

Jaryk promised he would deliver the report, but there remained the excuse of the dinner party. The guests, he said, were starting to arrive, and the professor had asked them to serve as greeters.

"But first," Jaryk said. "I'd like you to meet my Indian saviors."

Jaryk found the Pals debating the proper choice of clothing. After he'd complained that he couldn't sleep in Misha's old room, he'd been given his own cabin, while the entire Pal family had been stationed in a musty room with walls that smelled of ammonia and a semifunctional ceiling fan. It was here that Avik was holding up two outfits: one was a schoolboy's suit and the other was the kind of toga Lucy had seen Indian men wearing.

"Is this dinner party a formal occasion, Jaryk?" Mrs. Pal asked. "And if it is formal, shall we look like Indians or, instead, like colonials?"

Lucy said, "You can't go wrong if you look like yourself."

Jaryk introduced her to the Pals as *Lucy, from New York.* He didn't say *"Lucy, my girlfriend and future fiancée."* Nothing remotely intimate, Lucy thought. Just a name and a location. Then he expounded on the history of Jaryk-meets-the-Pals—or rather, he glossed over it. The other details, she assumed, would come in time. She found Mr. Pal immediately likable. He had what in Mebane would have been called a serious beer belly, but he moved as if he were liberated of all weight. A caterpillar-length eyebrow hair ran rampant, which she wanted to pluck. From Mrs. Pal, though, she received the aristocratic shoulder. It wasn't enmity, Lucy felt, just a hint of condescension.

"Look at you, princess," Lucy said to Priya, who was dressed in a sari, each knot perfectly done, the whole contraption a marvel of structure. "Did your mother tie that for you?"

"Oh, not at all," Mrs. Pal said. "Such trivial things they learn by themselves."

·················

Though the grand table had been dusted and expanded, most of the guests—an assortment of university faculty with their spouses as well as the foreign delegation, which consisted of three American professors of history, an old Finnish expert on Tagore's life and work, and a few scholars from Cambridge and Oxford, specializing on everything from literature to botany—remained standing in the dining room to mingle. Small earthenware plates were provided ("made in Gopalpur," the professor announced), and the spread itself consisted of a mélange of vaguely European dishes: potatoes au gratin, a broccoli casserole, cutlets placed next to bowls with red and green sauces.

At first Lucy spoke only to Mr. Pal. He regaled her with tales of the area. A few generations ago, a spiritualist had meditated under the great banyan tree by the gates of the university and decided this was to be the Tagore family's retreat. "And that spiritualist, Dwarkanath, was quite close to the Bose family. Part and parcel. And so Rudra Bose's great-grandfather built this house."

As Mr. Pal talked about the evolution of the university at Shantiniketan, Lucy studied Rudra Bose. The professor was moving among the guests with Jaryk in tow. To each camp, he introduced Jaryk as "our honored guest," and while Jaryk mumbled a few words, the professor studied the room for his next destination; in between, he got the pianola to play Brahms, berated the wait-staff for not replenishing the cutlets, and festooned the lintel with flowers.

It was only when Jaryk's imploring glances turned sour that Lucy came to his aid. She knew he couldn't tolerate parties for long. While the idea of a party excited him, he quickly tired of the repartee. He couldn't understand the purpose of small talk, couldn't imagine that a flit about the weather or the news might turn into something serious, even a friendship. The time she'd taken him to her office Christmas party, he'd later confessed he'd only stayed because she was having fun. It had meant something then, that he'd endured a little for her sake.

Professor Bose was moving Jaryk toward the foreign contingent, a group of mostly elderly men, perhaps with an interest in either Rabindranath Tagore or the history of Warsaw. There was even a reporter in the mix, taking notes while sipping from a tumbler of whiskey.

"Darlings," Lucy said to no one in particular, "I'm stealing him for a minute."

The professor had decorated the corner windowsills with forget-me-nots, and away from the crowd, Jaryk thanked her by tying a flower into her hair. "They've been grilling me. Only reason I'm still here is because of you. And the chicken," he said. To prove it, he took a large bite of the saucy concoction on his plate.

They watched the foreign contingent pass around a bottle of Black Label; heavy pours overfilled silver cups. Outside, the walnut tree shook its leaves to a cool breeze. The engorging heat had lifted, and inside the dining hall, the grand windows open, Lucy sensed the crowd, its collective voice soaring above the bells of the walnut tree, celebrating the arrival of unseasonable weather.

It was the time for rain, she'd been told, but the monsoon was late. For the moment, they were alone with each other.

Lucy remembered the tightness in her chest the last time she'd seen Jaryk's old super, Roger Garcia, who'd unfolded his palms and said simply, "He's not here." Then climbing up to the fifth floor, where she'd found his apartment empty and she'd felt humiliated, as if what they'd had wasn't worth more than a letter. "I deserved a goodbye in person," Lucy now said. "I know you were going through so much, but you should've made time for me."

"You're right," Jaryk said. "I'm sorry."

But he said it too quickly, she thought, almost reflexively, as if "*sorry*" were the way to fix any difficult situation.

"You're here in India now. It was hard for me to even imagine."

"You know, this was all Misha's great idea. Misha arranged for the passports. Misha made the itinerary. I'll show you our guide-book. Cover to cover, his terrible handwriting. We were going to help the people of Gopalpur, and then we were going to travel. From the south to the north. Tea estates, beaches, and temples. See it all on two cheap motorbikes. What a plan it was! Except, I never intended to go—not ever. It was only when he died that things changed."

When Jaryk mentioned Misha's handwriting, she remembered the girth of his hands. She had named him *Woolly Mammoth*. The memory of Misha wrapping her in a bear hug tempered her feelings toward Jaryk's disappearance; she understood it couldn't have been easy for him, grieving alone. Still, she asked, though more softly, "But you didn't tell me about any of this even before Misha died—why not?"

"Because I didn't want to burden you," Jaryk said.

"That's not good enough," she said, struggling to keep her voice down. "Not good enough for the person I want to share my life with. You left your apartment in New York. You didn't tell me any of it."

"I didn't think any of it was going to pass. Look around! I'm in a village in India. Professors are asking me about a play I performed in Warsaw thirty years ago. I'm knee deep in the problems of people I'd never heard about before I came here. Would you ever have thought up any of this, Lucy? I could never have imagined. I thought I was going to get Misha's ashes and come right back home."

"Why haven't you?" she asked quietly.

"I have a job to do here," Jaryk said. "I finally have a chance to do something good."

She didn't know what to make of this side of Jaryk. She stared at him a long while, hoping to see into his heart, but the professor found them by the window and led them back into the party's swell.

Encouraged by the flow of Black Label, the party shifted into a noisier din. The waitstaff retreated into the kitchen with a *salaam* to the professor while the butler danced from person to person, refilling empty cups with a cheeky grin. A northeasterly wind blew the Victorian curtains from their restraints, knocked down glasses, and overturned a potful of curd.

The old Finn caught Jaryk's attention. "Are you the gentleman from Warsaw?"

The group had arranged itself in a rectangle, with Lucy and Jaryk on opposite sides. Lucy could feel Jaryk looking for an escape route, but there was no easy path out of the conversational phalanx.

"Won't you tell us about your experience of the play in '42? Won't you tell us how it feels to be here in the land of the author? Do you feel you are reliving that time?"

"No, I'm not reliving that time," Jaryk said.

"I'm led to understand *The Post Office* was also performed in Paris the night the Germans took the city."

"And in Bangladesh during the crackdowns of General Tikka Khan," Rudra Bose added.

"Well, I'm here because *The Post Office* means something to Bengal right now," Jaryk said. "I'm talking about what's happened to

Gopalpur. This play protects the villagers' future. Their story is what I'm thinking of now."

"In 1942, you were the hero of the play, weren't you?

"And it was performed in the ghetto, under the most horrible of circumstances, was it not? Under the expectation of execution? With a lack of food? In the thick of the deportations?"

"Yes, in the thick," Jaryk said.

"Is that a pianola?" Lucy asked, trying her best to politely change the subject. She didn't know these men but knew they didn't have the right to grill Jaryk.

"Yes, yes. But won't you tell them about those long days and nights leading to the August of 1942?" Professor Bose asked Jaryk.

"Didn't you say you got the pianola from the British?" Jaryk asked, ignoring the professor's bait.

"Yes, it's an Aeolian, purchased straight from the British Raj by my father in 1942."

"Lucy plays. She learned since she was a kid," Jaryk said.

"May we have the honor of a performance?" Bose offered.

"We'll see," Lucy said, walking to the pianola. She ran her hands along the keys, feeling all the eyes in the room on her. The pianola had a knob on its side that she turned to stop the waltz. Then it was a regular piano again, and she sat down on the piano bench, laying her hands as her mother had taught her. Even so far from home, there were habits that would guide you: the way to sit, for example, the way to let the fingers rise above the keys, where exactly to place the feet. She could play a prelude and fugue by Bach from memory, and that was what came to her now, all the notes her mother had given her, emerging from a place of uncomplicated joy. Playing a long composition from memory was like hiking a trail her body remembered without a map, its inner choreography a compass for the next note and the one after. When she stopped, she noticed that everyone was watching her.

The professor led a cycle of applause, but she hadn't played for the attention, only wanting to feel a little at home, as if she were sitting next to Mama, staring out at the dogwoods. It took a moment to come back to the room. Jaryk's eyes were focused on hers. She could tell he was admiring her anew.

"That was beautiful," Jaryk said. "You know, I've never heard you play before."

"I've thought about getting a piano, starting to practice again. Someday, when there's time." She wanted to deflect the attention. "Hey, will you introduce me to your cast?"

The cast, their families, and the Pals were in the parlor room, separated from the rest of the party. Here the food had been scooped onto banana-leaf plates, and a line of children eating on the floor consumed most of the room's walking space. There was no Black Label to be found, and the children seemed unusually well behaved.

Jaryk introduced her to the play's main actors, a crew of four stiffly dressed children. There was the Flower Girl, who true to her role had pinned a forget-me-not onto her dress; there was the Village Headman, who was played by a chubby boy with dimples; there was the Good Uncle, played by a bespectacled boy with an infectious grin: and, finally, there was Amal, who was played by the tea bearer she'd met at the professor's office.

"It's Neel, isn't it? *Neel like blue*?" Lucy said.

"Yes, madam."

The boy didn't strike her as being the likeliest of stars. With his mother in tow, his head resting on her shoulder, he seemed ill equipped for a public performance; but then, none of the play's cast seemed to be from acting ilk, at least not the way she'd known actors to behave in her school. She herself had participated in theater with a series of uninspiring supporting roles, and had been told by Mr. Roberts, the drama teacher, who doubled as gym teacher, "The number-one rule of acting is enthusiasm." These children would never have survived a day with Mr. Roberts.

Jaryk whispered into Lucy's ear, "These kids have been through tough times." But she didn't need him to tell her that. She'd been watching the way Neel shared space with his mother. Even when he ventured away to play with the other kids, he'd hang on to the hem of her sari. While deep in play, he'd give her sari a tug, and she'd reciprocate with a pull of her own.

The professor joined them in the parlor. "I see you've met our stars," he said to Lucy.

"Did you hold auditions?" she asked. "How did you find them?"

"Auditions? Well, let us say they were for the most part—informal. Let us say that each and every villager has a part to play. They are all witness to the atrocities, that is. They are all fighting for the right to their land."

Lucy looked over at Mrs. Pal, who was frowning as openly as she was.

Lucy excused herself from Jaryk and the professor's company. She didn't know the first thing about the history of Bengal, but neither had Jaryk. She supposed she had come to India with a lover's mission: to find Jaryk and bring him home. He didn't seem amenable, though, to so simple a plan. The professor had explained that the play would be performed in a few months, but Lucy worried that Jaryk might want to stay even longer. What he loved about the Lower East Side, he had once confessed, was how he could wander the streets without needing to think, every mail-box, street sign, and phone booth a marker of home.

She hadn't told him about the baby. The time just hadn't felt right. But these last few weeks, she'd walked around with a feeling of presence. "*Moonflake,*" she would say, touching her belly, remembering a story her mother had told her about a factory where children were grown from the tiniest particles. "*And each day, Moonflake gets bigger,*" her mother would say, and she would imagine it as a luminescent snow particle, growing as it fell from the sky.

Mr. Pal joined her in the courtyard. "I'm not long for parties," he informed her, leaning back against the trunk of the walnut tree, pointing his girth toward the clouds.

"Care for a cigarette?" he asked. "Actually, it's a *bidi,* a stronger, more local equivalent."

The bidi looked more like a hastily rolled joint. The sharp smell

of the tobacco struck her fiercely, and she remembered the first
week she'd given up cigarettes. Her diary had memorialized that
time as *the Autumn of Desperation*. At work, she had chopped away
at her caseload, biting her fingernails until she left tracks of blood
on her paperwork. She'd done it for Jaryk. Rather, she'd done it
to mark the seriousness of their relationship. Inherited from her
father, the idea of a necessary sacrifice—that to gain something
good, you had to give something else up, a kind of zero-sum game
to happiness. Except, that had been in New York, and this wasn't
a cigarette. It was a local variant—did it count?

"Proper Indian tobacco," Mr. Pal said. "You will not find in
America."

She waved him away with a smile. Rules were rules, she told herself, even if no one was watching.

....

In the parlor, Jaryk helped Professor Bose serve his guests dessert
from a giant brass tureen. The banana-leaf plates, upon which the
children had feasted with grim determination, had been piled and
collected. Later, the whole bundle of leftovers would be tossed
over the fence for the wild boars and their offspring. But now it
was time for the sweet treats. Jaryk watched the professor scoop
a mound of rice pudding into little clay bowls. The children ate
each grain with delight, licking their fingers afterwards.

When they were finished, the professor announced, in English
and then Bengali, "Now we eat with our minds! We tell each other
ghost stories. We sing monsoon songs."

What ensued was a kind of collective bargaining; no one wanted
to sing, and yet everyone wanted to sing. No one wanted to tell a
story, but each of the children, Jaryk could tell, was dying to tell
a story. The Flower Girl had her hand raised in the air, as if she
were answering a question in class, but the honors were given to
Neel, who began a song in Bengali. Mr. Pal translated into Jaryk's
ear. The song was about a fisherman going out into a storm. The
winds at his back. The night beginning to descend.

The boy had a good, sure voice, not terribly melodious, but he could project his words to a much larger room; he wasn't afraid to be heard. As Neel sang, the academics from the dining room wandered into the parlor. The old Finn gaped. At least one of the Indian professors joined in the song. Lucy followed them back into the room.

"If the fisherman dies in the storm tonight," Mr. Pal translated, "then he wishes to see everything for what it is. He wishes to smell the mud on the riverbank he will not reach. He wishes to feel each splinter of the boat he has made with his own hands."

After the song, the professor announced it was time for the families to return to the village.

"I'll see you tomorrow, okay?" Jaryk told Neel.

"Okay," Neel said, though he didn't seem convinced.

"He's got a lovely voice," Lucy said to Neel's mother, who squinted in response, quickly gathering her son.

When it was only Jaryk and Lucy left in the room, Lucy stroked his neck with her fingertips.

"That was beautiful," she said.

"It was about a boatman in a storm, but somehow it felt close to home." He wanted to tell her about the pull of the village. Jaryk now believed that even before he'd come to India, on that evening when Misha had clutched his chest and Neel's mother had settled his head on her lap, he'd been bonded into their service. Misha, taking his last breath, had passed the torch. Now it would be Jaryk they'd first have to kill before they could reach Neel or any of the others. All this he wanted to tell Lucy, though where could he begin?

"I have to tell you a story," he said.

Lucy leaned into his chest. The house grew so quiet he could hear the wind through the curtains. "Me first," she said. "There's something I need to share."

Dinner at the Orphanage

(Once so grand a table, it stands now woefully meager—bereft of candlesticks, bereft of baskets of freshly made bread—though still full with children. There are perhaps a hundred of them seated from one end to the other. Pan Doktor serves them from one side from a giant tureen of watery soup; Madam Stefa serves them from the other. The children indecipherably murmur.)

PAN DOKTOR: Come now, Stefania, let us not put on such a dour face. I myself went begging to all the wealthy Jews and poured upon them such guilt that they could not refuse a portion. There is simply not enough. But the children need not know. Let us make a game of our lack.

STEFANIA *(plopping onto each child's plate a dollop of soup)*: I can count the potatoes with two hands. I can count the loaves of bread with one. Is that the kind of game you mean?

PAN DOKTOR: Precisely, Madam Stefa—quite brilliant, really. Children, we have an announcement! *(The children pause their murmuring.)* For the main course, Madam Stefa has secured ten very special potatoes. These are not the normal potatoes you are used to. No, these are from the planet Rho. Eating just a bite of a single potato, you shall feel terribly strong. You shall not feel hungry for hours. Your mind will become sharp, and you shall study your books with joy. What say you children to such potatoes?

(He cuts a single potato so finely he nicks his thumb, but covers the blood with a napkin before anyone can notice.) Who shall be the first to try this magical tuber?

(All the hands raise.)

STEFANIA *(whispering into Pan Doktor's ear):* But what will happen in two hours, Panie Doktor? Will they eat the honey of your words? How long will these games last us?
PAN DOKTOR: As long as we allow.

(After the meal is served, Pan Doktor retreats to his attic room. During the day, the room can become so hot as to dissuade visitors. The old doctor is thus surprised to find a bearded old man sitting at his writing desk.)

PAN DOKTOR: You there—announce yourself!
R. TAGORE: At your service, Rabindranath Tagore.
PAN DOKTOR: But sir, did you not die last year, upon your bed in India?
R. TAGORE: That I did, good Doctor, that I did. However, let it be known that time has remade itself within the walls of the ghetto. I do not mean anything cosmic. It is simply the result of the ingredients. Did you know that Shiva doesn't appear until his disciple submits to thousands of years of sacrifice? But how can a human being live long enough to sacrifice so much? You see, it is a matter of time bending upon itself to accommodate beauty. How else can the perfect thing be made?
PAN DOKTOR: Ah, but the perfect thing cannot be made. Of that, I am quite sure.
R. TAGORE: Are you, though? Are you entirely certain?
PAN DOKTOR: Consider, for example, the matter of our play. Rather, sir, *your* play. The performance won't be shabby, I

hope, but how can it be perfect? Hanna, who is to play the Flower Girl, has no flowers and must therefore use scraps of cloth sewn to resemble flowers. Mordechai, who is to play the Headman, has all but lost his voice, a strange bug having crawled into his throat. And Jaryk, who is to play Amal, barely knows his lines.

R. TAGORE: You don't say! Then why perform it at all, if so enfeebled? So altered from the source?

PAN DOKTOR: Obvious, sir. How else to learn of death? How else to teach a child of his own impending—

(A knock on the attic door.)

PAN DOKTOR: Sir, would you mind hiding under the bed?

(The assistant enters the room.)

MISHA: Is someone here? Good Doctor, with whom were you speaking?

PAN DOKTOR: Not a soul.

MISHA: Indeed, then. I have received the words for the invitation. Szlengel was happy to provide his voice for the occasion. He has given us three lines. Esterka and I have made copies for everyone who will attend.

PAN DOKTOR: Let me see it. Let me touch the ink with my own hands. *(He reads.)*

It transcends the test—being a mirror of the self.
It transcends emotion—being experience.
It transcends acting—being the work of children.

MISHA: But what is this test of which Szlengel speaks?

PAN DOKTOR: *The* Test. Not *this* test. For it is *the* Test that you will find in your life, dear Misha, as I find now, awaiting death with a bum knee. For it is *the* Test that will seek your heart, rent as it may one day become, and then we shall see—I will at least see from my own little perch in heaven—how you answer the call, what kind of man I taught you to become.

(Curtain.)

The News

O n the town's main road, they walked in long stretches of darkness and starlight. Jaryk asked Lucy to close her eyes as they moved farther from the row of shops. She gripped his hand as he steered her past potholes and cow manure. Once they were far away from the few street lamps, he asked her to look up. Above them, the blue dazzle of the stars, all those constellations that Pan Doktor would pretend he could name: *Fortress of the Heart,* he once called what Jaryk later learned was the Big Dipper.

He told Lucy the story. "I like Pan Doktor's version," she said. "What a blessing to see the night like this."

He remembered a power outage in New York during the summer of their first dates, how the lack of light in the city brought to their lovemaking a quietude. Hardly a noise—everything he'd felt he kept inside until the final moment—and she, who other times was as loud as the rush hour, remained with him in that silence. If she'd been otherwise, she might've startled him from falling in love.

He believed that if there was anyone who could understand what kept him here, it would be Lucy. At the dinner party, she'd pulled him away, saying she had important news, but for these last minutes of their walk, she'd grown quiet. He'd filled the space on his own, starting at the beginning.

"So I ended up in jail," he said, which he'd meant to come off as a joke, but which alarmed her, so he explained how he'd ended up in a prison hospital in Calcutta, only to be rescued by the Pals.

They'd turned up the lane that would lead to the Bose mansion. No matter how slowly he walked, Lucy walked even slower, until finally she stopped. There were moments when Lucy wanted to be embraced, but he didn't think this was one. The weight of her thinking kept him at bay.

"So it's been a difficult few weeks for me," she finally said. "When I say *difficult*, I mean it's like I've been balancing on one leg. It's like everything that was solid before isn't."

She whispered into his ear, "Jaryk, I'm pregnant."

The idea seemed so strange to him that he almost smiled, but there was enough light that he could make out her face. What it was telling him was that he should listen deeply, which he was trying to do: he was to become a father.

"Me?" he said, because that felt like the only word he could muster.

"You're going to be a daddy," Lucy said.

He felt an awakening, as if a precious gift he'd saved since childhood, kept hidden from Poland to Germany to America, could finally be unwrapped. Mixed with this came an old fear. What right had he to bring a child into this world of suffering? An orphan, a survivor, a friendless refugee—what right had he?

"Okay," he said. *Okay*. It came to him like a mantra, and he said the word again and again, until he believed it was going to be all right.

·················

At first the idea that he would be a father seemed impossible. With fatherhood came a moneyed job, a yarded house, a plan for the future, but he had none of these and so had assumed he was beyond the prerequisites for the role.

"I'm exhausted," Lucy said. "Just telling you has worn me out."

He began to feel protective of her. They headed back to their cabin, where she slept the night, and he watched her, afraid at any moment that she would require his services. The next morning, he brought her breakfast in bed. She accepted his overfried eggs, which he'd had to prepare in the near-darkness for fear of waking the butler.

"Thank God it's not spicy," she said.

"What now?" he said.

"Now we figure things out, one day at a time. I want to see what you do here, how you've been keeping yourself busy." But as soon as she said it, she began to feel queasy. He led her by the hand to the bathroom, where she threw up her breakfast.

"It's okay," she told him afterwards, gulping down a glass of orange juice. "A few more weeks and this thing they call morning sickness—which, let me tell you, is not just in the morning—will be on the way out."

The professor found them at the dining table looking at each other with a mix of what must have been fear and wonderment and expectation. "Is everything all right?" the professor asked, and almost as one, Lucy and Jaryk said—"*Mostly.*"

....

When they reached Gopalpur, he wished he could announce the news to the village men, but Lucy had told him to keep it quiet. It would have to be just the two of them who knew, at least for a while.

He began by showing her around the village. The communal area of Gopalpur, where the football field had been turned into a theater, was in the center of the little valley. The residential dwellings were spread out on upper steppes to reduce the chances of flooding. There were sixty houses arranged in an elliptical shape up the top face of the slope.

"Three hundred or so people live there," he told Lucy. He held her hand. He kept her close as they walked up the steep face, pausing every few steps to ask if she was all right.

"I'm pregnant, not old and weak," Lucy snapped.

He took her to Neel's house, which was half the size of the professor's living room. Lucy sat on the cool mud floor while Neel told her about his school life.

"The town children are jealous because we are performing this play," said Neel. "The town children have money, but we have our play."

"They have to walk ten kilometers to get to the nearest school," Jaryk added. "That's part of what we're trying to do here. If people know about this community, we can raise money for a school in the village."

"A school? I thought you wanted to raise a racket, let people know what's going on here," Lucy said.

"The professor's trying to raise a racket," Jaryk said. "And I'm thinking about their future. To have a life, you need schools and jobs."

Neel came over and interrupted. "Come, Auntie, meet my baby goats."

After their morning together, the boy had developed a ritual with Jaryk: whenever he saw him coming up the path to the village, Neel would run to greet him. He would take Jaryk's hand, as if he were a bodyguard, a tiny protector, and would lead him to the stage for the day's work. Maybe, with Lucy here, Neel had felt too shy for that, though now he again took Jaryk's hand and led them to the back of the house, where twin kids had been born the week before. The mother eyed them warily at first, but after sniffing Neel, allowed Lucy to cradle her newborns.

"You're a natural," Jaryk said.

"Don't start," Lucy said.

Down by the football field, Jaryk showed her the stage and the bleachers. All this he'd built with his own hands, he told her. They still had to sand, prime, and paint, but otherwise the space had come together.

"In Warsaw, we used the dining room of the house and made a stage out of rotting wood. Windows came from scrap metal and twine. For costumes, we used pillowcases, cutting them into what we thought were Indian dresses. But here, we're doing it properly. Everything is going to be just right."

"It's really something," she said.

An old goat wandered down to rub its nose on the side of the stage, sending shivers through the structure.

Lucy pulled Jaryk close and whispered, "Also, a man was murdered on this field. What have you gotten yourself into, Jaryk Smith?"

Every newspaper in India was beginning to cover the event, which meant that *The Telegraph* and *The Statesman* were all reporting about the three hundred people of the valley, about Neel and the death of his father. In Warsaw the play had been the prelude to death, knowing as they did that the performance meant the cattle cars were not far behind, but here *The Post Office—Dak Ghar*, as they called it—meant life.

Every time a newspaper ran an article about the upcoming performance, every time a luminary from the city promised to attend, the professor would celebrate by pouring a glass of his prized Johnnie Walker whiskey. *"L'chaim!"* he'd exclaim—*To life!* Still, Jaryk had developed the nagging doubt that the performance might also have the opposite effect, leaving the villagers worse off. In Warsaw, Pan Doktor didn't believe till the very end that they'd send a house of children to the death camps, and yet the German authorities had done exactly that. You could never know what men in power would do, what evil they'd commit. When the time was right, he'd confront the professor about his doubts, but now there was no reason to worry Lucy.

"My being here is good for them," he said. It sounded grand, as if he were their ombudsman now.

"It's also good for our baby to be close to daddy," Lucy said.

Her return to the States was less than a week away, but he harbored the secret hope that she would remain longer. They hadn't discussed when he would return; he'd been avoiding the subject. If he headed home before the play's production, he would be reneging on his duty to the villagers; but if he remained, Lucy would go back to America alone. Every week, she would head to the clinic by herself, and every week the child inside her would grow without him.

"I've traveled thousands of miles to see a village. What else do y'all do here for fun?" Lucy asked, trying to lighten the mood, Jaryk thought.

They headed back to Shantiniketan to tour the grounds. The Pal children led the way around the Tagore estate, showing Lucy the Aston Martin Tagore had driven to Calcutta, sitting her on the steps of the house where Mohandas Gandhi had come to break his final fast.

"These are the small moments of history," Mr. Pal said. "One great leader giving another a glass of orange juice."

The children laughed at some joke they'd been exchanging, and soon Mr. Pal joined in. They were always sharing anecdotes, riffing off one another. When Jaryk dreamed of his own family, laughter around the dinner table was what came to mind. To have that with Lucy, they'd need to be married, wouldn't they? Later, he would ask Mr. Pal for advice. He needed a guide, even if Mr. Pal had been married in a different tradition.

At the town's center, they showed Lucy the centuries-old banyan where Tagore's grandfather had found spiritual largesse, where he'd forsaken his possessions and put down roots in wild country. Priya scaled up the limbs of the tree with ease, and when Lucy followed, it took every ounce of his will to keep from telling her to stop. He moved closer to the tree: in case she lost her footing, he would break her fall. But she was a natural—soon she and Priya had scaled up ten or more feet to a steady limb, where they gazed down at Jaryk with a shared look of mischief and delight.

During the war he'd come to believe it would've been better if they had all perished, every single Jew and Gentile, so that their story wouldn't have to be retold, the horror of it relived. It had only been over the last year that gratitude for living had returned to him, all those mornings with Lucy waking in the tangle of her hair, and now in the village, the good mud settling into his nails. Why then did it feel as precarious as Lucy's foot on a tree limb— this thing called *happiness*—this ache in the center of him? There were moments when he wondered if it would have been better if he'd never met her at all, never accepted this risk of love.

"Come up!" she cried.

But he couldn't move. He shook his head, feet planted into the earth, arms extended should she fall.

The Rehearsals

For the next several days it rained. The family of boars by the Bose estate retreated under a canopy of garbage, the frogs chorused louder than the crickets at night, and the field was too waterlogged, Lucy was told, for work to continue at Gopalpur. Instead, the professor drove to the village and returned with the main cast. With everyone cramped into the den, the rehearsals began in earnest.

At first it seemed like a comedy of errors. The children did not know their cues or when to approach the stage, or how best to deliver their lines. Lucy's mother, who'd taught the piano with a combination of fierce grace and tough love to dozens of students over the years, wouldn't have approved. The professor was too easy on them. Instead of correcting mistakes, he would smile and wave the scene on.

She'd read *The Post Office* in New York, but it was an altogether different experience seeing it performed by children. Thirty years ago, Jaryk had done what Neel was now doing. Neel was also, it seemed, the only actor to not only have grasped the plot of the play, which was simple enough, but also the emotional pull of the scenes.

Watching Neel rehearse, Lucy understood why Janusz Korczak had chosen this play, why he'd wanted it performed in the ghetto, facing starvation and the fear of the camps. She saw it in Neel's expression—what dignity the boy had. The art that mattered was about sustaining this sense of self, even when everything else in the world demanded otherwise. At night in the cabin she wanted to talk about the play's meaning with Jaryk, but even when they touched he still felt distant from her. They'd pulled their bed close to the window to listen to the rain. It was never the same music, perennially moving into new rhythms.

"Pan Doktor had this belief that you should never surprise a child," Jaryk finally said. "Not in the bad way, at least. I remember when I had to get my vaccine shots. Pan Doktor told me days before what was going to happen and why. Then he showed me how he was going to do it and explained it was going to hurt, but only for a second. The play was one big rehearsal for Treblinka."

Jaryk grew quiet again. "It's making me remember how we spent our days, and I feel hungry all the time," he said. While she'd battled nausea ever since she'd become pregnant, and stayed away from most of the food on her plate, he'd eat his own meal and move on to her leftovers.

"And it makes me think of what happened after. Me and Misha were the only ones who performed who lived."

Back in Brooklyn, she'd been chastised for wanting to know about his last years in Warsaw, but neither Jaryk nor Misha had told her the whole story; the gap between what he was willing to tell her of his survival and what she wanted to know had remained a thorn between them. She tried to clear away these thoughts by listening to the downpour, which sounded like a village of drummers calling across far distances. She heard the wind's rattle against the walnut tree, all its bells in fury. She wanted to take Jaryk home.

"Jaryk, let's go to the city tomorrow," she said. "Let's find you a return ticket. We can get a last-minute cheap seat."

He said, "Actually, I was thinking you could stay on a bit longer."

Years later, sitting in a café, she'd remember his face as he said those words, her child dozing in her lap. How earnest he seemed, how full of some boyish belief. It would be difficult to refuse him but impossible to lie. "Can we go out in the rain?" she asked, keeping her answer at bay.

It was a denser, heavier rain than she'd ever seen. It felt like a thousand little fists pounding on her skin. Soaked through, she ran back inside and dumped her clothes by the door. She burrowed into the bed, and soon Jaryk was next to her. His warmth felt so familiar, so essential for her and for the child that would soon come.

The Ruined Temple

J aryk was sanding the stage—the sharp edges of the bamboo smoothed down—when he heard the commotion from the steppes above. All the children had gathered around Neel's hut, with Lucy among them. She was wearing a bright yellow blouse, celebrating the return of the sun, he supposed. After three days of rehearsals at the Bose estate, it felt necessary to be outside, though the grass was wet, and a palpable lethargy still in the air.

When he climbed up to the huts, he found the children had presents in their hands. The boys had little soldiers and the girls dolls in glittery dresses; in their excitement, they were circling Lucy, who in a moment's time had become the most popular person in Gopalpur. He imagined Lucy combing through the bazaar at Shantiniketan until she found exactly what she wanted. She was picky in this way; she believed that the right gift announced itself.

Days before her last birthday, which felt so long ago now—February, the streets of New York covered with the gray of city snow—he'd scoured the vintage shops on the Lower East Side. What would make her happy? Impossible questions to ask of objects, but he knew better than to ask her what she wanted. Usually she was the one who knew exactly what to make for dinner, what to do on a Saturday afternoon, but other times she needed him to be the one to know, without asking, just what she wanted. If he asked her then, it was as if he'd failed to listen, though she hadn't actually said anything. He finally found a shop that sold LPs of 1940s jazz. *Songs for the Moon* was what he bought her. It had a woman's face on the cover, a woman with a long nose and a full, mischievous smile. A face that reminded him of Lucy's mother, from the one black-and-white portrait Lucy had propped on her nightstand.

Listening to the scratched record and the honeyed voice, Lucy danced softly around the room, kissing him hard on the mouth only after the third song, keeping him in suspense whether he'd done right. Only now did he understand that it hadn't mattered so much what he gave her. She'd never been a woman charmed by expensive things. She'd only wanted him to go searching, to consider carefully what would fit the shape of their love.

....

That evening, he found the professor in his courtyard office. A wild dog poked its nose in, but the professor didn't seem to notice. He was writing to editors of different newspapers to see if they'd cover the production.

"I was going to hire an assistant for this, but the funds are with Mr. Pal's position," the professor said.

It wasn't the first time the professor had alluded to his kindness in securing Mr. Pal a position, and Jaryk found himself thanking Rudra Bose again.

"Listen, Dr. Bose—"

"Why do you insist on calling me that? I am Rudra to you and to anyone else who's spent an afternoon with me."

"Okay, Rudra." It still felt odd to call the professor by his first name, and technically the man was his boss. After all, he'd arranged Jaryk's plane fare and was paying him a small stipend, which meant he was about to ask his boss for time off, something he'd never enjoyed doing for fear his job might be taken from him; and so, while in the employ of the fish market and, later, of Beth Israel, he had neither asked for nor taken much leave. But he did so now, for Lucy's sake, telling the professor he needed a few days away from the play's production.

"Of course, I understand," Rudra Bose said. "But I hope you are not planning any drastic actions?"

"What do you mean?" Jaryk asked, trying to keep his tone neutral.

"Please, sit down," the professor said.

He took the seat across the table, which was lower than the professor's own, so that despite being several inches taller than Rudra Bose, he found himself staring the man in the eye.

"The people of Gopalpur have formed a relationship with you. The children see you as an uncle. Their mothers are looking to you for something. A promise."

"A promise?"

"Of what your art will deliver. Of what change will come."

"I understand," Jaryk said. "The play is their publicity. The publicity holds the government's mercenaries at bay. You've told me this all before. I'm your token American, and I'm your man from Warsaw."

"There's no need to get upset," the professor said. "We are friends, are we not? I was going to tell you something beyond what you already know. Not only are the cerebra and celebrity of Calcutta coming to our little production, we shall also be receiving the sarkar in the form of Rajan Datta. Mr. Datta is the chief minister's right-hand man. We shall be able to exert influence on the state. We shall be able to send a direct message to everyone in the government."

That morning he'd seen the professor and the butler conferencing in a dark corner of the house, and though they were speaking Bengali they ended their conversation when he approached, as if what was being discussed wasn't fit for public consumption. *A direct message.* Sometimes the professor's words inspired him; other times they left him feeling afraid. There were times when they bore some resemblance to words that had come from the loudspeakers in the ghetto, recounting in German and Polish all the injustices he and his brothers had supposedly committed. But this was not about Rudra Bose. This was about Neel and the people of the village.

"I understand. I won't disappoint you," Jaryk said, taking his leave, though he felt as unsure of his next step as he ever had.

....

After breakfast the next morning, he pulled Mrs. Pal aside.

"I'd like to buy a piece of jewelry," he said. "For Lucy. As a gift. I would like your help."

"Indeed," said Mrs. Pal, as if she'd expected his request all along; and what a relief it was to ask for help, to have the Pals still with him. They walked to the village market, where local artisans had come to show their wares. Healthy lambs were on tether. Jackfruits larger than his head were being weighed. A corner was kept for textiles and for handmade jewelry.

"It's not a vast selection, but perhaps we'll find something to your liking."

The villagers had brought humble selections of brass earrings and iron bracelets, though in one stall he found a dusty old ring, which after considerable polishing seemed extraordinary in the light: three ruby stones, red, orange, and a deeper red. "From the caves of the south," Mrs. Pal translated. He was thinking of the outer two stones as the two of them and the gem in the center, the deepest red, as the third body. Someone they could feel but didn't yet know.

He didn't haggle the price down, though Mrs. Pal found his accepting the first ask to be bad form. The jeweler wrapped the ring in what looked to him like tinfoil, and Jaryk wedged it into his pocket, where he checked for it every few moments.

As they reached the Bose estate, Mrs. Pal touched his wrist. "Jaryk, you should know there is talk of unrest. Of Professor Bose spreading word of the production in a way that has incited certain government peoples. If you were to return to America, you would avoid any ill that might come of the professor's publicity."

What had once felt distant was now all around him. He could taste the danger in the minerals of the well water, see it in the way Neel's mother clutched her sari hem, feel it whenever he touched the professor's hands, shaking from what he'd first thought had been too much coffee but which he now suspected was simply fear. Danger grew on the trees here, spread along the canopy wall, and sank back into the rice paddies. He'd lived that life once. For good cause, he would do so again.

"The spirit of this country is of peace, I think," Jaryk said finally.

Mrs. Pal stared at him evenly. "Yes and no," she said, allowing him to continue past the gate and into the mansion.

....

He had imagined proposing to Lucy like Cary Grant in *An Affair to Remember*, atop the Empire State Building with the view of the city all around them, and he had imagined proposing to Lucy at Montauk beach, to the tune of sunset and crisp, clean air, and he had imagined proposing to her on one of those beaked boats he'd seen in Venice travelogues. He hadn't imagined proposing to her in a village in India with a ring he'd come by in the local market. It didn't feel perfect, but then, nothing in their story had come the way the movies promised.

Mr. Pal had suggested a romantic spot. *Suggested*, perhaps, was the wrong way of putting it. Jaryk had cornered Mr. Pal on campus and grilled him on quiet, reclusive places accessible by rickshaw.

....

They headed away from the town on a rickshaw driven by a turbaned man—hard to say *man*, maybe closer to *teenager*—who smiled coyly at Lucy from time to time. She was wearing her blue chiffon dress, the one he'd seen her in when she'd first come to Gopalpur, the mud cleaned from the hem, the wrinkles magically gone. He felt for the three-gem ring in his pocket—*still there*—and they talked first about Neel, how the boy had learned to say the Southern *y'all* with the right intonation, and then they reminisced about their first fancy dinner.

A whole paycheck must have gone toward that evening, full of French dishes and expensive wines, but he was glad to have planned it. Lucy had had a hard week at work, and he wanted to surprise her with something nice. He remembered their waiter's name was *Colson*, which seemed to him like it belonged to a more genteel time. When Colson asked what he'd like for his entree, he ordered the second-least-expensive dish on the menu, figuring that was a fair compromise between his budget and his desire to experience the finest the city had to offer. Lucy had no qualms getting the porterhouse steak, medium rare, with a half bottle of Merlot that poured so perfectly red it seemed there were jewels inside. She *belonged* at the restaurant, flirting easily with Colson, while he'd felt, all the while, as if he were trespassing. When the meal came out, she sent hers back—twice—and Colson apologized and smiled both times. She was a woman who wasn't afraid of asking for what she wanted, which felt important to him but also terrifying.

Now he had only a picnic basket of sundries he'd bribed the maid to cook. A few pieces of paratha warm in his lap, some curried potatoes and peas, and a tiny jar of jam. Lucy asked him again what this was all about, though he could tell she was enjoying the surprise.

"Just a night on the town," he offered.

As they approached the hill that led to the ruins, he felt a chill in the air. It was cooler here than it was in Gopalpur, the humidity a half step behind, but underneath his shirt, which he'd ironed for the occasion, he was sweating. More than once he had imagined they would get married *someday*, but it was a someday in the sweetly distant future; now he felt his hand had been forced. He loved her, but still, the idea of fatherhood had not settled. *How could he bring a child into this world?* he asked, but again only silently, afraid to share his worries with Lucy.

Mr. Pal had sketched him a map of the place. He tried to study it, but his hands shook. No matter; he remembered the general outlay. He asked the rickshaw driver to wait for them and led Lucy onto a cobbled path that had once been the gateway to a temple where acolytes worshipped a dark goddess who was depicted with her tongue sticking out. Nowadays bats slept along the temple's rafters, and from the nearby forest a gang of macaques announced their claim to the land.

"There are three natural sulfur pools where devotees came to cleanse themselves," Mr. Pal had explained, and Jaryk now relayed that to Lucy. He led her toward the nearest pool. Its water rippled in the light of the sun, low now above the horizon.

"Whatever spirit gave you this idea, I thank her," Lucy said, testing her toes in the water.

For years, he would remember her as she was in that moment. Full of energy, awaiting his surprise—*did she suspect?*—her toes grazing the water ever so slightly, her hair curling down about her shoulders, her slip showing through her dress, and that smile, which said *yes* or *no* depending on the weather of her and you just had to sense it, you couldn't ask or try and figure things out as if it were a puzzle, because life with Lucy was not a puzzle at all, but a mystery that didn't need solving.

"Thank you for coming to India," he said, though it didn't feel like it was enough; it felt more, in fact, like an apology.

She must have sensed it then, how he was in a bad way, his fingers made into fists so they would stop shaking.

"What is it that you're afraid of?" she asked, almost a murmur.

He couldn't have told her then. What words were there to describe it?

He kept the silence, and when the silence seemed intolerable, he stripped down to his boxers, holding the ring in his hand, and plunged into the pool. It wasn't deep, but he could sink all the way in, keep his head under water. He stayed down for a while until he felt Lucy's hand pulling on his hair. She was worried he was under for too long, but he could've held his breath even longer.

"You know I can't go in with you," she said. "The water's too hot for our special friend." She rubbed a circle around her belly.

"I'm sorry," he said. "I didn't think about that." The three-gem ring was still in his hand, and he could've gotten on one knee and asked for her hand in marriage, except he was overcome with a terror that sent chills up his spine. He didn't know anymore what he felt about fatherhood, what he felt about caring for a child he'd brought into this world, except he believed it wasn't his right, it wasn't his due. He plunged once more below the surface and let the ring fall into the deep.

That night he felt lighter. He'd returned to the Bose estate as unmoored as ever. Nothing to hold him. When he and Lucy had dinner with the Pals and the professor, Jaryk told them the story of how they'd met, described the subway as if it were some sort of mythical beast that had refused to crawl any farther, and how then they'd had to walk, hand in hand, from the darkness of the tunnel into that sallow light.

"You must have been terrified," said the professor.

"Not at all," he said. He felt giddy with the lie, sure somehow that no one could tell from the fix of his face how scared he'd been then, how fearful he was now.

....

The next night, they had an argument, which he imagined had been coming since their time at the ruins, when he'd failed to do what he'd set out to. They were sitting by the walnut tree, watching the priest play along the line of bells. Lucy had been silent for most of the trip back from the temple and the day after.

"Tell me one thing you notice about me tonight," she said.

Her eyes were firmly on his, and he didn't dare look away. But he didn't need to. He noticed her from smell to smell, from sight to sound. He noticed when the cycles of her breath became disturbed, and the temperature of her.

"I notice you're wearing your mother's earrings," he said. "The ones you found underneath the bed in her bedroom after she died. Like she'd hidden them for you. Like she wanted you to find them only after searching." The earrings were jade, finely cut triangular drops.

"You're not coming home with me, are you?"

He looked her in the eye. "No," he said. "I have work left to do here."

"Guess I should've known," she said.

He reached his hand to touch her cheek, but she said, "Don't. Don't even talk to me right now."

That night Lucy skipped dinner and went straight to bed. He tried to get her to talk again, but she turned away from him. He lay next to her, afraid to touch her for fear of bringing out her anger. In ten hours, she would be driving back with Mr. Pal to Calcutta, in twelve hours sitting on a plane headed first to London, then to New York.

"Lucy, will you hear me out?" he whispered. He wanted to tell her so much—his past, their future together, how he feared but also believed in it.

She turned to him. He'd never told her about those August days at the orphanage. He hadn't even told Misha the truth about how he'd survived. It had felt to him always like a great shame, though he knew, when he could feel distant enough from it, that it was only survival willing him on.

"I have this nightmare about our last day together. It takes different shapes, it's never the same. It was the last day I was together with Pan Doktor and Madam Stefa and Esterka, and my brothers and sisters from the orphanage. When Misha asked me about that day, I lied to him."

The moonlight coming through the window illuminated her bare shoulder. In three days, the moon would be full again, with the rains likely to return.

"We don't have to talk about this right now," she said. "It's all right."

"No, I want to tell you the whole story," he said. "I want you to know what it was like."

He told Lucy what he'd kept from Misha. He told her about the day from its start, how they'd been awoken early and dressed in their best clothes. He told her how Esterka had brushed his hair until it nearly shined. They rarely felt like beautiful children, though that morning he saw how loved he was when he looked into Madam Stefa's eyes, that frown that knew the world. He told Lucy how they'd marched to the trains as one, while the entire ghetto watched. He told her of the stink of the cattle cars, of the false promise of a loaf of bread, a pot of jam. Sixty miles east was the place he'd heard spoken of in whispers, whose name had gotten stuck in the cracks of the house, and when the train stopped midway, when he saw the window big enough for him—when he looked at Pan Doktor, the heart of his old, good life, when Pan Doktor winked back at him—he jumped on the old man's shoulders and squeezed through to roll into the fields and run into the woods.

It didn't matter which version of his story was the truth. What he'd wanted to tell her—what he hoped she now understood—was that he'd left his only family, everything he loved in this world.

"I remember the smell of that grass," he said. "I could smell the cows who must've once grazed there. I was in the woods when everyone else was gassed."

The clouds once again hid the light. He could no longer see the expression on her face. What would a woman like Lucy think hearing such things? He gulped for air, felt high from the telling, as if he had just surfaced after a plunge into cold water. If she was to carry his child, she should know who he was.

All those evenings in New York, when he wasn't with Misha, when he sat in that axis of hallway where Chopin's sonatas sounded as pure as if his beloved composer were playing in the flesh. He had no wish to repeat those evenings. To live as he had. Those years without shape.

"Jaryk, you've suffered more than anyone should," she said. "You were just a child."

"You don't understand," he said. "I could've stayed. They were the only family I had."

"I know who you are. You are a good man, Jaryk Smith."

He heard her but didn't accept her words. "Sometimes I lie awake and pretend Pan Doktor is telling me what to do with my life. There's no God, but Pan Doktor and Stefa are watching me, encouraging me to do good in the world."

Lucy burrowed into him. He couldn't tell if he'd lost her. "Will you stay with me, Lucy? Will you stay for the play and for after?"

"Hush," she said.

PART 4

Labor Day

Labor Day weekend the city feels deserted, and for once Lucy thinks she could walk up Fifth Avenue all the way to the park without the jostling she has become accustomed to, the bursts of noise from storefront stereos and disgruntled traffic, and that feeling of always being in a hurry, which she'd first assumed was a by-product of efficiency, but sees now as something else—a desire to keep running, to not slow down and smell the city: the flowers along the sidewalks, the garbage left to rot. These days her sense of smell is working overtime, so there are mornings when she doesn't want to leave home at all, except there's work to do, groceries to be bought.

More and more, her evenings are filled with social calls. Through the summer her girlfriends have found new places to meet and people-watch: sidewalk cafés in the West Village, museums, and bars on the Lower East Side where she must clutch her purse to her chest, drinking tonic water by the bottle while her friends Julie, Margaret, and Renée drink chilled white wine. It must be the kind of life her Mebane crowd imagined for her, though until she returned from India she couldn't have imagined it for herself.

When Jaryk was in New York, so many of their nights had been spent together, but now Renée and Margaret and Julie fill her calendar, the stories of their lives recast with degrees of embellishment or modesty, depending on the when and the how. She has grown to love their ease at being single, of navigating the city as if it were theirs alone.

Then there is Jonas. Soon as she'd returned to the office, he'd pursued her friendship.

"India," he said. "Well, you are a cosmopolitan Christian." This phrase alone is enough to get him grinning.

She's headed to see him now. He'd suggested the New York Botanical Garden in the Bronx, and "Why not?" she'd said. "For once, it'll be roses and hyacinths instead of mildew and trash."

The only person at the office she's told about India is Jonas, simply because it's hard to lie to his baby face. So she's told him the truth, at least partly.

"I went to visit someone dear to me," she said. She didn't say *boyfriend*—that word felt insufficient now. The rest of the story she'd kept to herself, and Jonas had the goodwill not to pry.

She makes it as far uptown as the Diamond District, at which point her feet might as well be walking on the hot pavement; her sandals are a year out of fashion and worn to their last walk. Past the displays of jewelry, past the pale man squinting into his microscope to guess the price of a gem, she descends into the subway, which even now, after a couple of years as a New Yorker, feels fraught with danger.

Especially on this day, when there are so few riding the trains, she can see, through the gaps in human traffic, the graffiti in all its grandeur, the scrawls that she assumes to mean *"This gang was here,"* and the murals of civil rights martyrs baking underneath the fluorescent bulbs, half of which are blinking out of sync. Scattered on the platform lies the *New York Daily News* with articles of robberies and acts of violence so seemingly mindless that she can't believe the printed word. This is her chosen city, where entering a subway car, she feels she must keep her eyes to herself, though she won't—she doesn't have it in her to ignore the people with whom she shares space—glancing up to see a businessman, a teenager immersed in his comic book, and a woman without shoes, her bare feet scratching the floor of the car, exposing the cracks. This is the city she has chosen, and she will not look away.

Her last day in India had felt full of miscues. *"Mission failed,"* her father would have said. That morning, she rose early and walked around the village. What a privilege it was to breathe the kind of fresh air alien to New York. *"It was a little bit like Mebane,"* she would tell Timothy, though only years later. On her way back to the Bose estate, she watched a deer cross the road, following an errant cow who'd escaped pasture. She'd heard cows sometimes walked the streets of India, but that deer could be seen in broad daylight still surprised her.

When she returned to the Bose estate, she found Jaryk had made her breakfast. Eggs, sunny side up, though for once she thought she would have liked the local cuisine, a last hurrah of sorts. They stayed in their cabin and ate with the windows open, the morning flies crawling over her leftover toast.

They didn't talk about what he'd told her the night before, his story of escaping from the train. To raise that again felt like a grave undertaking, appropriate only at certain hours in the night, available only in moments of extraordinary intimacy. This meant they talked little at all, preferring the sunshine, the solitude of their own company. Still, she felt warmly toward him with the dull thud of love not far behind.

She'd come with expectations. Different ones, depending on the day. Mostly, that he would return to the city with her to practice for parenthood. That he would ask for her hand in marriage, then for her father's permission. That he would allow himself to bury his grief—Misha's death and the loss of his childhood. None of this had happened. He'd shared a story of his old life, brought her closer in a way she felt was a kind of gift in itself, but that had been all.

When it came time to leave for the airport, then to part ways at the departure lounge, he'd remained speechless but passed her a paper bag, which she waited to open until she was on the plane.

It was a meal of bread and vegetables, the sort of fare one would take down to the trenches. She'd forgone the food the attendants brought around, savoring every bite of Jaryk's last meal.

But then somewhere over the Atlantic, the plane hit a patch of rough air, even the flight attendants pale and grimacing. After the turbulence had passed, she'd grown angry at Jaryk, because he hadn't been next to her to tell a joke or even to hold her hand. Her compassion for him began to dry up as a new wound opened.

Back home, it hadn't been simple keeping her pregnancy a secret. To account for the nausea that had affected her so fiercely the first twelve weeks, she'd invented simple sicknesses—a stomach ache, an ear infection, a problem tooth—preferring to keep the excuses close enough to plausible in case a divine justice avenged white lies. It had been difficult to be alone with the news, though perhaps her girlfriends had guessed it from her choice to stop drinking wine, which seemed to have fooled no one at all; but still, no one had asked and she hadn't told them outright. Soon there would be no choice but to tell. No amount of loose clothing would hide the fact of her changing body.

....

At the gate of the Botanical Garden, Jonas has his hands on his hips. Something about the way he's tilted his torso suggests he might topple over, though Jonas is often graceful—the time he opened the door of her taxi and bowed mockingly, for example, even that carried grace. He has the kind of blue eyes that comes with big sky and livestock, and perhaps in another life he'd balanced on bulls, but in this one he's more Gypsy than anything else. And he's tall, maybe even taller than Jaryk, though narrower across the shoulders.

"Is my clock off?" Jonas asks. "Could it be that Lucy Gardner is on time?"

"Don't get used to it," she says. He's forever pestering her about the first time she'd agreed to show him around the Lower East

Side, a tour to which she'd been an hour and a half late. But he'd waited, which she thought was either a flaw of character or a saving grace.

The rains haven't been as fierce as in India, but the city's gotten a few decent swells and the flowers look it. She tries to memorize the names of the roses from foreign countries, searching to see if there are any from the Far East. The first few times she stops to inspect the flowers, Jonas clicks his heels, impatient to track the rest of the place, but she waits him out and he heeds her pace. He's into the bonsai house more than she is; he loves to study the minuscule worlds, appreciate the attention the artist gave to each plant.

"Could you imagine doing that? It takes hours to get it right."

Her mind feels like a motorcycle on ice. "Not a chance, but I bet you couldn't neither."

He opens his palms to the sky, closes his eyes, and preens a long "*Om.*"

She pinches him hard on the arm.

"Ouch!" he says, not kidding.

She doesn't like him joking about India. He'd tried something or other with "*holy cows*" a while back, and she'd punched him. He'd reacted much the same—a little girlishly. Still, he's good company, a good listener, and she doesn't feel conscious about letting her Southern drawl out around him. He doesn't mind himself, either, interspersing his pent-up *y'all*s with every other word.

Jonas has brought sandwiches, which they eat on the lawn, surreptitiously and quickly because eating isn't allowed in the garden. He's even brought some wine in a flask, of which she entertains a few gulps. It's one of those days of summer she had looked forward to through the whole winter. She presses her hands into the barely damp grass to feel the give of the good earth.

"Your friend that you went to see. Is he back?" Jonas asks.

She's told him bits and pieces about her trip, about Jaryk. She's certainly not said she's carrying their child. Instead, she told him curtly on their first encounter, "Just want you to know, Jonas, that I am not available—this is strictly friends." He'd nodded, not asking for more.

"I'm not sure if he's coming back," she says now, though as soon as she says it she feels as if she's hurt Jaryk in some way. She doesn't know if it's true, and it feels spiteful to say it, though Jonas seems buoyed by the news.

He slides off his edge of the blanket to rest his head on her lap. The motion is so fluid, the weight of his head so comforting there, that for a long moment she doesn't move. He locks eyes with hers, for once serious. She has no choice then but to make light of the situation, pulling his ear, chiding him, "Get off now."

"Yes, ma'am," he says, rolling off into the grass, arms and legs spread-eagled. He doesn't seem to care whether his light-blue shirt will stain from the grass; he is as far away from worry as any man can be.

"Hey, I got something for you."

"Unless it's an icicle I don't want it. I'm too hot for anything."

"It's nothing special," he says. "But it's no icicle neither."

In one motion he ties a necklace on her as if it's a lasso trick. Before she can gasp, she notices the gold trim and fine inlay of rubies.

"Are you thick of head, Jonas? I can't take this from you."

"That's a reaction," he says. "Look, I've been trying to get rid of it. I won it at a poker game. It ain't anything. Don't flatter yourself."

"Too late, I'm flattered, but I'm giving it back."

"Man can't wear a necklace," he says, sliding back onto the grass.

"Don't ever do this again, you hear?"

Her mother had this belief about alternate lives. A few low times in her life she'd broken down, shared how she could smell the other lives happening around her—her life as a pianist touring the halls of New York, Chicago, and Boston, her life as a wealthy man's wife, her life as a teacher in a school that so needed her. Lucy rubs the necklace and catches herself wondering now of a life without Jaryk—how simple it is to forget!—when Jonas snaps to attention.

"Oh, I have an idea," he says.

....

She once revealed to him that she's never seen the Statue of Liberty up close, which Jonas says is un-American. It's a journey and a half, the IRT line from the Bronx all the way downtown to Bowling Green. Then he leads them onto one of the tourist boats, which takes a long view of the Brooklyn Bridge and the underpass, where she's heard artists and drug dealers roam freely. The boat cruises along the South Street Seaport, then heads toward Jersey until finally they turn back toward Staten Island and circle Lady Liberty.

It's a day of clear sky. Lucy imagines taking a quick, sweet dip when she sees the statue in the water, the throngs crowding around the pedestal, climbing up her bones. It is as if by her floating in the water, holding the torch alight, that the city can bear to do its daily work. The sight moves her, though she won't let Jonas see that. He's brought his Polaroid, and she allows him to cradle her back while they pose for a picture with sky, sea, and Lady Liberty in the background.

Thirty years ago, Jaryk would have seen the same, or maybe for him the view would have been entirely different. She can only guess what it must have been like to land ashore, having escaped from a train sent for death, and to see the image everyone spoke of as if it were their freedom carved into stone.

....

After Labor Day she can feel the city return to its sound and fury. It's a town of always doing, she's learned, and with the summer behind them, the pace of life shifts toward the hectic. The men who barbecued and brawled their summer away return to her for employment advice, but sometimes it feels to her as if they've just come to confess their wayward habits, their misspent dollars. The days are long and the paperwork longer, but the morning sickness has begun to abate. She's bought a new wardrobe of flowing dresses she can wear even into the third trimester.

Jonas, too, has seen his workload increase. She'd always assumed city employment served more men than women, but now as many women come into their offices and seem to love chatting Jonas up. His office is always full, and he looks so comfortable in there—as if he's propped his feet on his desk, though he hasn't—smiling away, gunning for their trust.

Miles has been given a promotion. He's now officially her supervisor, though to be fair, he'd always lorded over her. The day she announces her news in the break room he doesn't say a word; the next morning he steps into her office and tells her with so much magnanimity that she could sock him in the gut, "This is a beautiful thing that's happening to you, Lucy, a beautiful, extraordinary thing. Don't worry quite as much about work right now."

She knows the words are meant to sound sweet, but she doesn't trust him. What is it about Miles Norton that awakens the animal in her, the one who'd wring his neck at first chance? Whenever she sees his beer belly and his eyebrows, which are so long that they give him a look of perpetual electrocution, she feels an inexplicable fury. More than once he's told her he's too educated for this job, with all his graduate study and postgraduate whatnot; but standing next to her desk with an endless supply of theories on the working life, he seems perfect for the profession.

She smiles, says she appreciates his understanding. "Oh, and I'll be late again tomorrow morning," she says, as he's leaving the office, thank you very much.

....

The clinic that confirmed her pregnancy referred her to a Dr. Malhotra, who, they say, is king when it comes to delivering babies, so effusive were the nurses in their recommendations. Dr. Malhotra practices on the Upper East Side, a few blocks from Lenox

Hill Hospital, where Lucy imagines she will be giving birth in five months. The morning clouds have given over to a steady rain, and without an umbrella Lucy begins to feel a chill.

She waits in the reception of Dr. Malhotra's office, which is bereft of basic waiting-room necessities—no magazines, no children's books, not even brochures. For someone who doesn't enjoy waiting—and who, anyway, enjoys waiting?—it is a kind of torture, though productive, because she decides she will call her father that evening and tell him about his upcoming grandchild. He might give her the lecture of her life. So be it—better that he knows. She waits long enough to curse Jaryk three times over.

When Dr. Malhotra finally meets her in the waiting room, Lucy first mistakes her for a nurse.

"I'm Elizabeth. So sorry to keep you waiting. We were having some technical problems."

Elizabeth Malhotra doesn't have the accent Lucy grew so accustomed to in India that she herself started using it, hoping it would help. Lucy mentions her recent trip. She's surprised when the doctor informs her that she's never been.

"Medical school, then residency. Guess I never had the time," she says.

Dr. Malhotra is of this country in a way that Jaryk never will be, which feels comforting somehow; the movement of generations can remove obstacles, if not for Jaryk, then for those who go on after him. Lucy feels free to tell Dr. Malhotra about the pregnancy, that the father is still somewhere in India.

"Well, maybe we could send him a picture," Dr. Malhotra says, explaining that there is a new kind of machine that can see the baby inside her womb by sending tiny pulses.

"But will it hurt the baby?" Lucy asks.

"It is perfectly safe," the doctor tells her, leading her to the ultrasound machine, one of the first of its kind in the city. The machine is grandiose with its dials and symbols. Its screen shows a gray-black nothingness that begins to shift as Lucy's own body comes into focus, and there, in the gray-black space, says Dr. Malhotra, is a large white bubble that soon enough will develop eyes, a mouth, unborn weaknesses, desires she will not always understand, hopes she will not dare to crush.

Elizabeth Malhotra prints a picture of that light-filled center and hands it over to Lucy, who cradles the image to her belly. It is the first time that the child inside her has felt like its own being; until now, it had been a source of nausea or an inconvenient chapter in her love for Jaryk. But now it is of the flesh, *hers*. She cradles the picture as if the child were already born.

"The baby is developing just fine," the doctor says, but Lucy barely hears the words—she feels an extraordinary loneliness at being given such news without Jaryk alongside her.

....

Around ten o'clock that night she calls Timothy. It's too late to call her father, who is early-to-bed-early-to-rise, though even if he were awake, on this night at least, she couldn't tolerate being berated by him.

"A child out of marriage?" he might say. "This what I taught you?" He might say that, or he might cry for happiness; she doesn't know which, and doesn't dare to risk it. So Timothy Norwood it is.

It's true that Timothy was married long before Lucy came into this world, long before her father even made his acquaintance, though there was no child from that union, as far as Lucy knows. The most he ever showed her about that time was a black-and-white photo of a young woman with plump cheeks, which he kept pocketed in the middle of his copy of *Moby-Dick*.

"Who's that?" she said when she discovered the picture.

He'd snatched it away. "That's my old girl," he said.

She can't imagine what a man of his age and experience might say of her situation, but who better to listen? Maybe the gout's gotten to his leg again, because it's one more ring before he makes it to the line.

He sounds so old when he answers. Older than when she visited last Christmas. "I am going to be a mother, Timothy."

"Oh, my," he says, for once grave, the line between New York City and Mebane gone as silent as the country night. "Well, you have my full congratulations."

He sounds formal to her, perhaps even displeased, though she can't tell if it's simply an effect of the phone line and the physical distance. "Oh, and I might have to raise the kid myself."

"What happened to the father?"

"That's a complicated story," she says.

"Well, it isn't true," says Timothy, after a long pause. "You will not have to raise the kid yourself. Your father and yours truly will be there. We'll live under your bed if we need to. I have changed some wet clothes in my time."

She can't picture Timothy ever having changed a diaper, but still his words are what she's needed to hear—what she wants from home, where she cannot be unloved, no matter what.

"Oh, and Lucy? If I hear the complicated-story father of the child doesn't do his duty, I might just load up my pistol. I still have decent aim."

"Thank you, Timothy," she says. "You get some rest, now. No more staying up late, okay?"

"Yes, darling," he says.

It's the silence again, the room she rents for a fortune, the unread books on the bookshelf, the half-washed dishes drying dutifully on the rack. Soon it'll be morning in India, the sun rising over the farms and the hills, the cows lowing out to pasture, the hips of the sari women moving to some ancient beat, and soon Jaryk will wake into his own life. The walnut tree will shake its eaves, and the smell of her will be long gone from their cabin.

The Butler's Disappearance

J aryk learns to sleep on the roof even when it rains. He learns that all he needs is a mosquito net, which Rohan the butler has rigged to the fronds of a coconut tree; he learns to count the stars through the million eyes of the mosquito net, learns that when it rains it is a warm rain, like being in the shower, only he can't control when the water stops. He learns to keep a beard, which in the mornings is wet and heavy like a dog's fur. If he wakes in the night, he hears the professor's flute rising from the recesses of the house. Never the same melody, complex riffs, melancholy minors flirting with birdsong, music that surrounds the property whether he's listening or not.

Two weeks into his new sleeping arrangement, he finds himself awoken by Mrs. Pal. For a long moment, he stares at her turmeric-stained palms, confuses their color for that of the sun. It's early enough that he feels the damp from the night's rain, turns over to feel his sheets are soaked through.

"You need a proper shave," she tells him. "And why do you still sleep out here? There is so much rain."

"The mosquito net catches most of it," Jaryk says, though it isn't true—after a monsoon, he and the net are equally drenched. Sleeping in the cabin reminded him too much of Lucy. He could've claimed another room in the house, but whatever room he chose, Misha's ghost would've found him. On the roof the rain discourages the ghosts. He can feel the tides that rise larger than his life.

"Also, it is too hot to keep a beard," says Mrs. Pal.

He nods. Though she's right—during the day it becomes too hot for even a T-shirt—he hasn't been able to shave. Not that he hasn't tried. He's lifted razor to chin, held it there until the warm water in the basin turns cold. Something in the ritual, which he'd performed every day of his working life, now repels him. Besides, the month-old beard makes him feel like a different person—not beyond recognition, but capable of new identities.

"Your husband said you are leaving," Jaryk says. "I'm sorry the position at the college didn't work out." In another week, the substitute position Mr. Pal had been given will run its course. Anyway, the children have their own school to return to, so now it'll be him and the professor, carrying the performance to the end.

"I will tell you once more," Mrs. Pal says. "Now that the sarkar is involved, it's best you leave." She's warned him of rumors that mercenaries are bent on disturbing the performance. Their little village theater has become confused with issues of larger dissent and has attracted the eye of the government.

"I have to see it through," Jaryk says. At first, it was enough that he had come, as Misha had before him. The mercenaries wouldn't bother a village with an American, wouldn't risk the bad publicity an incident would bring, but now that the professor has appeared on radio shows and in newspaper columns, spoken at over a dozen rallies in Calcutta, the little village of Gopalpur looms large on the map. Even the prime minister, Rudra Bose has claimed, knows of their story.

"See this," says Mrs. Pal. She shows him a copy of *The Statesman*, where Rajan Datta, the chief minister's right-hand man, has made mention of them, responding to a question about the fate of Gopalpur: "'Not even the Academy, not even American transplants, can deter the hand of justice.'"

"Yes, the professor showed me," Jaryk says. "All day yesterday he was gloating that we'd made it onto the big stage."

Mrs. Pal adjusts her sari to kneel beside him. He moves the mosquito net out of the way and offers her a seat on his wicker-mat bed, which she refuses. She's no longer glaring at him, that's good, but something's still screwed up in her face. Spending time with the Pals has absolved him of some illusions surrounding the serenity of families. He's never had one, a proper family, that is, nothing after the orphanage, at least, so he'd assumed that when both father and mother give their love, the resulting happiness multiplies with each child they bring. Except they bicker, the children fight, and Mrs. Pal often seems at the point of exhaustion. It's right when he thinks she's about to scream that he'll see, as he does now, the look of a woman who's not wholly there, who lives an alternate life with a perhaps younger husband, a different set of unruly children, or maybe no dependents at all, maybe nothing to keep her on the narrow path. If she catches his gaze, she'll fix herself back into matriarchy, and the moment, as it does now, will pass.

"What about you, Mrs. Pal?" he asks. "What's next for you?"

"For my family everything will be as it was," she says, her face fixed again into austerity. "And yourself? That day, why did you not go home with Miss Lucy?"

It's been a couple of weeks since Lucy's departure, yet he often finds himself replaying their last day together, the order in which things happened. He remembers rising before dawn to kiss her belly and listen for a heartbeat, though it's too early for that—their child remains more concept than person. He'd come so close to proposing to her by the ruined temple, but he hadn't.

When Lucy awoke that morning, she found him staring. He tried to look away, but felt her gaze drawing him back, the tenderness of the night when he'd told her about the train to Treblinka. "Are you coming home with me?" she'd asked.

He'd shaken his head no. She began to pack her clothes, spending long moments folding the salwar kameez that had been gifted her, making sure her blue chiffon dress was rolled tight into a bun to avoid getting wrinkled. He remembered all the colors of her open suitcase, all that evidence of a life lived in hues and shades, the slope of falling light from the window illuminating her fore-arm as she pressed on the suitcase till it groaned and closed.

He'd made her lunch for the plane. Warm, good food for the two of them—Lucy and the child. His hand had lingered on hers as she took the paper bag, the last sign of his love.

"I ask myself that question, Mrs. Pal," Jaryk says, bringing him-self back. "Why not go home with Lucy? It would've been easier, but what about Neel? What about the safety of everyone in the village? Every day that I'm here is a day without guns."

"You sound like Rudra Bose," she says, gripping his wrist. "Don't let him fool you. They'll come when they'll come. He has his own fish to fry, Jaryk, but it is not your concern. I wish we could stay. I thought it was our karma to protect you."

"Don't worry," he says, loosening her grip on his wrist. "I've been through worse, much, much worse."

"I know," says Mrs. Pal. "That's why we wanted to take care of you."

His gift has always been to attract the best protectors. First, Pan Doktor, then Misha, and now the Pals.

A week later the Pals leave. He promises that he'll call them when the date for the play is set, and they agree to return for the performance.

⋯⋯⋯⋯⋯

The problem with the date of the play is that it keeps getting pushed back.

The first time is the professor's doing. He's decided they'll per-form the play in English to appeal to an international audience, which initially means chaos for the child actors, who've studied little English at the local school. Still, he tries his best to train them to speak English phonetically, an exercise in irony, the English language never having been his strong suit.

The second delay is due to one of the main actors, playing the Fakir, coming down with jaundice. They don't have backups, so losing the Fakir comes as a shock. The professor scrambles to find a replacement, but there are few children left in Gopalpur who can carry the part.

"Why don't you play him?" the professor asks Jaryk. "The Fakir is an older character, and, besides, in Warsaw, your leader played the part, no?"

"Yes, that was Pan Doktor's role," Jaryk says. Sometimes, he thinks he's told the professor too much of the way the Polish production had been staged, how Esterka had directed them to speak the lines, many of which come back to him the more he rehearses with the cast. She'd been the first woman he loved, at an age when love soared past boundaries of the romantic or the familiar, and remembering her has given the work of rehearsal—which is often more of an English lesson than anything else—the feeling of homage. If there were a heaven, which he did not believe there was, but say there were some place afterwards where good people could winnow their hours, she'd be looking down on them, clucking her tongue at every missed gesture, though even in the scolding you'd feel a little adored.

At Gopalpur he tries a mix of loving sternness but lacks Esterka's gravitas. When the children want a break, he always concedes, and without Mrs. Pal there's no one left to keep the discipline. Certainly not the professor, who's been less and less a part of the play's production as the weeks have worn on. He's busy giving interviews to journalists and speaking at conferences in the city, retelling the story of the village and the story of the play. Sometimes he encounters the professor only if he wakes at night and happens to hear the flute from the house, the etudes becoming more frenzied—or is that only his imagination?—and then if he wanders into the house, stands by the staircase, Misha's ghost shoves him back to the roof: *I died here. Don't let me have passed for nothing.*

He thinks of Lucy less and less. It was only a month ago that she was here, her long blue dress trailing in the field at Gopalpur. Perhaps it's the way remembering Lucy comes with memories of New York, a city that now feels as faraway as the North Pole. Instead, his days are filled with Neel. Like most children at Gopalpur, Neel is subdued when he's outside the village. But at Gopalpur when he's with Jaryk playing by the well or the goat shed, his smile comes easily, and Jaryk can see the gap between Neel's two front teeth.

Neel loves to teach him things. He leads Jaryk into a forest of *taal* trees, where anteaters have built their towers as tall as men, and rattles off facts he's gathered from library books. *"This tree has been here thirty years,"* he explains. *"Just count the grooves and you'll see."* From Neel, Jaryk's also learned a few words of Bengali. *Accha*, for instance, which means, depending on the situation, *okay*, or *go on*, or even *maybe*.

In turn Jaryk helps Neel with his math homework. A good morning is teaching Neel about fractions, cutting a mango into sections to demonstrate a half, a fourth, an eighth, then enjoying the fruit together, the juice sticky on their chins.

"What is the point of math?" Neel once asks him.

"If you know math, you can decide your own life. If you don't know it, then you have to trust other people to tell you how much you've earned."

"I trust my mother and my aunt. And now you," the boy says.

"Trusting too many people isn't good," he says, though he's pleased to be part of Neel's circle. "Sooner or later someone will put on a different face."

"Like a mask?"

"Like take off their mask," Jaryk says.

He begins to share stories of the performances in Warsaw. "We performed it twice," he tells Neel on one of their walks in the forest. "The first time was during Passover, and everyone came to see it." It's a detail he hasn't even told the professor, and in telling Neel he feels closer to him.

"What is Passover?" Neel asks. Jaryk explains the story of the exodus as best he can: Moses and the Israelites, the plagues, the flight from Egypt. "Kind of like your people running across the border from Bangladesh," he says to connect it back.

"We didn't run," Neel says. "We walked." It's a point of pride with Neel that his family left of their own accord, though from what Jaryk understands, they'd barely avoided a forced fate. In Bangladesh, Neel's family had been small landowners. They worked with men and women of a different religion who, when the time came, decided to drive the family out. Now they are just as penniless as he'd been crossing into the DP camp in Germany.

"I know you didn't run," Jaryk says. "Most of us don't." He doesn't mean it as a compliment but says it gently enough that Neel can take it as one.

"Why do you think all of this has happened to us?" Neel asks.

For much of his youth Jaryk railed against the iniquity of the world. Why had his mother died after childbirth, why had he been born into a poor family, why had they come for the Jews? None of his childhood wrongs—a stolen piece of cake, or the time he shoved a cousin into the mud—seemed to justify his lot. So many had it better, and it was only in the orphanage, surrounded by children whose stories were like his own, that he stopped asking "*Why me?*" When he did feel that way, he learned to hide his feelings. He thinks Neel has mastered the same trick: little that happens seems to depress him, though it should by almost any standard. He knows the boy misses his father. Every afternoon he sees Neel dust the few good photos he has of his dad before setting them back beneath his bed.

"I don't know the answer to that," Jaryk says. "But here's a trick: when you say your lines, imagine that they can take you from this place to somewhere beautiful far away." That had been Esterka's advice to him, but he thinks it carries just as well for a boy who's lost his father and his home.

They walk to the stage. Last week he sanded and painted the bleachers, secured bamboo poles to stake a perimeter of lights powered by a borrowed generator. They can fit hundreds in the space, and if the professor's outreach is any indication, that many will come. They've turned a football field into an amphitheater, he's proud of that, of leading the men and children from the village to do the work of building a stage. He squeezes Neel's hand. "Tell me how many can sit in the space. Count the number of rows and columns of seats."

"Four hundred exactly," Neel says. "It is a wonderful sight."

It's nothing like the stage he built with Mordechai and Chaim and Misha, which they'd imagined out of nothing. Hollowed-out wood became windows. The Flower Girl's flowers came from sewing together brightly colored pieces of cloth. No one had a proper costume, so they all wore mismatched clothes—as many bright colors merged together as possible—because that was what they thought children in India would do.

Days before they were to perform the play, an SS officer had come to inspect the orphanage. Pan Doktor was out on one of his trips, begging the last of the rich Jews for food, and Madam Stefa was taking her afternoon nap, so Misha and Esterka were left to show the officer around. He remembered the cleanliness of those boots, how they shined in the hallway light. The officer's cap was without a crease, and he smelled of a leathery perfume. After visiting the girls' and boys' dorms, the officer noticed the set. Chaim had just finished putting up the curtain, which was nothing more than unwashed bedsheets tied together. Behind the curtain, they were to change from one costume to another.

"What is this?" the officer had asked, indicating the hung sheets and the windows of thread and the scraps of cloth.

"It's for the children," Misha had said, but he didn't protest when the officer told them to take it down. They had suspected from the beginning that the most disobedient act was the making of their art, and so had been prepared for this very moment. Along with Chaim, Misha took down the sheets and the windows hung with string and the watercolor pictures of the Indian sun. All the children watched. When the officer had left, they began putting everything back together. Jaryk remembered how Esterka had joked about the black boots not being fans of theater. A simple act of defiance. Esterka's voice in his ear, asking him to help Chaim with the curtain. In the end it didn't matter what they'd done, the Germans had their unbreakable plans, but still it'd felt powerful to pick up the pieces, to go against what they were told.

"Yes," Jaryk now tells Neel, mussing the boy's hair. "It is wonderful. And you, sir, are good at numbers."

He likes giving Neel compliments—the harder-earned ones, mind you—and watching the boy's face catch into a smile. He's begun to think of himself as an uncle, an imperfect one, but still. He's even daydreamed about taking Neel away to America, showing him the Statue of Liberty, then taking the boy to his favorite pizza spot on Staten Island, watching him eat with glee. He knows this is unlikely, but it doesn't hurt to dream.

It's only when he's alone at night that he's beset by doubt. What if performing this play does the opposite of what they've imagined—what if the black boots come to take Neel and his mother to a worse fate? The performance in Warsaw hadn't protected the orphanage; alone at night, he can't be sure that now it'll guard Neel and the others.

Still, during the days as the mist clears, there are the demands of their production, the bits of carpentry and rehearsing left to be done. There's an energy to the affair, an unbridled optimism that breaks the night's fear. During the days things go well enough that he can forget both his life in New York and the tumult outside their village. Each morning Rohan brings the newspaper to the breakfast table, but he's learned the front page isn't for him. On Saturdays, he scans the comics. He prefers *The Adventures of Tintin*, which he'd read even in his youth, and is surprised by how little the plots have changed.

One morning he finds the professor alone at the dining table. There's a coffee stain on his place mat, and Rohan, who'd normally clean the mess, is nowhere to be found.

"They've taken him," the professor says. "Rohan's gone."

The professor rarely refers to the butler by name, but there is an intimacy in the way the syllables come off his tongue. *Rohan*. He enunciates with force. "Abducted," he says. "Taken by the police when he went to fetch the paper."

"Why would they take him?" Jaryk asks.

The professor gazes at him pityingly, as if during this time he's learned nothing at all. "To provoke me, of course," he says, cleaning the coffee stain with his sleeve, not caring that he's wearing one of his long white shirts. He stares into the middle distance between the rice fields and the horizon, gives his mustache a few good tugs. "Rohan was a sympathizer, and when I taught at Calcutta University, he was also one of my students. Back then, he used to do some work for the Naxalites. Mind you, he didn't make bombs, nothing like that. Mostly, he handed out pamphlets, organized rallies. The police put his name on their list, and when he found out he came to me. He was a remarkable student. I wasn't going to let them put one more boy in prison. I let him stay here. I didn't think they would look for him outside the city."

From the first day Rohan hasn't seemed like a butler. He eats his meals with everyone else, often wears the professor's shirts. Sometimes, when Rohan carries coffee up to the professor's room, he lingers awhile, and Jaryk hears the two of them engaged in what seems like lively debate.

"We're not going to just sit here, are we?" Jaryk finally asks.

"No, we're not," says the professor, though he remains ensconced in his thoughts.

"You took him in. I know you meant to keep him safe," Jaryk says.

The professor glances up from his coffee, but his sleepless eyes refuse to meet Jaryk's. Here is a man who keeps few friends, though Rohan had found a place in his heart. Perhaps the police discovered this. They wouldn't do anything to an American, but a hideaway rabble-rouser was another matter.

"I'll help you," Jaryk says. "I'll help you bring him home."

....

They nearly drive past the prison. There's a hastily arranged barbed-wire fence around the property, and through a gap in the fence the professor steers his jeep. Several guards emerge from what appear to be barracks, wearing only shorts, bare-chested pot-bellied men staring at them with suspicion, hands close to the revolvers on their hips. Next to the barracks there's a pool filled with dead water, where clumps of mosquitoes hover on the sur-face. One of the men converses with the professor, and they are led farther down the path.

As they walk past the pool, a swarm of flies hurries their prog-ress. A guard accompanies them to a building with a sign that hangs askew: *42nd Prescient of the Police, West Bengal.* It's intended to read *Precinct,* he assumes, but the spelling only imbues the place with more of a strange aura.

They wait. Occasionally a guard emerges to have the professor complete a form. Sometimes it's the same form handed out again, and though Jaryk protests, Rudra Bose puts pen to paper every time he's asked. *"The warden is out and about,"* they're told. *"It's best to have all documentation."* Some of the guards speak English well enough to try to enlist Jaryk in a hand of gin rummy, which he refuses.

"Why is he being held?" Jaryk asks variants of the question throughout the morning.

The response remains the same. *"There is always a reason. Only warden will know the reason."* The guards smoke so much it's diffi-cult to see into the back rooms, where they're told Rohan is being kept.

The professor grows despondent as the day wears on. At one

point he tells Jaryk, "I don't have a family. I suppose Rohan was the closest, someone who needed me for food, shelter, and even guidance. All he'd done was put up some flyers in the city, and he ran to me to protect him. In the end, I failed him."

"You protected him as well as you could," Jaryk says. He thinks of all the rooms in the mansion that remain empty, all the covered history from hall to hall. In ways that matter, he and the professor are of a similar breed. It's been easy to get along with a man who holds his past at bay, makes few allowances for love or fellowship. He won't ever know Rudra Bose deeply, and there's a pleasure in this distance, at least some comfort.

Were it not for Lucy he might've lived his life by the same rhythms. No one to look or judge. At night when the professor drapes the boudoirs with sheets, it's as if he's putting curtains over the eyes of his ancestors; Jaryk can understand this desire—this need to burrow into oblivion.

"We don't know why they picked up Rohan. We don't know if it has to do with the play."

The professor nods, as if he's been tossed a philosophical argument. "Time will tell."

After four hours of waiting, Jaryk says, "Maybe we should just try and force our way." It's the kind of thing he would've expected Rudra Bose to say. In truth, he has no desire to storm the guards. Though they're smaller men, he's seen a whole barracks' worth of them, and his treatment for roughing an officer would likely be worse than what he'd received at the military hospital. The comment's more to prompt the professor to action, but it doesn't have an effect.

"Don't even think about it. They'll only beat him more if we do that."

"Are you sure they're mistreating him?" Jaryk asks. "Wouldn't we hear something?"

"Oh, he's not here," says Rudra Bose. "They've got him holed up somewhere else. They'll bring him around when they're ready."

The warden comes to see them as the sun begins to set. "Sorry to keep you waiting," he says. The warden's snow-white hair and the glasses that sit on the rim of his nose make him seem like an academic, as if in another life he were a dissertation partner with Rudra Bose. "Any tea for you?" he asks. It's the first time that day they've been offered anything, and though he's thirsty, Jaryk answers for them both, "We're fine, thank you. We just want to see our friend."

They're led past the dirty pool, where the guards have dumped their fruit peels. A crow skims the surface and takes a mango skin in its mouth. They follow the warden to a small hut that's anointed by the falling sun in colors of burn.

"You remain outside," the professor says.

"We go together," Jaryk says.

He's seen enough in the ghetto, men degrading other men with spit and fists and batons and rifles, children following suit, playing out the ways their fathers and mothers tortured the Jews. Still, it comes as a shock when the warden lifts the curtain to the hut and says, "On his way here your supposed butler fell once or twice."

Rohan lies on a straw cot. His hands are covered in poorly tied bandages. One of his eyes is swollen shut, and the one that isn't looks at them with a dreamy scorn, as if he isn't ready to receive them after all. His shirt's been ripped; blood has pooled and dried at the base of his sternum in a heart-shaped pocket. The professor squats by Rohan's side, strokes his hair, says something into his ear.

"Why have you done this?" Jaryk asks the warden.

"Section 377 of the Indian Penal Code," the warden says. "This fellow has been engaged in illegal acts. He has also written subversive poetry. He has also put up advertisements against the state. You come from a country without morals, sir, but here we have our limits."

"You'll have hell to pay," the professor says under his breath.

"Who will? Who has committed the act?" the warden asks. "I

have simply brought you to see your friend. I did not punish him in any way. None of my men laid a hand. Though we were in the right to incarcerate him for years, we gave him breakfast. Afterwards, if it happened that he opened his mouth and insulted an officer, then that was dealt with accordingly. If it happened that he insulted yet another man of rank, then that was also dealt with. Now, it is only my job to return him to you."

Rohan swats away a fly that's landed on his neck and closes his one good eye. His carotid artery pulses like a trapped snake, the work of his heart in plain view. Jaryk looks at the professor to see what can be done. He wants to punch the glasses off the warden's nose, spill a little blood. When the terror had come for them in the ghetto, he'd been only a child. Perhaps that can be forgiven, but now he's a grown man. "What do we do?" he asks the professor.

"We leave," Rudra Bose says, helping his former student to stand. "Please tell Rajan Datta and his cohort that the message has been received."

"Excellent," the warden says. "Please also know that your foreign friend no longer provides you cover. One could even wonder about his visa, for instance, whether it remains valid. Shouldn't he return home to his country? One might wonder about his general health here."

The warden's lips are so thin that when he smiles they stretch indiscernibly into his face. He scratches his snow-white hair, releases a plume of dandruff. "Good evening to you all," he says. Bare-chested officers escort them to the jeep.

The professor drives, and Rohan and Jaryk sit in the back. Though it's warm and humid, Rohan shivers against him. He tries to avoid looking too closely at Rohan's face.

Back at the Bose mansion, the professor helps Rohan into his room. Jaryk waits at the dining table, keeps seeing Rohan's bloodied face in his mind. Whenever Misha had gotten rowdy enough to punch someone at the bar, Jaryk had stepped in. Violence sobers him, salt on sunburnt skin. But he's come all this way for a purpose. He's let Lucy return to America alone. As the night wears on, he drinks the professor's coffee to stay awake, considers what he can still do to save Neel and the village.

When the professor returns, he pours himself the last of the coffee and slurps it down, getting his mustache wet in the process. Then he says, "I'm sorry you had to see that. Today's politicians are not like the ones who fought for independence. They sow terror in the soil. It used to be different."

"Is Rohan going to be all right?" Jaryk asks.

"He has a bruised eye, a split lip, possibly even a broken jaw, but I have handled worse."

The professor stares into his cup, then continues. "This whole government is rotten. The Naxalite boys had the idea to tear everything down. Were they so wrong? You need a proper revolution. You can't have incremental progress and hope the disease will be dealt with. You can't elect the same kind of crony over and over, hoping for magic. That's why City Hall needs to burn. Only then can you get to the beauty underneath."

"But what if you burn the good?" Jaryk asks. "Not everything was made by the corrupt or the greedy."

The professor looks at him a long while. "Did I ever tell you about the time I saw Mahatma Gandhi as a child? It must've been winter, because he was wrapped in homespun wool, walking along the main avenue of Dehradun, where all those who loved him waited to touch his feet. I was a boy of seven, beside my mother, who was screaming hysterically, "*Bapu, Bapuji*," and as the Mahatma stopped for a moment, his sandal strap came undone. I rushed past the security and helped the old man hobble back into his shoe. When I held his hand, I could feel the thinness of him, the hallowed bones. Nowadays all we have are our loudspeakers, our cronies, and our capitalist Communists."

Over the many hours at the prison Jaryk has had time to think about what he'll tell the professor, what'll he say to set their course. What he knows is that he won't quit now. He let Lucy go back to America so he could save a village. A brush-up with the police isn't enough to set him back. "What about the play?" Jaryk demands. "Rohan's beating means we have to go forward sooner than we thought. No more delays."

"Look at you," says the professor, peering at him through the hair falling over his eyes. "You've grown to be a little like me. But nothing is without cost, as you've seen for yourself. If we hold the play, they'll surely be there. Rajan Datta surrounded by his men. We'll hold the play. You don't have to worry, Mr. Smith. Just know that no one takes my friend from my home and walks away unscathed."

"Are you planning something?" Jaryk asks.

"Do your part," the professor says. "Then we will have met our obligation to each other."

The play's purpose is to give Gopalpur a voice, but now he understands there's another intention, a more personal one. He can feel the professor's agitation, as the man's knees knock in time against the wood of the table. *Stop*, he wants to say. *Stop, before you bruise.*

They're closer to each other than he'd like to admit. It's simpler to settle scores than it is to raise a family.

Years later he'll wonder why he didn't press the professor, why he didn't ask about the retribution that's been planned, but in this moment there is the stained place mat and the silence between them. There's the memory of a young man's swollen cheekbone and the bruise under his right eye as he follows his saviors home. He'll always remember that ride in the jeep, Rohan's broken body against his, when the professor slowed down for each pothole and drove as if it were his first time on the road.

The Performance

The morning of the performance Jaryk gathers the child actors, and they practice their entrance, with Neel leading the cast. He tells them to walk as if they own the earth on which they stand. "Like this," he says, demonstrating with long, exaggerated steps so that they laugh.

"Uncle, we are feeling nervous," Neel says. Last rehearsal Neel forgot a few lines, and his timing has been less than perfect, but Jaryk doesn't chastise him. After all, he knows what it's like to stand onstage before a house of strangers.

"If you say to yourself that you're relaxed, then that's how you'll feel."

They're nervous not only because they will be performing before hundreds but also because of the rumors that have reached the village, whispers that what happened to Rohan will soon happen to them. Last week the Flower Girl's parents approached the professor; they're concerned about all the attention, and maybe they could begin the show by thanking the government for the use of the public land? Maybe they could even start with an apology?

"Absolutely no," Rudra Bose told them. He's assured the parents that no harm will come to their children. Anyway, it's for their collective benefit, he says. With all the journalists and dignitaries in the audience, no one will raise a hand against Gopalpur.

"What about the day after?" Jaryk later asks the professor in private.

"Perhaps they will get a permit to remain for as long as they like," the professor says. "But these things are unpredictable."

"What do you mean? I signed up for this because you said they'd have a better life. Are you saying all of this might not help after all?"

"Oh, it'll definitely help," says Bose. "It just may not help them right away, or it may not help Gopalpur but another village. Change is complicated. A shot fired in one village could mean justice in another. You can't look at this so narrowly."

The professor excuses himself to run an errand, and Jaryk spends the morning worrying about what will come once the media have left. Since Rohan's beating, his being here—the protection he believed he offered—seems to matter less and less, and he's no longer sure that the play will give them the cover that they need.

....

At six o'clock that evening, the cast emerge from the village courtyard and walk down the staircase of the hill, marching past the kerosene lamps that mark the football field toward the stage. Neel carries their banner: *Gopalpur Theater Players.*

Jaryk spots the Pals in the front row and waves. They have come, warnings or otherwise, though they've left their children at home. If Lucy were here with him, he might've felt a sense of accomplishment. Instead her absence strikes him as a sign of his failure. He searches for her in the audience but knows what he will find; she has chosen, as he has, the course of her own life.

Neel's hair has largely grown back for the role. Now he leads the cast into the dressing area, which is no more than an enclosed section at the rear of the stage, where they have hung sheets on bamboo poles. A few of the mothers are here to help the children with their outfits, and they treat Jaryk like one of their own. Despite his protests, Neel's mother applies makeup to his face, smudges it to blend with his tan. She dabs a bit of rose oil behind his ear. "Good luck," she says.

She has a name that he's learned means *gold—Hema.* "Thank you for your kindness," he tells her, knowing his smile will translate while his words will not.

He puts on a long gray wig and peeks out of the dressing area as the professor takes the stage. Almost every seat in the bleachers has been filled. The villagers are serving as ushers. A few have cameras on hand, awaiting their child's emergence onto the stage, pride visible on their faces. Somewhere in the ether, he likes to think, Misha is watching alongside Pan Doktor and Esterka.

"Welcome to art changing history," Professor Bose begins. "It is not often that I am able to speak to such a diverse audience. We have here represented men and women of the village, the city, and of many nations. I am so pleased to also have in attendance a member of the ruling party, Mr. Rajan Datta."

Heads turn toward a frail man flanked by two policemen. Disparate sections of the audience clap, but the reception is tepid. Jaryk looks to his cast; luckily, they can't see what's happening outside the dressing area. This has been the question on his mind—how do you protect the child in a world that means to malign, trade suffering for suffering? At Pan Doktor's orphanage, the charter was made by the children, but once they stepped outside they were in the land of their enemy, as the children of Gopalpur are now. Was there another way to save them, or was it only his hubris that had made him believe they were his to save? Now the first bloom of regret. All the warnings of the Pals, then of Lucy, gone unheeded; but there is no going back.

The professor is still talking. "For the sake of our honored guests we have prepared some pre-entertainment," he says.

A poet enters the stage and recites lines in a cadenced Bengali, the rhythm of Calcutta's traffic, the engines spurring up and dying down, no one going anywhere fast. Jaryk watches the poet's hands for meaning; he has a way of motioning that reminds him of the flight of birds in the middle of a storm. The audience waits for each line, and Jaryk feels the quiet spreading in the theater. Is this what it will be like for the actors?

After the poet finishes, Rudra Bose returns to the stage, framed by the beginning of a sunset that will soon be muted by the passing clouds.

"The poet you heard tonight is not from Calcutta," says the professor. "He is born and bred in a nearby village. He is educated at Presidency College and receives an honors in history. But he does not stay in the city. No, he returns to his family. He begins to run their farm, and he brings in techniques of science. In the early mornings, he writes poems. The poems he writes are of our brothers and sisters. Of those who have been here for generations. Of others who have fled recently from across the border. The poems he writes consider the crops, the water, and the land. The trees that were planted long before the British arrived. All of this is the real news of the day. Not what we read in the Calcutta dailies. Not what is told to us by our government radio.

"Now the boy who is playing Amal here tonight has his own history," the professor says. He walks across the stage in five long steps, opens his mouth as if to speak, then closes it again before continuing. "Amal's real name is Neel. He is ten years old. Less than a year ago, Neel arrived here with his family. His mother and his father. They walked from Maimansingh to Calcutta to finally here, to what we now call Gopalpur. Neel's father began to tend the land.

"He was not interested in elections or the changing of the government. After all, he had escaped one in total transition. A government in failure. He was surprised when representatives of our United Front visited him prior to the elections. They offered many things. Schools, better jobs in the city, relief from taxes. And Neel's father, like all the others, stamped his thumb *yes*. Let this government have their new power. All the seats of parliament filled with their names.

"But after the elections Neel's father and others asked about what they were owed. For a school in the village. For jobs they could walk to in the winters. That had been the deal, they said. Initially, they were entertained. Then, they were condescended to, but when they grew persistent in their protests—when one of them threatened to go to *The Statesman* with the terms of the deal— certain people began to visit this village. These certain people had heard about Neel's family. They said they wanted taxes to pay for the new school, but nobody in Gopalpur had money. Afterwards, these men said the land wasn't theirs at all. The land we stand on today, they said, is needed to build a new car factory. It was then that the gundas took action. The gundas, who as everyone knows, are hired and paid by our government."

It strikes Jaryk that the audience have come for this political theater as much as they have come for the play. All quiet, not a hand fan, not a sneeze. All waiting for whatever Rudra Bose will say next.

The two policemen who've accompanied the politician stand up. That's all they do: stand up. The professor notices and turns in their direction. "The gundas did things," he says. "All manner of things. Some of these led to the murder of Neel's father. Though the government has a different story. No official records. Like the Amal of *The Post Office*, Neel is without a father."

The policemen begin to clap. Just the two of them, clapping as the professor remains onstage. Not the beginning Jaryk envisioned. He looks into the faces of the policemen—faces so ordinary and inculpable in shape—and he feels the fear entering his knees. It is the ordinary men who are sent to kill. The ordinary men who sent Pan Doktor to his death.

"What is it, Uncle?" Neel asks.

"It's nothing," Jaryk says. "Go be with the others."

He's taken Misha's promise to the village farther than he could've imagined, but he's also brought the tar of his old life. It was only with Lucy that he'd begun to remove himself from his own story, only in her love considered another version of the truth, but she's nowhere near. The children of Gopalpur are alone with him.

The policemen stop clapping.

The professor continues, "What a pleasure to have appreciators of the arts in the audience, who applaud even before the play begins. But won't you all give us another hand? Most of these children have never performed before, so won't you make them feel welcome—won't you show them your support?"

Slowly, the audience joins in, and Jaryk hears the goats braying in the fields above the theater. Without their masters to keep them, they're on their own, wandering as far as their tethers will allow.

"There's nothing to fear," Jaryk says to his cast. "We've made ourselves ready, and now it's time to go on."

He says this to himself as much as to them. When Pan Doktor marched the children toward Treblinka, who knew that one would end up here? As it was for him, so it can be for Neel and the others—a life that surprises itself into being.

....

For many years afterwards, Jaryk will refuse to discuss the performance of *The Post Office* in Gopalpur. When asked, he'll say, "It was nothing special, I hardly remember it." Yet that day will remain for him, as the performance in the ghetto remains for him—a point through which he'll gather his bearings and say, *"This happened."*

Late into old age, he will remember mundane moments: before Neel first takes to the stage, he whispers into the boy's ear, *"Break a leg,"* then sees the expression doesn't make sense to a Bengali, so he hugs Neel instead, wrapping him tightly in his arms. He'll remember the sweet smell of Neel's ears and the spot of talc on his right cheek, which he wipes off just in time. He'll remember watching Mrs. Pal in the audience; she has a tic of turning over the bangles on her wrists as if she's counting rosary beads. He'll remember that the Flower Girl sneezes on stage but that no one in the audience seems to mind. In their silence, they support the children, will them to produce their lines with precision and clarity, and all the children rise to the occasion, turning to their mothers on their way off the stage to make sure they did good. He'll remember saying his own lines as the Fakir, the wandering Uncle, though in his memory the lines will seem as if they are the words of a boy, not of a man, the words spoken in Warsaw from an open throat. He'll remember the clouds that begin to clear as Amal lies on his deathbed. He'll remember the lanterns illuminating Neel's face and the boy's long shadow. He'll remember hearing the noise of the stage itself, the soft spots he failed to level. At times he'll feel he welcomed the devil to the village—and shouldn't he have known better?—but other times he'll remember the play and believe it was for the best. All of these moments will come into focus before the final scene finishes, which it never does.

Neel lies on the child's bed halfway into the afterlife, garrisoned by all the cast members, including Jaryk, and though he towers over everyone else, he no longer feels conscious of this. His lines are exhausted. They are all waiting for the Flower Girl's last words. Jaryk watches Neel and thinks of the fragility of life, of how much this boy matters, though only to so few—a handful in the theater and the village—and beyond that space, how little a life might matter. The same is true for his unborn child, a thought that brings him back to regret, but he steels himself; there is one more line for the Flower Girl to say.

As the Flower Girl approaches the stage, he holds his breath. No matter, it will be over soon, he thinks, and he will be able to breathe out the whole effort, once she climbs the steps with her basket of chrysanthemums, once she walks toward Neel, who strains to lift his head, who asks her, *"Will you forget me?"*

"I will not forget you," says the Flower Girl, holding Neel's hand.

Instead of an exit, Jaryk has staged a moment he hopes will stay with the audience. He returns to the uneven platform they've called a stage, stands next to Neel, and says, "Hello, I'm Jaryk Smith. I was born in Poland."

As he removes his wig, he can feel the audience waking from the spell of the theater. "You all heard the last line of this play," he says. "Tonight, we're going to have you say the line back to us. All the parents of Gopalpur are passing out notes that have the names of the children who live in this village. When I count to three, you're going to read the name on the paper out loud and say to your child that you will not forget them. Then you're going to take this name and this story of Gopalpur and share it with everyone you know. Got it?"

Last week he wrote the names of all the children in the village, one on each sheet of paper: *Neel, Megha, Dushyant, Soumya* . . . Toward the end he added a couple of extras: *Rohan* and then *Misha.* He waits for Hema to translate his words into Bengali.

"One," he begins to count, trying to steady his voice. Whatever he's done to help them, he prays it's enough to last. "Two . . . When I say 'three,' you'll read what's on your paper back to me." He studies the audience, as taken aback as they are by his commandeering of the last scene. He takes a breath and says *"Three"* as the sound of gunshot fills the amphitheater.

The Flower Girl, her open mouth, the child's body on the bed. All this he sees but he does not move.

He will remember little of what happens next. The versions of what remain in his memory will begin to confuse him. Mr. Pal calls to him from the audience, though he can't make out the words. Then everyone scurries, the bleachers come undone, and for a moment he thinks of the great waste of their effort. The Flower Girl is the first to exit the stage, though he can't remember whether it's her mother who carries her off or if it's the professor himself, who seems then to be everywhere at once—pleading for calm on the microphone, leading the children offstage, righting fallen chairs—but Neel and Jaryk remain as they are.

First, he'll think it was the Flower Girl who was struck. Then he'll see that it's Rajan Datta, the politician, who's been shot, who's surrounded by policemen attending to his wounds.

He won't remember whether it's Neel who comes for him or whether it's he who carries the boy, but either way, they will end up underneath the stage. He'll wait there, whispering again and again *"Are you okay?"* but will be refused a response. He'll rub Neel's shoulders and his feet. He'll say, *"We wait until everyone leaves."* He'll say, "*Soon we run*," but for hours they'll remain without another word.

Underneath the stage the darkness smells of cow manure. A certain sweetness from the wind traveling through the rice plateaus. Even after the constable cars have come and scoured the area, even after the only sounds he can hear are the village goats, who've wandered down to graze, they still hide, falling asleep in each other's arms.

················

When he wakes, moonlight is passing through an open slat of the stage, and he risks coming out. The stage still stands, the set almost as it was, as if they were preparing for an encore, but all the lamps that had been staked to the ground have been knocked free. The generator snores for no reason. The dressing area is strewn with torn garlands, the smell of burnt hyacinth in the air. A crow lands on a collapsed bleacher.

He carries Neel, still sleeping, up to the village huts, which are so quiet he's unsure if anyone's home. After the fourth knock, Hema bares the door. She's holding up a lantern, and in her face he sees anger and fear but also relief. She takes her child from his arms, and Neel begins to stir, waking from his sleep.

"Hello, Uncle," says the boy, still half asleep.

He wants to tell them he's sorry for his part in the trouble that's come to pass—the trouble he feels still coming. "Come with me," he tells Hema, gesturing toward the fields. He can take the two of them to the Pals', where they can stay until it's safe to return.

"No," she hisses.

"Please come," he tries again, this woman who held Misha as he clutched his heart and took his last breath.

"No," she rejoins. She raises her rifle from the hem of her sari up to the moonlight and speaks rapidly to her son in Bengali.

"This is our land," Neel translates. "This is our fight."

Hema strokes her son's cheek, removes a smudge of dirt.

"Goodbye, Uncle," Neel says.

Goodbye. He kisses Neel, his sweet sweet smelling hair. Then he leaves the boy who let him love this land that wasn't his own.

Under the light of the moon, the stage is well illumined, and he surveys the damage to the collapsed bleachers. All his work wasted now. By the dressing area, he sees movement, remains crouched in the shadows until he can make out the man as Professor Bose. The professor signals for silence, and they walk together toward the road.

"I was searching for you." The professor leads them to his jeep, parked in a clearing of *taal* trees above the turnoff to the village. "Now, that was beyond my expectations. That was extraordinary."

Jaryk stares at him. He is not sure what to make of the professor's celebratory mood.

"What we achieved tonight is the beginning of our revolution," continues Rudra Bose. "Tomorrow, all the papers will be writing about us. What we did through art. What we did through nonviolence."

"But someone was shot," Jaryk finally says.

"Yes, it seems Rajan Datta was shot, but not by us. At least not by me."

"What do you mean? You planned this in some way, didn't you? This was your revenge for Rohan and everything else in your life. Isn't that so?"

"Of course not," the professor says. "I keep my personal life outside of my political aims. Look, unfortunate as Rajan Datta's shooting may be, it gives us the press we need, the press Gopalpur needs to keep its story alive."

He thinks of holding Neel in his arms and of Hema's words: *This is our fight.*

"Listen, it is best we be off soon," the professor says. "I'm afraid that you also are a persona non grata now. We shall head to the house, gather some supplies, then Rohan, you, and I will lie low for a few days somewhere. After that, we shall plan our next move."

"What do you mean, 'our next move'?"

"This is what we have worked so hard for. Revolution not just for Gopalpur but for all the poor peoples of India. Now is our time. Come," the professor says, opening the door to his jeep, "let us continue our mission."

The man Misha met in New York last autumn, when the idea of India was just that, is asking Jaryk to continue. If it had been Misha here instead of him, the performance might have gone differently, though who knows how Misha would have responded—how he would have met these words of revolution?

He remembers now that he saw the professor as the strangest person to have entered Seven and a Half Dimes, so outside the spectrum of the bar's regular personalities that he had trouble staying with the conversation. Now, he and this man are balanced on a pendulum. After they went to free Rohan, he saw Rudra Bose in a different light, felt his flaws and desires. Now he believes the professor, whether by his own hand or through accomplices, shot Rajan Datta, a man he barely knows, who somewhere in the city might have his own family to keep. Rudra Bose has traveled past a boundary that he will not cross.

Leaves rustle underfoot as the professor waits.

"I've made my mistakes," Jaryk finally says. "I wanted to help Gopalpur. I wanted to help Neel and his mother. I thought this play would give them a new life, and it still might."

"Yes, it certainly will. They've learned they're not powerless. They've learned they can alter their fate with art. Come on, let me give you a lift," the professor says.

"Goodbye, Professor," Jaryk replies, as he turns and walks deeper into the forest, from where he knows he'll reach another clearing, and from there, a kilometer north, he'll find a turnoff onto the main road, heading back to the city. He finds the North Star and, keeping it in sight, begins to run.

....

The Sabbath. He's lived thirty years of his life without celebrating the movement of the week into the day of holy rest, from sunset to sunset. The rules of the Sabbath do not permit running unless for good reason, but he has good reason. He is heading due north, nothing more dependable than the direction of heaven.

Misha, barely eighteen years old, is running beside him with his long legs, and he is doing his best to keep up, and the others—Chaim, Mordechai, Hanna—are calling his name. and there is no rain anywhere, just the weightlessness of sky.

For all his preparation he could not have known what it would feel like to stand before a foreign crowd, introducing the play from his childhood. A stone on the heart, a taste of salt on his tongue. When he said his lines, they felt as if they were emerging from a city deeply submerged. It did not matter that he was standing on a stage, being watched. Nothing mattered but the glint, the faraway memory, retracting and again emerging, that moment before they had stepped onstage, all the audience holding their breath, right before he and the other children announced their play. Holding Hanna's hand, letting go of her fingers so he could walk alone into that bright room.

After the Train

GERMANY—SPRING 1945

After two weeks in the displaced persons camp, Jaryk spotted Misha in the back of the soup line. At first he kept a safe distance because he thought it was only a Misha look-alike. The outline of the man's face matched what he remembered of his oldest friend, but over the gaunt cheeks a dirty beard had grown, with wispy, lifeless ends, where bits of food tended to lodge from meal to meal. This man shuffled along after he had collected his portion of soup and bread: every few steps he would pause and look behind him, as if he were afraid of the bowl being snatched from his hands.

Jaryk sat one table to the left to steal glances. He thought he was only seeing things, but when Misha slurped down his soup, then licked his bowl clean and produced a look of such contentment, showing everyone who cared to see his gap-toothed grin, Jaryk couldn't deny who was before him. He walked to Misha's table and tapped his brother on the shoulder.

"You didn't save me any soup?" Jaryk asked.

Misha stopped chewing his bread mid-bite. He looked at Jaryk but didn't speak, and he supposed Misha was digesting Jaryk's own transformation in those two years. He had lost weight; he had grown an older boy's voice; he, too, had endured.

"You!" Misha finally said. "How did you live?"

Jaryk had imagined that as soon as Misha recognized him, he would be wrapped in a bear hug and carried around the camp like a jewel of the past. He wasn't prepared for this question. It was earnestly asked, but he wouldn't tell Misha the truth, then or ever.

"The morning they came to take us, I got separated from Pan Doktor," he said. "I looked for the others, but I couldn't find anyone I knew. So I ran to the countryside. There, I did what you taught me: I found the right food."

················

Up until the last days of September 1942, it had been possible to live by Misha's training. Where Jaryk had escaped from the train was a long stretch of forest, and he found himself tracking the sunlight to sources of water and discovering, as Misha had taught him those weeks of summer camp, which fruits to eat and how to make a shelter. Nearby, there was a farm, and at night he would steal into the chicken coop and leave with a handful of eggs.

Then it began to get cold. The first time he awoke with frost over his fingernails, it was a Sunday. He knew this because the farmer's family was wearing their churchgoing clothes, and it meant he might be able to sneak into their house for a bowl of hot soup, the kind with beets and thick strips of meat, or perhaps even some baked bread. He could barely wait until they were gone. They had a son a little older than him, and perhaps he would borrow the boy's coat. His arms were freezing fast. He counted the screws that jutted from the wall of the barn door, where he hid until the family settled into their donkey carriage.

When the carriage left, he crept into the house through an open window, but he found that the grandmother had been left behind. She was sitting in a high-backed chair by the fireplace that took up half the room, and when he landed on the floor and locked eyes with her, it seemed that she had been waiting for him.

She didn't say a word, but it was as if she knew exactly how many eggs he'd taken, as if she were counting in her head the price of his thievery. She rose from her chair and produced a switch from the folds of her skirt. He tried to escape, but she was quicker than she'd first appeared. She held him by the ear. She beat him so fiercely on his bottom that he forgot to weep.

But the next week the cold only crept deeper into the earth and the shelter he had made from leaves and branches wasn't enough. It was the first time he awoke in the middle of the night wishing to be dead. He had known hunger on Chłodna Street and Sienna Street, but this was a different kind of pain. Now he was hungry, but also alone, and loneliness sharpened hunger's bite. That week, he raked his nails against the maple trees to see if he could release their sap. His fingers came away bloodied, and he blamed Pan Doktor for giving them hope when none was to be had.

Next Sunday, he returned again to the house, wishing for the same: a coat and a portion of soup. The grandmother was sitting exactly where she'd been the week before. This time, she looked at him like she was disappointed. She watched him for a while, and as he stood there, he took note of the singular silver braid that curled down her neck, the heavy gullet that swayed as she rocked in her chair, and those eyes as blue as the sky above the river Vistula.

When he made for the vat of soup, she grabbed him and brought him back to the rocking chair. She pulled his trousers down and beat him thirteen times with the warm end of the rod she'd used to stir the fire. This time, he wept with shame. He wept for his own fate, for the fate of his community, for the fate of everyone who would soon be born into this wretched world. As the blows landed on his bottom, he felt a little grateful for the warmth of the fire, and his cheeks burned with the weight of such miserable gratitude.

The fourth Sunday he saw her, he could barely walk, so great was his hunger. It had been eight weeks since he'd talked with anyone, and his voice was parched, but he cleared his throat and spoke. "Your soup," he said, pointing at the simmering pot from which he could smell the meat and vegetables, "smells so good."

When she stood up to her full height, he didn't take a step back. He only wanted a taste. Then he would leave. He wouldn't bother them again. He wouldn't even bother to make his shelter of leaves. Instead, after a taste of her soup, he would allow his body to float in the stream, where tiny sheets of ice had begun to decorate the surface with crystal rainbows.

She grabbed him by the ear. There was no hint of mercy on her face, but this time she did not beat him. Instead, she dragged him to the yard, all the while yanking on his ear, as if her purpose was to separate it from his head, dragged him to the barn, unlocked the padlock, and threw him in with the goats. A minute later, she came by with a cup of soup, grunting as he watched her for signs of his turning fortune. He didn't wonder if she could speak. He didn't wonder why the rest of the family didn't take her to church. Instead, he drank the broth with his remaining strength, coughing as a strip of meat became lodged in his throat. She hit him hard between his shoulder blades, and he fell forward and kissed her feet.

Over the course of that winter, she beat him fourteen more times. Each time, it was done differently: an old wooden cane, a long paintbrush, the ladle with which she served him soup, even her callused palm. Each time, he cried louder and turned to look at her, but there was nothing in her face that resembled remorse. He began to believe this was the price of survival.

He never saw the rest of the family up close, and he supposed that was for the best. She had made him a warm corner in the goat shed. There, he would lie next to the two kids, while the mother would look at him suspiciously, but in the night he would sometimes find her nuzzling his chin, warming him, and if there was anything that allowed him to live for the next morning, it was the regularity of his beatings merged with the experience of those animal heartbeats, which were growing surer with each day, and the long white chin hairs of the mother goat, who steadily and with increasing pride would huddle as close to him as to her children, as if it were her duty to keep all three of them warm.

This was how he lived the twelfth year of his life. And with the spring and the thawing of the road, he saw a line of men and women. It was the longest line he had ever seen. For a while, he simply counted the arms and legs: thousands of the bedraggled passed the farm, smelling of rot and dirt. No one bothered to stop, but when he had counted as high as he could, he kissed the goats and ran to join that great zigzag. What finally pushed him—*two thousand and thirty-two*, he still remembered counting—a slow welling of terror, some old spirit who rose up as fierce as hunger, commanded him: *Go*.

He never looked back at the farm. He never wondered about why the old woman had kept him, barely alive. When Misha asked *"How did you live?"* it wasn't possible to answer with the ungodly details. He had already rolled off the train. He had already left the goat shed, the smell of that soup, the taste of its spices on his tongue, and he had left the silence of that old woman, who spared no mercy in her beatings but who, for reasons he'd never know, showed him the way through the hardest time.

....

It seems he is the only one on the road. Perhaps there are others at this time of night who fade like wolves into the hills above the villages. Once, he thinks he sees the shapes of families huddled on the grass, but he does not stop running. At this hour the night has given up its pretense of wariness, and as he covers more ground the light of the North Star becomes the road itself. The body's directive to keep adrift. Breathe on.

Who knows how long until his lungs beg him *"Stop,"* until his knees plead *"No more,"* until he pauses at the boundaries of his own moonlit shadow. That lonely grandmother. A silver braid. What justice had caught her up? What had moved her to give him shelter, even as she mixed his chance at life with the kind of suffering that he would always remember?

A good thing he can't remember her face. Just the pooling fat underneath her chin, and the thick, slippery, silvery braid, which would weave in and out of his vision as she beat him without remorse. A small price for what he had gained when he rolled off that train to Treblinka.

....

In the warm Indian night, his sweat breaks through his clothes. He leans on a lamppost to catch his breath, feels a sudden coming of peace. What he is grateful for is only ordinary. The bamboo plant Lucy once bought for him, the baby-soft skin of her wrist, the way she can roll her tongue and whistle, stopping traffic for a block.

It is her he wants now. He has never liked the word *regret*, believed no choice is without reason, and now, sweat soaked and exhausted, miles away from any city or town, he worries what he's done cannot be undone. The Lucy he knows is fire and light, and fire and light wait for no man.

"For family you must fight like a tiger," Misha once told him.

He begins to run again. A thousand miles till home.

Second Trimester

She's never been good at secret keeping. Back home, when Jeannie's daughter Emily told her she'd had enough of their small town and was planning an escape, up north somewhere or maybe even Nashville, Lucy had tried to keep quiet, but Emily's secret had come undone; soon the whole town knew about it, so that when Emily showed up at the bus stop around midnight, Jeannie was there to meet her, and her uncle, and her two brothers—half the town, actually—even Lucy's father had gone out that night in his flannel just to call Emily home. She thinks of how kind he was that night, helping carry Emily's suitcase, telling her the sadness would leave come morning. It's time James Gardner knows of his grandchild.

His best moods come Sundays after church, so she calls him then, hoping the Lord's grace will make the telling easier.

"Lucy, I was looking at our albums," he says, answering the phone. "Saw one of you climbing Timothy's oak. You must have been up sixty feet."

These days when they talk on the phone, she can find herself overwhelmed by the tenderness in his voice. Part of her wants to ask *"Where have you kidnapped my father?"* but mostly she's grateful that old age and her mother's passing have left James Gardner less bitter, more forgiving. It's what she's counting on now.

"Daddy," she says. "I screwed up. I really screwed up."

"What's the matter?"

"You'll be a granddad is all," Lucy says. She's tried to be strong in her solitude, but her father's tenderness has surprised the toughness out of her. All the hope she had for a family with Jaryk, unraveling. The grief she's been holding at bay threatens to come out, and her voice shakes as she says, "So that's my news."

"Oh, Lucy," he says.

"I've been thinking that if I can't make it in the city on my own, I might move back to Mebane, just for a while."

"Say when," her father says. "I'll come up there and drive you back home."

He doesn't ask any questions about how it happened, and for this she is grateful. Maybe Timothy has prepped him, but she doesn't think so. He's coming into his own, her old man.

She's halfway settled on Mebane. Most mornings, rising out of bed, then hugging the handrails on the subway to City Hall, she can't imagine how she would manage here as a single mother, though there are moments, when she gazes at all the boats on the Hudson, or when she steps into the cathedral of Grand Central, that she also can't imagine forsaking the city's great rush.

She's had to ask Miles Norton about maternity leave. On her lunch break, she followed him out of the office to his favorite hot-dog stand. She waited in line with him, offering office talk, and right before he was about to order his dog, she said, "Miles, I'll need to take some time this winter away from work."

The request put him off his routine, which she'd believed would work in her favor. "Around Februrary. That's when I'm expecting my child."

The hot-dog man slapped Miles's order in his hands, no questions asked.

"Oh, my," said Miles, nearly forgetting to pay. "This is a new one for me."

The next week he alternates between leniency and strictness, offering first to help with some of her clients, telling her she can take an extra break in the mornings, then walking into her office and announcing he must keep fair standards for all and how many clients has she seen today?

"Oh, I believe I'm still the most popular counselor," Lucy informs him.

"I'm just worried you won't have time for both mothering and work," Miles counters. Just another thing she now has to worry about, getting the boot at her job.

All the talk in the office has Jonas perked up. She agrees to meet him for dinner after work. It's his turn to choose, and he gives her an address on the Upper East Side.

"Got the best catfish in town," he says.

A dusty Creole bar is what she imagines, though it's an apartment building with an Old World inscription—*The Predwin*—and prewar architecture well beyond her means. Jonas greets her as she arrives.

"Why do I not think this is a restaurant?"

"Just wait till you see the white-tablecloth service," Jonas says. He's always seemed a carelessly careful dresser, but tonight his wardrobe draws a smile from her. He's got on a vintage vest and a linen shirt and ankle-high boots that match his silver belt buckle. His hair's slicked back, and he looks on the whole as if he might be about to perform a magic trick.

A doorman in a navy-blue suit greets him as *"Mr. Jonas, sir."*

Jonas high-fives the doorman and says, "Right this way, madam."

Oh, he's a charmer, Lucy thinks, as she allows herself to be steered into the elevator of the apartment building, whose antique door Jonas now gently slides shut. Close in the elevator with him, she smells his cologne, which has a whiff of forest about it, an element so outside of the city that she appreciates it.

"Mandy's been acting up lately," Jonas says of the elevator. "Named after the first lady who lived in this building." He presses the Up button half a dozen times before finally they begin their ascent. It's a crowded space, but not so crowded that Jonas has to press up against her, which he does, sliding his hand a little too close to her.

She weighs his intentions as they climb to the top. In the beginning of their friendship, she'd announced she wasn't available, that there was a significant someone, though perhaps, without any evidence forthcoming, he's been wooed to think otherwise.

That may well be the case, she thinks, following him into an apartment that's at least twice the size of hers, where's he's folded a white tablecloth over his dining table, arranged a yellow rose in a glass jar. and opened a bottle of wine. The ceilings, too, are several feet higher than what her rent could afford.

"You sure you don't have a second job, Jonas?"

"Before I moved up here, I started getting some money from my grandpa. Gets me a decent-sized place."

"Grandpa Goldshoes?"

"I'm still working, all right?"

"You didn't have to go to all this trouble."

"Before you say anything, know that I love to cook and rarely get the chance. In this city, we're always eating food some half-mad person slapped on a plate. I just thought we could relax, slow down, and eat a meal at the pace of home. And hold on—" he says, rushing to the oven—"I have baked-from-scratch cornbread."

The bread stirs from the heat. She inhales the buttery smell that forms its core. "Okay," she says. "But you're going to let me return this favor."

He's made catfish in a style he learned from New Orleans. A few spices she can't name and tarragon. Nola is where he fell in love with music, Jonas says, pointing to his guitar, which shares space in the corner with his shelf of LPs. Records are stacked on the floor, books arranged in formidable towers. Little Russian dolls line the sill of an unusable fireplace. He may be a nomad at heart, she thinks, but Jonas loves to nest.

"I know, I'm a little messy," he says, serving her another piece of cornbread.

She butters it thoroughly before eating it with relish. Now that the nausea isn't prominent, she can enjoy the taste of food again, and she is often hungry. Maybe Jonas has noticed her extra snack breaks throughout the work day and the way she's wolfed his meal down this night, but she doubts it—he's got his nose in his food as much as she does. Still, she's decided she wants to tell him about her pregnancy. Miles wouldn't have leaked the news—he doesn't have a gossipy bone in him—but it's only a matter of time before people see her showing. Anyway, when she tells him, it'll be a kind of boundary between them. If his intentions are more than being just friends, it'll put a stop to it. Something about this makes her feel a loss—she doesn't, after all, want to lose the gentle flirtation they've enjoyed—but she can't help telling him the truth.

"It's very sweet, you making this whole meal, putting on the white tablecloth. All of it," she says.

"Madam, it's my pleasure."

"Who taught you to play that thing?" she asks, pointing to the guitar.

He tells her he followed a minstrel in New Orleans. She likes the way he says "*minstrel.*"

"I spent my youth following him into bars," Jonas says. "I don't mind playing you one of his tunes."

Lucy was born with the gift of perfect pitch, and she can hear the same in Jonas's voice when he sings to his strum. First he sings her an Appalachian tune about an orphan girl, his voice suited to the notes of mourning, and then he sings her a boot stomper about moonshining on the mountain.

They head up a flight to the roof, from which she can see the neighborhood changing. Jonas's building is prewar, but around her the other old residences are being felled. In every direction, bulldozers are awaiting orders. Large dugouts of land prepare for skyscrapers that will soon house hundreds of tenants. Mayor Lindsay has talked about the city transforming itself, becoming again the jewel of finance, manufacturing, and even art, but the only art she can imagine flourishing here are the graffitied murals, ubiquitous and as diverse as the city itself. The sun slides low over the city, and for a moment even the wasteland of the city, the abandoned houses, the plots saved for skyscrapers, all of it is beautiful. She leans against the railing and summons her courage.

"Jonas," she says. "I'm so glad we met. We have a good time, the two of us, don't we?"

"Lucy, there's something I've been meaning to tell you," he says. He moves too close to her again, as if he's winding up for a kiss.

"I go first," Lucy interrupts. "Jonas, I'm seventeen weeks. Pregnant."

"Oh." He takes a turn around the roof, stepping gingerly over the antennae and the lines tying into the water tank. "Is it your special friend, the one who doesn't live here?"

"Yes," Lucy sighs. "It's him."

She can see him searching for his gallantry, but the news has caught him unawares. If he suspected something, he didn't put it all together, she's sure of that now. He looks defeated, and that's no surprise: men are so easily wounded. Jonas is a good man, and she has no wish to hurt him. She kisses him on the cheek, refuses to linger.

"Good night."

She walks herself down to the elevator, but it won't go on her command. A light's on in the vestibule, but she can't tell what it means. Jonas has come down after her, slips in. He has minty breath, like Mr. Pal.

"Mandy doesn't like quick goodbyes," Jonas says, seeming like he's got on right again, seeming like he's aiming for overtime. He slams the elevator cage shut, and they descend.

Walking her to the train, he says, "Lucy, I'm no fair-weather friend. I'm no fair-weather anything."

"I know that, Jonas."

"What I mean is that I can be a support to you and your baby. I'm just prideful is all—sometimes get a temper about it. I just want to know if we're playing the same song. I can really help you, Lucy."

It's been a night she wishes to remember for its sweetness. She doesn't want to push him into any confessions he might later regret, though still—*still*—it is good to be desired so recklessly.

"I'll see you at the office tomorrow," she says.

....

Alone in her apartment, she goes through her mail. It has always given her comfort, the sorting of wanted and unwanted things. At the bottom of her pile, she finds a package from her dad. It's *The Little Prince,* which he and Mama read to her as a little girl. A story about a boy, a flower, and a volcano. The inscription says: *"Ole Tim and I would like to read this to beansprout, as it was read to you."* Those words make her feel like a child again. She will be looked after. Her baby will be looked after. It won't be any ordinary family, but—Jaryk or no Jaryk—her little one will be loved.

Office Hours

He walks the streets feeling like a tourist. The long tail of Houston leading to the tenement buildings of the Lower East Side, which he'd admired for having preserved their immigrant history, feels as foreign now as the countryside of India had been at first. Delivery boys rush up the Bowery, and he sees the cycle rickshaws; at the supermarket he samples an heirloom tomato and thinks of the Pals' garden. Women cross the streets in miniskirts; he remembers the village wives who balanced the harvest on their heads, their saris faded from the sun. He is still between worlds, unprepared for reinvention.

He arrived three days ago. Without a place to live, little left of his savings, he headed to Temple Beth Israel. Old Rabbi Samuel greeted him as if there'd never been a separation. Ten years in the temple's employ, Jaryk had rarely sought the rabbi's counsel, but now he did, asking where he might find a room to stay in for a while. The rabbi led him to the basement, where next to his beloved library was a study little bigger than Jaryk's holding cell in the military hospital, but until he found another apartment it would have to do.

He spent most of his first day in the congregants' chamber, attending to the bulbs that had burned out in the chandelier. The High Holidays would soon be upon them, and he wanted the hall to be filled with light. His first night he slept on the pews and was awoken in the early dawn by Rabbi Samuel's hand.

"Morning to you and morning to me," said the rabbi.

Before he left for India, Jaryk had begun to smell the age of Rabbi Samuel; as his employer settled into the pew, he could smell the sourness that reminded him of the next life.

"I wouldn't mind hearing a good story," the rabbi said. "Do you have one in you?"

"I feel it's hard to put what I've experienced into a story."

"Try," said the rabbi.

Once there was a man from Warsaw . . .

Once there was a play in India . . .

Once there was an orphanage in a ghetto . . .

He didn't know where to begin. Whether with Misha's death or the taxi ride into the country with Mr. Pal; cycling toward Shantiniketan; his hours in the police hospital; grieving for Misha, alone; all the afternoons at Gopalpur, building the stage; the force of the rains; Neel's face breaking into a smile; Lucy coming to visit him, trying her best to take him back home.

Once there was a man from Warsaw who loved a girl from Mebane . . .

The morning light had fallen onto the pews in a widening trapezoid. Rabbi Samuel had fallen asleep against Jaryk's shoulder. He could smell the dab of perfume the rebetsin had once each morning put on the rabbi's ear, which in her memory the rabbi now applies himself.

....

His last night in India he ran as long as he was able. The Pals found him sleeping by the side of a road, a wanly lit lamppost marking his shape.

"They'll be on the watch for you," Mr. Pal said, dark shadows under his eyes, worry in his voice. "We have to get you out now."

Even in the rush, he made the Pals stop at the estate so he could retrieve Misha's ashes, but forgot his statue. Once again it became lost to the world. In the months after, he'll imagine Neel returning to the Bose house, claiming it as rightfully his.

Afterwards, Mr. Pal instructed Jaryk to hide in the trunk, at least until they were closer to the city. He apologized profusely for the kerosene smell.

"Is it really necessary?" Jaryk asked.

"Well, you were the leader of a play that culminated in a government honcho being shot," answered Mrs. Pal. "We'd prefer you to avoid any and all interrogations."

"I promise I'll drive slowly," said Mr. Pal.

He squeezed himself into the trunk and lay huddled for what seemed like hours. At times the car would slow to a crawl, and he'd hear muffled shouts, his heart racing, but each time they'd start moving again.

Eventually they stopped closer to Calcutta, where he was brought into the backseat.

"I'm terribly sorry for that indignity," Mr. Pal said. "But as we suspected there were several checkpoints along the way. Each time they were asking about a tall white foreigner. We, of course, feigned ignorance."

They made it to the airport but all flights out were booked. No choice but to hunker down in the Pal estate, far enough off the thoroughfare. He worried about everyone's safety and tried calling the professor, but there was no answer. Finally, on the second day, he reached Rohan, who explained that the professor had headed to Bangladesh and was going to be away for a while.

"But no worry," Rohan said. "Professor soon come. He soon come. Many papers at Gopalpur."

"What about your safety? What if they come for you again?"

"No worry," Rohan said. "Very many journalists. They won't touch now."

The press had invaded Gopalpur and its surroundings, so for the moment the villagers were safe. He told Rohan to pass on a message—that he was heading back to America first thing tomorrow. But he would never hear from the professor again. He would send letters to the university but receive no answer. Years later, cleaning up his mailbox, he'd find a flyer for a new play in India:

It was to be about a blind king, and a sightless child was to play the lead role.

Once there was a blind king.

Once there was a blind boy who played a blind king.

He'd stay in touch with Neel, though. Two months after the performance he'd receive a letter: *"Uncle, we've been given our permit to live here,"* it began. All their hard work had turned into a claim to the land. Over the years, he'd keep up a correspondence, stuffing comic books into packages that traversed the oceans to end up in a village and later in the city as Neel grew older.

When it came time for him to catch his flight, he told the Pals he would write from America. He thanked them for their kindness. Mr. Pal sauntered out to the garden, bending gingerly to retrieve a handful of tomatoes from the vine. He was having a hard time of it, complaining about the ache in his knees, the pain in his lower back, when Mrs. Pal lifted her sari and helped him. All the while, they joked to each other in their secret language of love. Through a gap in the trees, the sun illumined them as they were, older and younger, incompletely suited, on the verge of some uncommon happiness.

The sight of the two of them in the garden would become his last memory of India.

················

He wonders what Lucy now thinks of him. In India he dwelled on the play, the professor, and the children of Gopalpur, but now that he is here, she consumes his waking hours. At times he thinks it would be simple to walk to her apartment on the Lower East Side and say hello, but other times he cannot bear the thought of being turned away. A possibility that grows larger the longer he is gone.

Now when he thinks of letting her leave India alone, he feels the weight of abandoning his unborn child, and when he thinks of himself in this light, it is too much to bear. What will she say to him now—what will he say to her? Pacing the synagogue at night, he practices. *Forgiveness* is a word he often uses, though he is not sure if he is simply rehearsing a script or if his asking for it comes deeply from the heart. How can he be certain—what is the test of his intention?

In India, he thought he might bury the ghost of Misha and the ghost of Pan Doktor and the story of the house on Krochmalna Street, but this is no more possible now than it had been thirty years ago, stepping off the barge into this city that sheltered him. He will keep his ghetto memories. They will weary him. They will question his time on this earth, and they will challenge his love for Lucy. This he cannot change, though with the years, he might grow a second heart: he might love this world more than his ghosts.

With the Jewish New Year approaching there is much to do. He must collect donations and assign seats. He must contact their caterer with the numbers of all who've confirmed and arrange a special menu for the children. He must speak with the new cantor; the old cantor, who'd known Jaryk for fifteen years, has retired to Florida. Here there is enough of a life to keep him busy, and of course there are the boys from the docks—maybe they're cooking up a game now, and they could use his gunner's arm on the field. But thoughts about Lucy keep coming back. When he cleans the pews into a dull shine, he sees her face in the light.

....

He makes a plan to visit her at the city employment office, where he will say *"Lucy, please forgive me,"* where he will make amends for leaving her for India, for not choosing to return when she asked. The next morning he gets on the 4 train between a suit and a man with dreadlocks, is reminded of why the *rush hour* is so named; many push to board the train, though so few seem to be happy about the dawning of the new workweek. Lucy had talked about moving up-country to start a family, leaving the clock-in-clock-out behind. He'd told her he could learn how to build a cabin, told her he could build anything with his hands.

He enters the Municipal Building at nine o'clock in the morning. A receptionist with a cone of blond hair greets him.

"I'm looking for Lucy Gardner in employment admin," he says.

"Do you have an appointment?"

"I don't," he admits. He wants to say that he knows her, that in fact he is the father of her unborn child, but in the next moment she's thrust a clipboard of paperwork his way.

"You're lucky she's got a light morning. She can see you at nine thirty."

He takes a seat in the waiting area. Sandwiched between two men with frayed fedoras, he fills out the forms. There are questions about his history. Where does he come from? What jobs can he do? What are his strengths?

Outskirts of Warsaw, he writes.

Bookkeeping, accounts receivable, handiwork, minor construction.

For strengths he writes: *endurance.*

At nine thirty, the receptionist leads him into Lucy's office, but in Lucy's chair there's a man with his feet up on her desk. He's wearing a gray blazer, hair slicked back, a big smile aimed at Jaryk. "Pardon, didn't realize she had a client coming in." In his voice Jaryk hears a Southern accent, like Lucy's but more pronounced.

As he collects himself, Lucy enters. She's wearing a long, loose dress, no makeup, and the pair of bangles she found shopping with Mrs. Pal. She seems lost in thought and at first doesn't notice him. Then she stops in her tracks and looks from the man at her desk to Jaryk and back again. "Can I help you?" she asks.

At first, he's not sure if she's directed her words at him. They sound so foreign, callous even. He holds up the paperwork. "I thought we could talk. I even made an appointment."

"Jonas, will you give us a minute, please?"

Jonas whistles under his breath as he leaves. It feels as if he's being mocked, and who, anyway, is this man who puts his feet on Lucy's desk?

"I wanted to see you," Jaryk says, after Jonas has left. "I wanted to explain things."

"I just got out with Glenn Adkins. I'm in no mood, and I can't talk about us at work, Jaryk. I have clients to take care of."

He remembers Glenn Adkins, the musician-turned-security-guard that she'd once spoken of as someone she might reform. "I understand. Can we meet sometime? Maybe at Veselka? Tonight, tomorrow, the day after?"

"I don't think so," Lucy says slowly. "I don't think I'm ready for that."

"Of course, I get it. I dropped out of thin air."

"Yes, you dropped out is right."

She's tapping her nails on the table, a nervous rhythm, and everything in him says, *"Run."* Says, *"She won't have you back."* He sees himself out into the clamor of the lobby, then out into the noise of downtown.

"I'm not ready for that," he hears her say again and again. There's a wedding rehearsal being held at the synagogue, which means he can't be back until the evening, at which point he'll help the cleaners with the dishes, reassemble the bibles into neat piles. For now, he's left to wander. From City Hall he fords the walking lane of the Brooklyn Bridge, heading south, unsure where he'll go.

Lucy's coworker Jonas troubles him, or maybe the man isn't a coworker at all but an intimate friend; either way he knows their connection is more than happenstance. That look they shared said he means something to her. Of course he might well have expected it, had he set aside more time to think about Lucy and not his troubles in India. It's been more than a month and without a word from him, what is she to expect? If she's moved on, found another partner, it wouldn't be strange. But he can't hold this thought for long; soon it's broken by a fear that he has missed his chance. All good things which come in time. All good things which come only at certain times, not for long when they do come, and if one does not love when called—so the rabbi has said—then what is lost is often lost for life.

Come Brooklyn he boards the train to Green-Wood Cemetery.

Misha's grave bears fresh flowers. A bunch of yellow roses, long stems of lavender, a few lilies. But in Jaryk's absence who would have tended the grave? He can't imagine any of the men from the docks stopping to pay their respects. Not that they didn't care for Misha, but they have families and long commutes and who would make the time? Still, he's grateful for the flowers. He's grateful for the silence that the cemetery offers. All this noise of the city and now, finally, a moment of quiet with a brother.

He's never had a gravestone to come to; everyone else he's lost remains without testament. Everyone but Misha. He checks the knapsack the Pals gifted him, where in a sealed container he's carried Misha's ashes thousands of miles home. To his dearest friend he wants to say that the summer hasn't gone according to plan. He wants to say: *"Things fell apart when you left me."* The gravesite is pristine. In fact, the whole cemetery is a gorgeous landscape with hills of blooming grass, some evidence even of wildflowers in the thickets, the road far enough away to forget the city. He sits on the grass to hear whatever Misha's spirit will impart. The last edict Misha had was to start a family with Lucy. He gave it a go at first, there's no doubt of it, though later he lost sight of Misha's words: *"Most important thing is family, then food, then everything else."*

He hasn't eaten, so after Misha's ghost keeps the silence for another hour, he feels weak enough in the knees to take his leave.

"I'll come back soon, and often," he says to Misha.

He heads back to the city. He gets his own table at Seven and a Half Dimes and orders a plate of fried mackerel. In his knapsack, he discovers two of the green tomatoes the Pals gave him on his last day. They've ripened to a tender red now. Each has its own taste, a sweetness that makes him remember the confections Mrs. Pal made him, so dense and moist, like nothing he'd tasted before, the sweetness sticking to his tongue for hours. That last day in Calcutta they'd helped him arrange what few things he was taking home. Avik and Priya washed and pressed his shirt while Mrs. Pal directed the operation. How strange a life—that he'd met them at all, that he'd grown to depend on them, at least for a while, as family.

On his way out, he stops at the Fulton Fish Market, where Earl Minton is manning the books.

"Look at you, Mr. Adventurer," Earl says.

At Misha's funeral, Jaryk mentioned he'd be going far east for a while. The docks boys had given him their silent respect then, but now he's back. Surely, they'll want stories.

"I directed a play in India," Jaryk says. "Hundreds of people showed up."

"You did now, did you?"

"Misha was supposed to, but I did in his place."

He tells Earl about all the necessary repairs at the synagogue, how soon the halls will fill with families for the Jewish New Year. "Oh, and I visited Misha's stone."

"Did you like the flowers?" Earl says.

"So, it was you, then?"

"A bunch of us pool money. I just go and put them on the ground. Misha was more than a colleague to us."

He's sad to have assumed Misha would have been forgotten so easily, grateful for these old friends.

"And what about the lady of your life? The one Misha was always bragging about?"

"She's swell," Jaryk says. He wishes he could speak to Earl about his Lucy troubles, but he has no language for it. Not with Earl, from whom he learned the art of bookkeeping, nor with any of the men who'll start showing up at the pub as soon as the sun sets.

"And your boys, Earl, how are they?"

"The oldest is off to the polytechnic this year, will you believe that? He's good at math."

"Gets it from his dad, I know."

"Well, keep coming with that flattery," Earl says with a wink. "I'll tell the boys you're back."

Now Jaryk surveys the unvarnished stools where beer stains have seeped into the wood, surveys the long bar with its upturned mugs and the pool table with its canvas warped by time—all evidence of conversations had, drink consumed, lives passing through. He can imagine Rebecca down in the basement, double-checking her accounts, making sure no girl at the bar is frenching away the tips.

He heads outside to the pile of burlap bags where he used to lunch with Misha. In the clear evening, schooners practice their foghorns. It would be simple to live another life, to return to the docks, or bury himself in his work at the synagogue, though also impossible now—across the island, there is Lucy with his child. Maybe she is setting her laundry out to dry. Maybe she is penning a page in her journal. He closes his eyes, sees again the sweet chaos of her nightdresses on the floor. A little courage is all he needs. If she rejects him, then so be it. He'll still volunteer himself a father, no matter what else happens. As others have done for him, he will now do for his own. He takes a deep breath. What he has been unable to confront appears to him now—not the terror he once felt, only the possibility of the future, its alarming brightness subdued by the setting sun.

He dips his feet into the water, takes the ashes from his knapsack, and lets Misha's remains merge with the tide.

....

A little courage, he thinks, knocking on the rabbi's chamber. It's early enough into evening that the rabbi's likely awake, though he's been known to take the occasional catnap during "office hours." It was a tradition the rebetsin started many years ago when so many of the congregation sought the rabbi's counsel that a first-come-first-served list had to be posted. Nowadays, there's no need for a list. After the rebetsin's passing, the rabbi spurned his office hours at every opportunity, and whenever he was available, he grew a reputation for answering questions with cryptic puzzles; a few months into the new routine the office hours were returned to the rabbi for quiet and contemplation.

Jaryk knocks again.

"Yes, Mr. Smith," the rabbi calls. "The door is open."

"I'm here for your office hours," Jaryk says. "I need your advice on something."

"Yes, I guessed that," the rabbi says. "Shall we take a walk in my library?"

Jaryk helps Rabbi Samuel from his chair and slowly they walk toward the basement room known as *Books and Other*.

"What was it like to be in Tagore's town?" the rabbi asks.

"It was like being in the country," Jaryk says. "So many trees. Some deer running loose. Then there is this university, and the students seem happy to be there. It was like no other place."

"So the journey was long but fruitful?"

"It was, I think."

The rabbi fiddles with his key chain until he finds the right one. "What are we looking for?"

"A personal memento," the rabbi says. He has Jaryk take down a stack of scrapbooks. The rebetsin called these their "*yearbooks*," because they would chronicle the life of the congregation—all the auspicious events, with a few good pictures to help memorialize the year. They skim through several volumes until they reach 1939.

"It's in the center," the rabbi says.

"What is?" Jaryk flips through and there in the middle of the scrapbook is a picture of Rebetsin Sarah and the rabbi, their faces pressed close to the camera, both grinning fiercely. The rabbi doesn't have any gray in his hair, and the rebetsin looks like she's just graduated college.

"I had been meditating on this picture," the rabbi says. "I had been trying to remember where in this fortress I put it. It took me a long time to remember. A couple of months, I'd say."

Rabbi Samuel slips the picture into his coat pocket and takes Jaryk's hand. They lean on each other heading back to the office. "What did you want to ask me?"

"Oh, it was nothing, really," Jaryk says. He doesn't want to trouble the rabbi any further. Soon, his employer will return home for the night, where in the darkness and solitude he'll witness again the rebetsin's beauty in the photo and perhaps remember what it was like, those first few months of love.

He helps the rabbi back to his office, bids him good night.

"It is a short life," the rabbi calls after him. "Don't wait too long."

....

What he wanted to ask the rabbi was simply this:

"Is it all right for me to bring a child into this world?"

Except he'd already conceived a child, so it was too late to ask that.

In the chamber of books, the right question seemed to be: *"After everything, am I capable of love?"*

It was simple enough, but not a question he would ask a man who thought so often of his deceased wife.

Down in the synagogue's bathroom he shaves his beard, revealing the skin underneath to be a shade lighter, and there's something comforting about the sting of the balm he applies to his cheeks and chin, a familiar hurt. Afterwards, he dons one of the suits he's saved in plastic, and though it's too loose in some places and too tight in others, still it makes him feel like a different person. There's an early chill in the air tonight. South along Second Avenue several garbage bins have been set aflame, and groups of young men huddle next to the warmth, eyeing Jaryk with a challenge he refuses to take on. It's not a neighborhood he could live in, and he never relished visiting Lucy in her apartment on Seventh and First, preferring instead her company at his place. Entering her building, he's stopped by an old woman who needs help getting her walker through the door. Her name is Mrs. Esperanza, and he tells her that Lucy is an old friend. Up the staircase, leaning on his elbow for support, she says, "Lucy's just darling. One of these days I'm getting her to play for me."

In the dimly lit hallway, Mrs. Esperanza needs his help to open the lock.

"You want coffee? I make the best," she offers.

"Another time, ma'am."

On the second-floor landing, he hears someone trudging up the stairs and turns to see her in the shadows. She's wearing a loose summer dress and heels. Her lipstick glows in the near-dark. Even at a distance, he can smell her perfume, though it's a scent he doesn't recognize.

"I always wanted to put some lights in here," he says. "I can hardly see your face."

She grinds a heel into the cawed wood of the railing, marking a decision, which one way or another will alter the course of his life. There will be no turning back, he thinks, when Lucy speaks.

A Choice

She dreams of *The Little Prince*. All this while, she's had premonitions of a girl, but after reading her father's letter she's not so sure. A beautiful boy, maybe, with a bowl of dark hair falling around his ears. A child content at times to be alone with his imagination. A child who'll do good in the world. A common wish, but that he'll help others, heal the sick. "*Oh, I always thought you were to be a concert pianist,*" her mother once said. Nothing goes exactly as one might imagine, but a child who'll use his hands to mend the world—is that too much to ask for?

She dreams of *The Little Prince*, then of Jaryk. She'd assumed that he'd be home before summer's end, begging to be excused for his long absence, but now that Labor Day has come and gone and there's no trace of him, except in her journal and in her thoughts, where she's begun to feel less of the love that sustained them their first winter and more of a dull ache, which sometimes, at night, could be called regret, not for the child—no, she's glad for motherhood—but for the time that she spent burrowing into him, that time which feels now as if it's come to nothing.

She gets blue enough thinking this through Monday morning, with the subway crowded and no one rising to give her a seat, that by the time she sees Glenn Adkins, her first client, she's in no mood for his complaining about the night shift or about the jazz show he couldn't play.

"Honey," Lucy says, "you need to tough it out. Now, quit being a child."

It's not what Glenn needs at that moment; she can see that as soon as the words leave her mouth. He doesn't have one of his quips ready, and the circles under his eyes look like they've been there for months. He's suffering, like she is, just differently. A little trick: she closes her eyes for a moment to stuff her worries into a giant purse. Glenn's come to be consoled, to know that he matters, no surprise. She reaches across the table to hold his hand, "I'm here for you, Glenn. I'm coming to listen to you play. We're doing this together."

She's not sure it's enough. He's still looking at her as if she tore up their covenant and burned it in the trash. So close to him, she can smell the coffee on his breath.

"Think of one good thing now," she says. She does this sometimes. She tells the men to close their eyes, imagine a place they could go. Maybe from childhood, a moment of extraordinary happiness.

Glenn closes his eyes. He tells her about a beach he once traveled to with his mother, the point stretching out like a long snout. On that beach, a stranger was playing a saxophone, his notes half-caught by the wind. He tells her about the feeling of his mother's hand guiding him to the sand.

"Perfect," Lucy says. "You hold on to that."

....

After Glenn, Jonas comes to visit. He's wearing a gray blazer over a white linen shirt. If someone were to put Miles with his over-starched collars and immaculate Jonas in a room, you'd think Jonas was calling the shots. In fact, Miles has become the butt of Jonas's jokes—the last one delivered within earshot, Miles turning beet red, not equipped even to retort.

"Thank you for coming over last night," Jonas says. "My cornbread tastes better with you around."

Oh, she thinks, *he hasn't given up his flirtation.* "I'm sure all the girls hear it."

"Maybe next time we'll try it at your place—making bread, I mean?"

"All right," she says. "But you're bringing the butter, the flour, and the sugar."

"Listen, there's a concert in Central Park tonight. I'll pick you up from your place, say around six?"

She considers the possibility of another date, but her head's still full of Glenn. She's not sure if she's served him the way he needs. It's harder these days to believe that she's done enough to help someone change. "Oh, I'll think about it. But now I got to get ready for my next client. And I have to go pee again."

When she comes back to her office, Jaryk's there with Jonas. It takes her a moment to process the two men in her office. Jaryk's got a beard that makes him look as if he's lived in a forest without a mirror. And he's even more deeply tanned. Now his neck looks to her like a fisherman's neck, gilded from the sun.

When Jonas leaves, he comes out with it, holding a clipboard full of paperwork. Will she meet him at Veselka? Oh, the nerve! She won't, she won't even consider it.

"You dropped out is right," she says, and just like that he's gone again. It's over so quickly that afterwards she wonders if he came at all, if instead it was an unfortunate trick of the pregnancy, a hallucination of sorts, but no, there it is, his paperwork on her desk. She reads it line by line. He lists his history, that he's from Warsaw, his date of birth, his job at the synagogue. *"What are your strengths?"* a question asks. He has written *"endurance,"* which she thinks indeed is true, and feels in herself a kind of softening.

On the bottom margin in his careful handwriting he's copied down some lines of Tagore's, which she recognizes from the book of poems he once gave her:

> *Trust love even if it brings sorrow. Do not close up your heart . . .*
> *The heart is only for giving away*

She sits for a moment with Tagore's words and Jaryk's handwriting. His smell still lingers in the room. It's not enough to bring around poetry, expecting forgiveness. She throws his papers into the wastebasket and readies herself for her next client.

....

What a privilege it is to listen to music under the canopy of dusk, so deep inside Central Park that the lights of the city do not permeate, only the waning sun and the few bulbs that illumine the stage, where a quartet is playing Brahms. Jonas knows the cellist, and after the concert he introduces Lucy as *my dear girlfriend.* She still doesn't know what to make of his solicitation. To anyone who's looking closely, she's showing, and what suitor would be interested in a woman who's due to give birth to another man's child? Maybe it's only friends he wants to be, though she takes pride in her good witchery to read a person's intentions, so if she's wrong about him, that's troubling for its own reasons.

After the concert, they stroll through the park. All around them, couples whisper in a dozen languages, the New York of it, the denseness of all romance.

"Try it barefoot," she tells him.

He's game. From time to time, he finds honeysuckle, which he collects into a bunch and presents with mock solemnity.

Maybe she'll ask Renée about a woman for Jonas, someone who will appreciate his kindness and his gestures of good faith.

"How about a ride in a carriage?" Jonas asks.

The horses are lined up against the edge of the grass. He points to the carriage driver leading the pack.

"I'm too full," she says. "With the music, I mean. It was lovely." Why, even now, does she hold him at bay, when all her options seem as thin as the ice over Mebane Pond? A man with means and an open heart. A half-choice, her mother told her, is not a choice at all, simply the soul agreeing to suffer.

"A walk, then?"

"No," she says. "Tonight, I need some alone time."

He has a bramble stuck in his hair that she would release were the moment opportune. "I'll see you at the office tomorrow."

He pulls close to her, "Lucy Gardner, have you been leading me on?"

"Have I been what?"

"I mean. you've been saying yes to every date. I thought we were playing the same tune. Are we?"

"I already told you, I'm not on the market."

"Oh, right," he says quietly.

He's a delicate man, this Jonas, he's got his tricks and his troubadour ways, and in one of her alternative lives she's taking him up on his offer, a walk in the moonlight, a walk down the aisle. Except she doesn't want to belong to anyone right now. Not Jaryk with his wild beard and his sunburnt skin, his lines of poetry come to reclaim some lost ship, and not this man who's come into her life with purpose and mystery.

"Well, I'll see you at the office, then," he says.

In the days to follow, she'll spot Jonas twice in the office halls but won't say a word. In a month, he will have left the office. Rumors will abound that he joined a band traveling south; alternatively, that he found a job with a fancy corporation. No one will be sure, and Miles won't tell her more than she already knows: he'll be gone from her life—for good.

Now, alone again, she digs her feet into the grass. If nothing else, the earth's still there. Jonas wanted more than what she was willing to give—she felt it from the beginning, she accepts that now. She's let him go, into his own world, free from hers. She makes good speed, the map of the park known to her feet. A cool wind sends shivers, so she walks faster. At moments when she's fearful, she rubs a wide circle around her belly. "*A flower and a volcano,*" she says, conjuring *The Little Prince,* until she's clear of the park. "*This is all I need.*"

....

When she turns the corner onto Seventh Street, she sees Jaryk again. At first, she thinks it could not be him but someone who only looks like him from behind, but when he stops to help Mrs. Esperanza at the door, she sees his face and notices that since the morning he's shaved his beard. She's close enough that he might turn and see her, but he doesn't. He touches Mrs. Esperanza on the shoulder. Mrs. Esperanza, the nightingale of Seventh Street, who sings for everyone from the rooftops in summertime, and there's Jaryk, guiding her up the steps.

Lucy circles the block, buying herself time. On First Avenue, a young man yowls verses from a poem everyone knows—Robert Frost, maybe—"The Road Not Taken," maybe. He's expecting money, but her change purse is empty. Back onto Seventh Street she turns. Ms. Esperanza and Jaryk are nowhere to be seen. She climbs up to the third floor, where she hears someone on the landing.

She invites him in for tea. She still doesn't know what to say to him, but a cup of tea seems like the decent thing. They sit in her kitchenette, his large index finger hooked into her mother's porcelain teacup. His sweat smells bruised, his skin a shade lighter where he's shaved his beard, the smell of aftershave wafting over the tea, and he's dressed himself in a suit, maybe one from the collection he keeps in plastic.

"You cleaned yourself up," she says.

"I figured the beard wasn't working anymore."

"So, is it welcome home, or are you gone again?"

"Home," he says. "Not gone again."

He lifts the teacup to his lips, the steam clouding his eyes. She knows he's not a talker, but if he's here to apologize for his absence, she won't drag it out of him—he'll have to get there on his own. She meets his gaze and stares back.

He says, "I had this dream. The two of us—the three of us. We were going to our cabin in the woods. We had a dog with a face like a wolf. We had a kitchen with many windows, and through each window you could see trees, nothing but grass and trees. Sunday mornings, I made pancakes. For the three of us. We kept maple syrup year-round. The porch smelled like vanilla."

"Sure, I know this dream," she says.

"I saw Earl Minton this morning. I visited Misha's grave. Earl's been setting out fresh flowers.

"And the rabbi, he's doing okay, getting old, really. But I'm working there again. Not as many folks come as once did, but lots to do still to get ready for the holidays.

"Oh, and the play, it went well, sort of. I mean, the kids did a good job. I had to get out of there. There was some unrest."

"What do you mean, 'unrest'?"

"A politician got shot, and they closed the roads. Everyone told me I should pack up and leave. I did."

"Are you telling me you left because you were chased out?"

"I left because my job was done. We staged the play like we said we would. We brought the media. The villagers now have a fighting chance of making a life. Do you understand?"

His words feel cold. If she could've held his hand while he spoke, maybe it would've felt different, but she didn't dare. There's the iniquity of his long absence that still feels like a tender bruise.

"Sometimes I understand," she tells him. "Mostly I don't."

There's something she wants to give him. It feels like a stroke of cruelty, but she can't stop herself. She pulls out one of Dr. Malhotra's ultrasound photos, where her baby's head and elbow and the tips of its feet are all visible. "This is what you missed," she says.

"Oh," he says, as if he's been punched in the gut. A fly alights on the picture, and he brushes it away. He cups the image in his hands. "Beautiful."

"Jaryk, I'm expecting someone tonight. You can keep that, though. It's nice to see you."

It takes him a moment to realize she's again asking him to leave. When he gets the message, he tucks the picture into his coat pocket and arranges himself. He reaches toward her—what, for a handshake? a hug?—then pulls back, afraid, perhaps, he's overstepped, and she doesn't encourage him.

"Welcome home," she says, though it sounds spiteful, not welcoming at all. While he gathers himself, she stares out the window. Down below the fire hydrant has been uncorked, and children squeal around its spoils.

"I realize I didn't get you anything from India," he says. "That was rude of me."

"I'll forgive you for that," she says, opening the door.

She sees him as a boy, crawling through the mud, searching for scraps. What he's lived through could break her. What he's lived through to stand before her—to hold what she feels now, as if it could be poured into a bowl, as if it, too, could be kept in his heart. He brushes a stray lock from her forehead. "Goodbye, then."

That night, she falls asleep in her dress and wakes to the sound of a telephone. It takes a moment to realize that it's her telephone that's ringing, and she crawls to it, manages a hello. Turns out, it's a wrong number, a lady from Russia trying to reach her cousin in Manhattan. With as much kindness as she can muster, Lucy tries to explain that one digit has been missed, but everything else is fine. A few minutes later, the phone rings again: 2:15, the clock says. This time it's only a caller's deep breathing, and she thinks for a moment it's Jaryk, about to say *hello*, but then she hears "*Sorry*" from the same Russian lady.

"Try again," Lucy tells her. She doesn't know why she's so encouraging. She's hopeful that the lady can reach her cousin for whatever intercontinental conversation needs to be had at this hour. Afterwards, it's unremarkably silent again, the white noise of missed connections.

The Piano

The city seems transformed into a place of muted objects, silent walkers. When the line of homeless approach him at Union Square, he fails to hear the rattle of their cups, and the traffic that flows up Fifth Avenue does so without disharmony—without any noise at all. The subway scudders below, and though he feels its vibrations along the arches of his feet, even that carries no sound. He thinks of Lucy, the way she guarded her teacup, as she banished him from their lives. He stares at the photograph of his unborn child and cannot imagine the future without the two of them.

Near the corner of Seventy-Second, though it's past eleven at night, he spots a lone food cart and stops for a knish, the smell of deep-fry rousing him from his numbness. The nocturnal street vendor takes his change and pours hot sauce at his behest, the smell of fire returning him to the sound of the city, which even at this hour is full of chatter that he can overhear from the open windows of the houses he passes.

Back into his hideout he retreats, the basement of Beth Israel providing the quiet of filial mice and leaky pipes, the detritus of old, collapsible buildings. With a bit of clear plastic tape he puts the picture of his child up on his wall. An elbow, an ear, the curved spine, and around it the elliptical barrier, protecting the shape— a him or a her, he still doesn't know but has begun to wonder— from the troubles of the world.

Rosh Hashanah comes on the ninth of September, earlier than

usual. He doles out prayer books, ensures that the new cantor, who is particular about drinking a hot cup of honeyed limewater before she sings and again halfway through the service, has what she needs. When the rabbi gives his sermon, Jaryk listens in the back pew. For once, the rabbi delivers in his old form; the entire congregation seems charged by his Torah reading, which quickly turns into interpretation and Midrash. Out with the old, in with the new. An embrace each day of what is holy, even if it does not feel holy. Keep your attention on the blue flame of this life, the rabbi says. Live this day and every day of this year with your highest purpose.

After the ceremony and the dinner, when it is only the cleaning staff and the two of them, the rabbi pulls Jaryk aside.

"You were weeping," the rabbi says.

"Not at all," Jaryk says.

"I just want to make sure you did not miss my point," the rabbi says. "You've been trawling for days."

Jaryk's heard the rabbi use the word *trawling* once before in answer to the simple question *"How are you?"*—which in fact is hardly ever simple with the rabbi, who has told Jaryk not only *"I'm trawling"* but *"Today I feel wobbly,"* like an untended flower in a garden. *"After seeing Lucy, I'm wobbly,"* he'd like to say, but he doesn't need to say anything—the rabbi speaks up. They should enjoy a piece of pumpkin pie, he says.

"Young people are always worrying about getting fat or being too thin," the rabbi says, "but really, this is nonsense. Especially on this day, we should eat what we want."

Pumpkin pie was the rebetsin's favorite. In her time, slices of pumpkin pie could be found in the pews, on bookshelves, on the stairs leading to the altar.

"I screwed up with Lucy," Jaryk says.

"Yes, I know." The rabbi scrapes the last piece of pie off his plate. "Listen, the best way to deal with such situations is to take your mind away from the matter, at least for a thimble. Anyway, I need you to do something for me. The cantor would like some instruments for day school, and there's a wonderful smithy who used to belong to the congregation, many years ago, who might be willing to give us something for cheap. Would you mind paying him a visit? His name is Amichai. Here, have the rest of the pie."

To have work in the face of Lucy's dismissal is no small consolation, a task as simple as a rendezvous with a tradesman a great relief, a reason, at least, to leave his basement room, which has begun to smell like his quarters in the military hospital, a little musky and a little dreary, on the cusp of arousing an unforgivable self-pity.

Amichai Belowski's shop on the Lower East Side, unmarked and nearly consumed between a school and a church, could easily be mistaken as another unkempt apartment in a neighborhood of low-cost housing, except that through the clean patches of a dusty, fingerprinted window, Jaryk sees that almost all of the space is filled with instruments. Violins lie balanced against each other's necks, and propped against the window are several guitars in various states of repair, the wood of the insides on some exposed while others seem ready to play. At the back of the room, there's a man working on an upright piano. What he knows of pianos is limited to what Lucy's told him, but even at a distance, he can see it's a beauty, made of Old World wood and sleek edges that give the instrument a sense of flight.

"Who's there?" the man calls from the innards of the piano.

"I was sent by Rabbi Samuel. He said you could lend us some instruments. For our Sunday classes. My name is Jaryk Smith."

"You're the boy from Warsaw," says Amichai Belowski, turning finally to face Jaryk. There's something in the country ruddiness of Amichai's face that reminds him of Misha, a sense of laughter, maybe, even though there's no joke to be told and even though Amichai is much older, maybe even the rabbi's age, though he seems to be nimble enough, clearing a path for Jaryk, moving instruments aside.

"I'm retiring," Amichai says. "So I thought why not give my old ones to the shul?"

"That's very kind of you."

"Rabbi Samuel said that in return you could help me with a few things."

"Oh, he did? I mean, sure. Not a problem."

"It's just that I need to clean the place for the next tenant, and I have no sons to help me."

"I'll be glad to."

In two weeks, the shop will be closing down. "Not enough people want things repaired anymore," Amichai says. "They just want to buy things new." Forty years he's been in the business, but recently it hasn't paid enough to keep the lights on. It's a shame, Jaryk thinks, to retire on a sour note, especially as Amichai's carried on a family tradition. His father in Vienna did the same sort of work, he says, tuning instruments with his ear so perfectly he was visited by concert pianists hoping for a little magic, a little something extra to enchant the audience—a good-paying job until 1939, when the family decided to flee.

"What good timing," Jaryk says. He doesn't mean it sardonically, but he can see Amichai wince—maybe the rabbi's shared the story of the orphanage, maybe he hasn't, though either way he would never begrudge the good fortune of others.

They talk of Amichai's first years in the city as Jaryk wraps the instruments and places them into boxes. It's a familiar tale and yet still feels miraculous to him—landing on these shores with no money, the father and son working together at a furniture company until they save enough to start a business. The American dream, predictable and comforting.

"We were lucky," Amichai says. "That we left when we did."

Jaryk nods. Was it luck that helped him roll off a train, or some flaw of character? He remains unsure, though in the presence of this man, who's worked all his life with his hands, listening for the most precise of sounds, that singular tone which means *pitch-*

perfect, he's willing to believe in something other than luck, a kind of grace, even, a kind of order in the choice of death and life, of all divine things.

After they've packed the instruments into boxes—a few of which he will carry back to the synagogue—Jaryk sweeps, sands, and then mops the floor with soap and lye. He washes the window of its years of stains. Hours later, it feels almost like a new storefront; all that's left are Amichai's tools and the upright piano, gleaming now from Jaryk's ministrations.

"The lady who asked me to repair this never came for it. It's a beauty, isn't it? Not a note is off." Amichai runs his hand along the scales. "Do you play?"

"No," Jaryk says. "But I know someone who does." He imagines Lucy with her hands on a piano again. How content she seemed in India, when after the struggle of the journey she'd been presented the colonial pianola and had performed Bach so perfectly that the chatter in the room ceased. Everyone had paused to take note. She had seemed to him irreproachably beautiful. Maybe it's not without reason that the rabbi sent him here.

"I gather the piano is very expensive, but if you are looking to sell it, then maybe I could buy it from you?"

"It is in fact very expensive," Amichai says. "It's restored to mint condition. I could sell it at auction. It would pay my expenses for a year, maybe two."

"I understand," Jaryk says. "I don't think I could afford anything so expensive, at least not right now, but maybe I could pay on a loan. A little every month."

"Help me sit," Amichai says, and Jaryk makes a chair out of the boxes in the room. "Your friend who plays, she must be very special to you."

"She is," Jaryk says.

"A boy from Warsaw," says Amichai Belowski, chewing his lip. "How could I refuse a boy from Warsaw? Listen, I might change my mind tomorrow. If you are to take it from me, best you do so tonight. Best you call your friends to give you a hand."

....

Outside Amichai's shop, he telephones Earl at the Fulton Fish Market and Earl sounds the alarm. "Jaryk needs a hand," he can hear Earl yell on the other end of the line.

Out of the subway they emerge still wearing the clothes of the workday, which hasn't finished yet, which means that somehow Earl must have secured them special dispensation. Five men in all, including Earl, all men he knows from his time at the wharves, at Seven and a Half Dimes, at the Dockside Players Field.

"We stopped for doughnuts, but otherwise we came as fast as we could," says Earl.

If only Amichai's piano had wheels it would be perfect. But no such luck. It requires men keeping an arm on each of its corners in order to labor it out onto the street. Before he leaves Amichai Belowski, Jaryk signs a promissory note that he will pay for the piano in small monthly installments, amounts so small that the loan is likely to outlive Mr. Belowski, a fact that's lost on no one.

As they steer the piano through Tompkins Square Park, troubling pigeons in their late afternoon droop, Jaryk exchanges a word with each of the men. If his memory serves, they all landed their jobs with Misha's help. Now they're here to lend a brother a hand. Around the statue of *Temperance* they go, cutting up toward Seventh Street.

Jaryk unlocks the door to Lucy's building, and there is Mrs. Esperanza.

"Lucy's not home, you know," she says.

"Yes, I was hoping for that."

"I'll keep an eye," says Mrs. Esperanza.

Earl leads them up to the second-floor landing, where the space is especially tight and maneuvering requires the men to collectively hold their breath and where the brunt of the weight is on Jaryk's shoulders, Jaryk who has insisted he bring up the rear, where it seems to him that he might give up the ghost, let go of his grip, but the men around him won't have it. Earl finds a way to steer them up with little injury to the walls.

There's no good place to set the piano in the apartment; almost the entire studio is filled with Lucy's things. Her nightdresses are on the floor along with her piles of books. They clear a space in the middle of the room, not knowing where else to put it. Jaryk leaves a note: *"For the music and for you—with all of my love, J."*

"I sincerely hope she plays it," Earl says. "And I sincerely hope you're about to buy us all a drink."

Returning

The city has begun to feel frenetic. The child inside her has begun to jab and kick. She still doesn't know whether it's a boy or a girl—who would want to know? Who would want to dampen that first surprise? Crossing the statue at Tompkins Square Park she acknowledges the knocking inside.

"Hello," she says. "I hear you."

At times the kicking feels playful, a testing of the waters; other times, a Morse code of sorts. Communications from unknown lands.

On the subway, men have begun to stand for her. If only they'd done the same a month ago, she wants to tell them. What a strange, private enterprise is motherhood. How it must have felt for her own mother, expecting Lucy, talking with her as she grew in the womb.

Mrs. Esparanza is sitting outside the building. She knows the comings and goings of everyone on the block. Before, she used to clean houses for professors at Columbia, but she always read eclectically. Octavio Paz. García Lorca. Foucault, who Mrs. Esparanza refers to as a paranoid Communist. Lucy didn't have to tell her that she was pregnant. She knew the way so many women in her life have known—who knows how exactly? perhaps by smell, perhaps by intuition—and immediately upon knowing conferred a blessing.

"Today is a day of love," says Mrs. Esparanza.

Lucy's come to expect these blessings. They have a ritual of hugging each other. This evening, Ms. Esparanza smells like licorice; waving goodbye, Lucy sees the candy stuck to her teeth.

Just a couple of years ago, she'd seen this hallway and couldn't believe the price of city life. Now, she hardly notices.

Even before she turns the doorknob she can smell the presence of visitors. Only Jaryk has her key, but it's not him, at least, she doesn't think so, because her apartment smells a little like fish. It's a Misha smell, really.

The smell of fish is stronger inside the apartment, though she doesn't feel afraid. Maybe it's Misha's ghost, she thinks, then sees the upright piano. It takes up nearly all the middle space of the room. She's seen quality pianos before, but she can tell that a master craftsman made this one. Someone who loves music as much as he loves the beauty of angles.

"For the music and for you—with all of my love, J." Next to the note, he's left her keys. Even the keys seem well tended to her, as if it's for her sake that he's polished that cheap steel.

She begins to play. Nothing specific, no exercise of her mother's, no proper composition. Just her fingers landing where they will, finding lost time.

....

The next day the congregation gather outside the temple in the waning sun. Is it a Friday tradition, she wonders, this lolling outside, this waiting for the last bell? She doesn't see Jaryk in their midst, doesn't see anyone she knows. This time she's not wearing a hat. She knows about white on the Sabbath. Her dress trails, it's so long, which is why she had to cab her way uptown, the driver treating her like a queen as soon as he noticed her belly. This state of motherhood gives her permission. Now she feels no awkwardness at the synagogue; some of the congregants treat her with deference.

She goes in with the others, who proceed en masse once the cantor begins to sing. Inside she notices the chandelier, every bulb casting a soft light onto the pews. She scans each row for a sign of him and, finding none, walks to the back of the synagogue. She's afraid he might've skipped the service. She's afraid she might not see him again, but he's there in the back pew, sitting alone.

He rises, seeing her. He's wearing his one silk shirt. Once he asked her how he should be ironing it, as if she had the first idea. Now it's bereft of wrinkles. He's neatly side-parted his hair and applied pomade; she notices he has more gray in his temples than before. He reaches out his hand, maybe in a hello, maybe to help her to her seat, but she declines.

At first she sits a few feet across from him, as if between them there is an invisible body who's claimed the space.

When the rabbi begins to speak, she moves closer to him. Again his hand reaches for hers and again she declines. It's only when they begin singing a wordless melody that she permits herself to move still closer. The whole congregation seems to know the tune, but Jaryk isn't singing.

"Do you know this one?" she asks.

"Yes," he says.

"Would you sing it?"

He sings so quietly she has to strain to hear. She's never heard him sing before. His voice is more melodious than she'd imagined it.

"Thank you," she says. She takes his hand, leads it to her belly, where their child is saying hello for the first time to a father.

"Oh," he gasps. "This is what it feels like?"

"Yes," she says. "This is what it feels like."

She doesn't know yet whether she'll allow him any more than this. An occasional visitation, a relationship of dutiful acquaintances. Returning to love is always the harder journey, and she doesn't know if she has the heart for it. Inside her, the little prince kicks and jabs, flops in seeming delight. Jaryk surprises her—he lifts his voice, joyously loud, to join the others in song—and it is so simple then to lift her own voice to make a harmony only they can hear.

NOTES AND ACKNOWLEDGMENTS

This novel came to be in community and in widening circles, and I am indebted to my mentors, teachers, and dear friends. To my parents, Kisor and Chandana Chakrabarti, who instilled in me a love of learning and stories, and my sister, Sukanya Chakrabarti, and my family still in India. To my Los Angeles family, Phil, Chana, and Michael Bell. To my writing teachers and mentors who nurtured this novel in its formative stages: Joshua Henkin and Ernesto Mestre-Reed from the Brooklyn College MFA program. To Elizabeth Gaffney and Mary-Beth Hughes, who guided me during my time as a Public Space fellow. To my writing community and my readers, Ruggero Bozotti, Peter Dressel, Katie Belas, and Mathias Black—this book is better because of you.

Thank you, Julie Stevenson, for your enduring vision and your kindness. Thanks to my Knopf family: Catherine Tung, Robin Desser, and, of course, the inimitable Tom Pold, whose patience, wisdom, and wit allowed this book to find its final form.

And to my first reader, poet Elana Bell—you've seen me through the hours—thank you for joining me in this life of books and love.

For research on the life of Janusz Korczak and his orphanage in Warsaw, Poland, I am grateful for the assistance of Dr. Robert Shapiro, Brooklyn College, and Agnieszka Witkowska, Historical Museum of Warsaw.

"It transcends the test—being a mirror of the self . . ." is a quote in translation from the poet Władysław Szlengel and was used in flyers to announce the performance of *The Post Office* in the Warsaw Ghetto in 1942.

The epigraph from "Childhood 1940" by Jerzy Ficowski was translated by Jennifer Grotz and Piotr Summer.

In addition, the following books informed the sections on Warsaw:

Selected Works of Janusz Korczak by Janusz Korczak, translated by Anna and George Bidwell, et al.

Ghetto Diary by Janusz Korczak, translated by Christopher Hutton

The King of Children by Betty Jean Lifton

The Warsaw Diary of Adam Czerniakow by Adam Czerniakow, translated by Stanislaw Staron and the staff of Yad Vashem

A Chronology of the Life, Activities, and Works of Janusz Korczak by Maria Falkowska, translated by Edwin P. Kulawiec

Who Will Write Our History? by Samuel D. Kassow

Who Korczak Was and Why We Cannot Know Him by Richard Lourie

Final Chapter—Korczak in the Warsaw Ghetto by Yitzhak Perlis

"The Religious Consciousness of Janusz Korczak" by Krystyna Starczewska, *Dialogue and Universalism*, vol. 7, nos. 9–10, pp. 53–71

While Gopalpur is a fictional village, there are historical correspondences to the social and political climate of West Bengal of the late 1960s and early 1970s. This material, along with some of the references to the life of Rabindranath Tagore and his time at Shantiniketan, were informed by:

Calcutta Diary by Amit Mitra

In the Wake of Naxalbari by Sumanta Banerjee

The Naxalite Movement by Prakash Singh

Rabindranath Tagore: The Myriad-Minded Man by Krishna Dutta and W. Andrew Robinson

The website sanhati.com

A NOTE ABOUT THE AUTHOR

Jai Chakrabarti's short fiction has appeared in numerous journals and has been anthologized in *The O. Henry Prize Stories* and *The Best American Short Stories*, and awarded a Pushcart Prize. Chakrabarti was an Emerging Writer Fellow with A Public Space and received his MFA from Brooklyn College. He was born in Kolkata, India, and now lives in Brooklyn, New York, with his family. *A Play for the End of the World* is his first novel.

A NOTE ON THE TYPE

This book was set in Legacy Serif. Ronald Arnholm (b. 1939) designed the Legacy family after being inspired by the 1470 edition of *Eusebius* set in the roman type of Nicolas Jenson. This revival type maintains much of the character of the original. Its serifs, stroke weights, and varying curves give Legacy Serif its distinct appearance. It was released by the International Typeface Corporation in 1992.

Composed by Digital Composition
Berryville, Virginia

Printed and bound by Berryville Graphics
Berryville, Virginia

Designed by Pei Loi Koay